Beauty

Secret

Blues

by

Sylvia Hardie

For information address: Crystal City Publishing, LLC.
P.O. Box 64-1181, Los Angeles, CA 90064

Sylvia Hardie
Beauty Secret Blues
Printed in the United States of America

ISBN: 978-0-9892485-5-6 (Paperback)
ISBN: 978-0-9892485-6-3 (Paperback –Uncensored)
ISBN: 978-0-9892485-7-0 (eBook)
ISBN: 978-0-9892485-8-7 (eBook –Uncensored)

Publisher – Crystal City Publishing, LLC.
www.crystalcitypublishing.com

Cover Design – Cre8tive Minds, Sam Adaslam

Editing – Dr. Judy Garcia and Crystal City Editing Team

All the characters in this book are fictitious, and any resemblance to persons, living or dead, is purely coincidental.

Crystal City Publishing, LLC
www.crystalcitypublishing.com

DEDICATION

I would like to first acknowledge God in my life and recognize that without his presence I would not have the strength and perseverance to accomplish all that I have.

Beauty Secret Blues

by Sylvia Hardie

Look for more books from
Sylvia Hardie

Coming Soon
Beauty Secrets 2

To enjoy more books from
Crystal City Publishing visit

www.crystalcitypublishing.com

Table of Contents

Acknowledgement

ACKNOWLEDGMENTS

I would like to thank my Mom and Dad for their continued belief in me and for supporting my dreams and aspirations, my 3 beautiful children for giving me the necessary motivation to accomplish all the goals that I have attained, Crystal Publishing and the support staff for meticulously editing my pages and keeping me true to deadlines, and my support team that kept me sane throughout this entire process.

Thanks to all of you, I could not have accomplished any of this without you.

↵INTRODUCTION

Mabel Holms, aka Big Mama is obsessed with power. Her every motivation is to get more money and more power. She was determined to never return to the impoverished life she grew up in. When she realized she could use her one asset to control men and get money, they became her weapon, and she waged war.

She soon has everyone in her pocket through one means or another. Her reign begins by invoking the supernatural, then gaining power over the Mayor, the city, the willing and the unwilling. Big Mama's power is felt by all.

During her war to gain all this power, she destroys the lives of many children and young people, including Barbra (who becomes known as Mammy), Samuel (Barbra's brother), Mabel's own grandson Rubert and of course all the children and young people in *The Hood*.

Barbra (Mammy), Samuel and Rubert go from their own lifetime of abuse and fear into a partnership with Big Mama. Their creation *The Hood*, under the guise of the nonprofits, "*Loving Holms*" for girls and "*Boy's to Men*" for boys, designed to help wayward girls and boys, caused a reign of suffering and terror which last four to five generations.

This book takes you through the lives and times of *The Hood* told in stories from Joyce, Mindy and Annie, who were born in *The Hood*. Their stories take you into the sex trafficking, murder, scandal and abuse that all who lived there went through every day. Highlighted are their personal struggles, friendships and their loves in the midst of all this hatred.

Determination and will take over freeing most of them, but leaving a ridge of anger and hurt between them all.

In the end, it's Synthia, the child that was stolen, who brings them all back together in old age. Her story tells the effects of how Big Mama and *the Partners'* terror still reign over them in the fifth generation. Although stolen when she was young, she ends up right back in *The Hood*, where the three girls, now older women, work separately to aid Synthia in her struggles for a better life.

The Secrets of Beauty begin now....

BEAUTY SECRET BLUES

SYLVIA HARDIE

Beauty Secrets

~JOYCE

I can still hear my mama screaming at the top of her lungs right before the sunset on hot summer days.

"Girls, it's time to come in!"

My best friend, Mindy, and I would shatter every time we heard the loud screech of my mother's big mouth. Her annoying high-pitched voice fell over the neighborhood like the warning siren on Dooms Day. All the kids in the hood could hear my mamma and knew it was time to go home. She had that type of voice that could stop you in your tracks and paralyze your up to no good thoughts, before you could even put them in motion. Once that call went out, it meant the streetlights would be on soon, and if the street lights caught you before the front door did, your ass was as good as gone.

"Those were the good old days, if there were any good days." I thought to myself, while sitting alone in our lifeless house.

My thoughts were my only company as I reminisced of happier days. With each new day I wish that I could go back and live those days over again. I missed the laughter of children and the fights between the aunties. I missed my idea of normal, but to be honest, I guess what I miss the most is not being alone.

13

Although my childhood was anything but normal, Mamma was here and her love shielded me from the nightmares that still play in my mind. My mamma was different and all the evil in this world could never change that. She made a home for us out of a shack, meals out of scraps, and she did it with love. I never once heard Mamma complain. She was grateful till the end, which is hard to believe because her beginnings were no better than her end.

Mamma never really talked much about her life because there wasn't much to say. As far as she knew, her mamma was a hoe who threw her in a dumpster to die at birth. Some homeless bums found her and took her to the police thinking they could turn her in for some reward money. They should've known that no one cared about another colored baby being thrown away.

Mamma was considered a ward of the state, which meant the state would provide you with the basic necessities until the age of eighteen, and then you were on your own. The state could care less if you had training or direction. All that was important to them was at eighteen you were no longer their responsibility. Wherever you lived on your eighteenth birthday was your last known residence because on that next day, you were homeless. If you were raised in the system, you were well-aware your death sentence started on your eighteen Birthday.

Poor city planning had caused lots of homeless children on the streets, especially girls. They wandered the streets until a street hustler, pimp or drug dealer gave them a job, or they joined a gang which took them out of life's game completely. Their perception was that life was pointless. Their reason for existing was meaningless. There was no reason to follow the law or have moral values. All that was important was survival. Life on the streets was dangerous and chaotic. It was like living in a no man's land. Between the fights, killings and drug overdoses, no day was promised. They lived each day like it was their last.

Then one day fast talking, scheming Mammy showed up out of nowhere with the opportunity of a lifetime. She told them of a better way, that they could be somebody and that their lives meant something. Her words inspired some of them

to want to do better. She quickly became known as the Savior of the Street's Lost and Forgotten. She painted a picture of hope and success.

Her motivating speeches were so convincing she became their god. Those girls would have followed her anywhere. They needed something to hang on to, and they truly believed she was a good-hearted mamma-type, who would go the extra mile to save them.

Mammy's evil plot was so convincing that even the Mayor saw her as a Savior. He gave her a grant and ten condemned houses. She used this to create the largest non-profit organization in the city called *Loving Holms*. The Mayor saw *Loving Holms* as an asset to the city. He felt her program would clean up the unwanted garbage, homeless youth, prostitutes and drug dealers. He knew it would move them from his beautiful downtown to Mammy's newly formed neighborhood. As far as he was concerned, she had created a new dump site for all his social problems, and he gave her full authority over her newly formed community.

My mamma was one of the first to get a home and to believe her life was going to get better. Mammy had planned it all out, even a way to keep the girls under control. She used the one thing a mother would give her life for--- her child.

Mammy had taken in four foster boys and raised them to be just as evil as she was. The oldest was Earl, and then there was James, Steve, and Charles. They all soon became known as the daddies, the pimps of *The Hood*.

Charles was the youngest of the boys and was considered weak because he had a kind heart. He didn't believe in Mammy's plans and gave her opposition. When he laid eyes on my Mamma, he fell in love with her and wanted her. Mammy told him to promise Mamma the world, if she only had his baby. He won't do it. Charles was different, his spirit was a lot like Mamma's and they fell in love. Charles knew that if he got Mamma pregnant, it would be her prison sentence. He told her one day they would run away together to have a real family. So, Charles and Mamma pretended to do as told.

Then Mammy realized she was being tricked, because my Mamma never got pregnant. Mammy got real mad at Charles. She told his brothers to teach him a lesson. But, Charles was a

beast of a man compared to them, and they feared him. So, one night Mammy's husband Rubert came in, raped my Mamma, and I was born. After that, real reality unfolded very quickly for Mamma, and she understood the true intentions for her life.

During the nine months Mama was pregnant with me, they gave her food, medicine, clothes and whatever her heart desired. For a while, Charles still came by to check on her. But the second I was born, they rolled up the red carpet and replaced it with bars and a locked door for which they held the only key. Charles was no longer permitted to come by, and I became their leverage to control Mamma. If she refused to do exactly as she was told, Mammy would make threats on my life. Mamma loved me so much she protected me with her life.

The girls were charged room and board to live in their small shacks. If they did not reach their quota by the end of the week, it was tacked on to their debt with interest. So my mamma, like the other girls, became a hoe to pay off the debt she owed to Mammy, the biggest pimp of all. The once perfect community quickly became the One Stop Shop for all sick perverted sexual fantasies.

The girls had to do so many johns per night just to break even. It was almost impossible to have any extra monies. The debt owed to Mammy was so great you would never be able to pay it off. You literally sold your soul or sold your child into child slavery. During the day our neighborhood seemed normal to the average eye, but at night the air changed and in swept a strange mood. No child was allowed outside after dark.

Our house was like every other house in *the hood*. It was a two bedroom and one bath with a living room, dining room, and kitchen combo. We had exactly six pieces of furniture - two beds, a couch, kitchen table and two small dressers. In all the years of my mamma hoeing, this was all she had to show for it.

Many years have passed now, and I can feel a new breeze sweeping through. Everyone is gone. Alone I sit next to Mamma's cold dead body, wondering how I ended up here. One by one everyone left this place for something bigger and better, while I sat in the window watching the day to day horrors of life. I could have been like everyone else and left, but

I could never leave the one who sacrificed her life for mine---
my mamma.

My mamma was not like any of the other mammas on our
block. No matter how many times she was beaten or raped or
degraded, she had a smile and a loving spirit so great that even
the worst evil couldn't wipe it out. Even as she lies here dead,
she still manages to take with her the world's best kept beauty
secret-- Love. My mamma was the true meaning of love and
Mammy, Daddy nor those hateful heifers--- my aunties could
turn her heart.

Each little house held its own dark secrets. Those secrets
formed a cloud that hung over our ten little houses like thick
smoke waiting to snuff us all out. The beauty of a secret is, once
you let it loose, it can blossom into something beautiful no
matter how horribly it was unspoken.

Here everybody's mamma was your mamma too. We
obeyed them all. Although their lives weren't perfect, they still
seemed to keep up their morale. We called them all aunties,
although not all of our aunties were nice. Some you knew to
stay away from, especially the ones who weren't the motherly
type.

Before all the strange men came rolling in with their big
cars and fancy shoes, our aunties would be dressed to the nine,
walking up and down the street like it was a runway fashion
show. Each one showcased their nightly selection.

The others would cheer them on yelling from their
window,

"Go girl strut it, show'em what you got."

"Put a little more swing in that hip girl. Tonight is your
night." They yelled.

Oh…. I remember working nights were always a big deal
in our neighborhood. The cars would roll in and there wouldn't
be room to park. Our aunties could have the men in and out in
twenty minutes, and the money roll would be thick! But we
never had enough to eat or any new clothes to wear, because
once a week they would give it all to our Daddies--- every dime.
Then he would pay them their share. It was less than a
sharecropper's share.

You knew when night fell it was your mamma's work time. You went in your room, and you didn't come out until the morning. We didn't have babysitters because our neighborhood was no place for babies. We all came into this world standing on our own two feet. We learned how to fend for ourselves from day one. We became the true survivors.

There were four children close to my age Henry, Annie, Rodney and Mindy. Annie being the oldest girl had it the hardest. Although she was only two years older than me, you would have thought she was our mamma. She bossed us. She told us what to do and how to act. She even reminded us how worthless we were.

Mindy was the youngest. Mindy grew up so fast you would have thought she was the oldest, because the men got to her.

Henry and Rodney were the only two boys. Henry was four years older than me and was in charge when the Daddies were gone. Rodney, on the other hand, had to spend his life living in Henry's shadow. This caused Rodney to despise Henry.

Henry would boss poor Rodney just like he was told to do. Henry bossed us all. That was his job. I was the only one who understood Henry and his planned life. And I loved me some Henry! Everyone hated him, but they didn't see his heart like I did. He had to do what his daddy told him, or else his own life would be in danger.

Henry used to be short and fat, but over one summer Henry got fine. He grew tall and muscles popped out all over the place! I don't know if it was the hot sun giving off all that vitamin D or what, but Oh…….. What a difference a summer made for him.

I wanted to be the cookie that took a dunk in that tall glass of goodness! I think he felt the same way about me, because I'd caught him sneaking a glance at me through my living room window. I fantasized about being alone with him like in the fairy tales, when the prince comes and rescues the princess. Then they are whisked away in a magical carriage drawn by white horses off into the sunset and live happily ever after.

As my mind slipped in and out of reality from past to present thinking, darkness fell over the house. My life had happened so fast I was losing it. Tears of sorrow began to fall and overwhelmed me. All I could think about was my mamma, what did she do wrong? Life sometimes is so strange. It is better not to ask why, you just do what you are told.

Mamma would say

"What you don't understand, you can't explain."

Just thinking about her seemed to ease my troubled mind. Mamma did the best she could to make a home for all of us children in *The Hood*. She turned our perverted neighborhood into a village of love, where she was everyone's mamma. They all called her Mamma Jean. She was like a mother hen keeping all her young chicks safe. She took the little food we had, and stretched it to make sure everyone have something to eat that day. It not only filled your stomach, it made our dreadful lives seem a little normal.

Mamma loved us all. It was hard to make my mamma mad. However, if you did, my mamma could put a whoopin' on you and cuss you out, so fast for being "a fast ass monkey"---- as mamma used to call me if I even thought of a boy. She didn't have much to worry about when it came to me, the only boy I ever thought about was Henry. I knew he would come and find me one day and take me away from here. Because we had a bond that no one could break.

Mamma knew my secret, and I knew hers. Now my secret, about Syn, lies in the mind of my dead mamma, never to be spoken again. No matter how hard I try, I can't get that dreadful day out of my mind. The day so horrible, it took my voice from me!

It all happened early one morning. I heard mamma talking to James and Steve. James was Henry's daddy, and Steve was Rodney's daddy. I never saw them, but I recognized their loud, rude voices, which carried into my room and woke me up from a dead sleep. I had just turned twelve. I couldn't understand much. What caught my attention was that I heard my name. These men accused mamma of stealing their plates. Mamma pleaded with them telling them she didn't do

anything. I heard the men tell her that her debt would never be paid if she didn't come up with the plates. Mamma again told them she didn't have them.

Then I heard them say,

"Joyce's life will continue to pay the debt once your body lies dead in the ground."

Silence came over the room and soon they left. Later on that afternoon when Mindy and I were playing outside in the yard, James and Steve came to our house to talk to Mamma again. I saw their shoes as they climbed the stairs. We never looked up, we just kept playing.

As soon as the door slammed, we heard my mamma's body being thrown from one wall to the other, like she was a rag doll. They took turns beating Mamma and there was nothing I could do, but hope the best for Mamma. In our neighborhood you were expected to mind your own business, no matter what was going on. If you interfered, you might be next. The price you paid for your interference could cost you your life.

After a while, I could no longer hear the sounds of them beating on Mamma. I kept my head down, and my eyes fixed on the cracked walkway. I could hear their footsteps as James and Steve walked down the stairs. I could feel both their eyes locked on me. I knew that it was my turn and there was nothing I, or anybody else could do or say to change my soon fate.

With one quick swoop, I was swept off my feet, and they took me to the back of our house.

James looked at me like I was evil itself, and said,

"Joyce you were always the one to play the innocent roll like your mamma, so now you're going to get punished just like your mamma."

I looked over at Steve. He had the look of death all over him. He looked like if he didn't do what he was told, his card would be the next one pulled.

"Don't just stand there looking stupid, you know what's next!" James yelled to Steve like he was his puppet.

Steve acted like a robot and ripped off all of my clothes like I was a rag doll. I felt ashamed as they looked down at my little childlike, undeveloped body. In unison, they pulled off their belts.

I closed my eyes, and began praying. I thought if I didn't see the hits coming, they wouldn't hurt as much. But each hit, pained even more than the next. With all their force, they beat me and beat me, until blood flowed out of each welt. I fell to the ground in pain.

I kept my eyes shut. The beatings paused, and a sigh came over me. I thought the nightmare was over. But I should of known that the beatings were just the Appetizer before the Main Course. I heard the footsteps of two others, and then I felt them hold my legs opened.

I felt the cold air on my private. The cool air felt good on my wounds. Then I felt my small opening stretched, then ripped as one of them forced himself inside of me. The pain was numbed by the aching of my welted back being pressed into the dirt. As he rocked back and forth, I could feel the gravel underneath me cutting into my skin even more. I knew the daddies were evil, but why did they want me when they had all of the aunties to entertain them?

I opened my eyes, just so I could see which of the daddies had invaded me and stolen my precious flower.

MY HEART SANK!

To my surprise, it was my Henry, the boy from across the street. The love of my life, the one I believed someday would take me from this horrible place! Tears ran down his face, he was only thirteen.

James and Steve poked fun at him saying,
"Come on Jr. You can do better than that! Tear that tail up! If you can't do it right, we are going to have to step in and finish the job."

Henry closed his eyes to block out my face, but I wanted him to see me. I wanted him to feel what he was taking from me. I wanted him to carry the pains that the daddies had

21

caused in our lives. I bound all of my fears, pain, misery and hate, then forced them all into one loud scream. I belted out a scream so loud, it could reach the stars in the atmosphere. It took all the strength I had left.

As my scream pierced the air, the shock waves passed through them. For a brief time there was silence, as if the sound has stopped time. Right at that moment, Henry and I connected. My thoughts became his thoughts and his became mine. I felt his heart beat, as its beats were as mine. His thoughts were as clear as my own thoughts. The pain I felt became his pain.

I looked deep into his eyes, and my heart spoke to his heart,

"I understand you're being forced into this. Just because you're a boy didn't mean that you're suffering any less." "We shared the same destructive life, we endured the same horrors. This is the price we have to pay in order to survive."

Henry looked back down at me, and a peace came over him. Then the feeling of love flowed so deep, so warm and so complete inside me. It calmed my fears and soothed my pain. I knew what he gave me was all he had. He gave me his heart.

As soon as the last bit flowed, Henry jumped up and ran down the back alley with his pants dangling in the wind. I watched him as he disappeared through the dust. I rolled into a ball and drifted in and out of sleep. When I woke up a blanket was over me, and it was my comfort for the night.

I never spoke of that day again. In fact, I never spoke a word again. I just pretended it was all a terrible dream that somehow came true.

Out of the all aunties, Annie's mamma was the finest! She was mixed with Puerto Rican and Black and had the most beautiful long, curly hair. She had freckles that spotted her face just right, and her shape was the envy of all the aunties. She wasn't a tall woman, but her beauty made up for every inch she was short.

They would say,

"You could bounce a quarter off her ass, because she was so fine".

Annie's mamma never paid them no mind because she said that one day she was going to leave this place and be famous. She had an air about her like this life didn't affect her like it did the rest of us. She had hopes of better things. The negativity and jealousy of the aunties wasn't going to get her down. She stayed to herself, and she never talked much. But she was notorious for picking a switch from the nearest tree and wearing your ass out, especially if she saw you acting ghetto!

She didn't care who was there or where she was, she would snatch you by the arm, brace her knee in your back, and go to city till she got tired. I don't think there was a kid on the block, who didn't fall the victim to Annie's mamma.

It was a sad thing, when Annie's mamma left. She never said a word, not even to Annie. I guess she became famous and left for better things like she said she would. One day she was there, the next day she was gone. No one ever said a word about it. Annie was all alone and motherless and had to go and live with Mindy.

Mindy's mamma was the complete opposite of Annie's mamma. She didn't give a damn about nobody and nothing, except a cigarette and a glass of gin. She liked to sit in the dark, so she never opened a door or a window to let the fresh air come through the shotgun house. She never talked nice to no one, and the house was filthy. The only time Mindy was clean, was when she came to my house, and Mamma cleaned her up. She never fed Mindy, kissed or even hugged her, and Mindy's attitude reflected it.

Mindy was a hard nut to crack. It was because of all the hurt and pain she had experienced in her short young life. Mindy was my best friend. Although we never talked much, I still loved her.

I sat in the window and watched as Mindy and Annie grew closer and closer. They began spending more and more time together. They sat on Mindy's front porch looking through magazines or playing with makeup. They spent a lot of time pretending to be runway models strutting up and down the

sidewalk, like they were in front of an audience of thousands. I sat there in silence, while watching my best friend become best friends with someone else.

As time passed, Mindy went from a tall, lanky insecure little girl to a tall, beautiful, flawless bodied, upscale and confident young woman. While I sat in the window and remained the same scared, alone and hopeless girl. I stayed in my own world looking out the window. Right now, I wish I had my best friend Mindy back.

I remember she would climb into my bedroom window to get away from our Daddy Rubert.

Shivering from fear she would say the craziest things like,
"We two broke ass black heifers sharing a twin bed. We're both too afraid to leave for something better."
If I tried to say something positive like,
"We should be grateful our mamma's is working for us, so we can have a place to stay."
She would get so upset and scream!
"My mamma ain't doing anything for me. She is only out for herself."
"You always trying to find the good in a heifer. But as long as she pees between two heels, and her ass points to the ground, she better not ever let my name come out of her mouth."
Mindy was full of so much hate and anger. She was so tough. I felt she could take on the world alone and win! But I remembered when she lost it. That was the day they found Rubert dead behind Annie's house.

The day daddy died, he took a part of us with him. I never knew Rubert, because I was conceived like a dog for breeding. But Rubert and Mindy's mom was an item. I guess they had a lot in common, drugs and alcohol. Plus, they both made Mindy's life hell.

Mindy was so strong. I never could understand how she let Rubert do those horrible things to her. She acted like she was obligated or something. It's a mystery to me.

After he died, Mindy was invincible! Her chains of bondage were broken. She was free and nothing could stop her,

not even life itself. Mindy knew she was the beautiful one. Within days of Rubert's death, Mindy marched like a soldier on a mission right down our single lane street in broad daylight, got out of the gate and left this place.

I still remember looking in her eyes when she left. The expression on her face was peace, and I knew she realized life's beauty secrets. The day Mindy left, she didn't just escape with all of our dark secrets. She also took a piece of my heart with her. After all, she was my sister and one of the few people who seemed to understand me. She was the only one I had to talk to.

The years of silence became my prison box and with each new day it seemed to shrink, getting smaller and smaller. I could feel the walls crushing in on me. I wanted to scream so loud that the world would hear me and come to rescue me from this silent enclosed box. Instead, in silence, here I sit next to my dead mamma.

Mamma was never the same after that terrible beating the daddies put on her. They broke her leg. I tried to fix it, but the leg never healed right and stayed full of infection. Mamma was in a lot of pain and it limited her mobility. She sat most of the time. Her happiness came from rocking Lil' Syn in her lap.

One day the Daddies came. They began to say she was good for nothing, and she had a debt to pay. Then they took Lil' Syn from Mamma. Mamma, with all the pain she was in, ran after that long black car, until her legs gave out. She collapsed in the middle of the street.

I waited until it was dark and tried to drag my mamma's limp body out of the street. Henry saw my struggle and carried Mamma in the house and laid her in her bed.

The next day Mamma was a different person. It was as if her heart was taken when Lil' Syn was taken.

She would cry out at night
"Me, me it should of been me."

I wasn't much comfort to Mamma, because it was all I could do not to roll up in myself and die.

Mamma was full of grief, missing Lil' Syn. In all, I guess the weight of life got too heavy, she had a stroke and never got out of the bed again.

The men kept coming. So, I had to take her place, to keep a roof over our heads and a little food in the kitchen. I got to see first hand what Mamma tried so hard to shield me from all those years? For the next five years, I took care of Mamma during the day and entertained her long standing clients at night. The last thing Mamma said to me was she was sorry. Then she died. Death took with it our horrors and debt. They all passed away with Mamma. She was all I had. Once the last breath passed out of Mamma, I knew her death sentence was over. It was time for me to leave here and find my own way.

The day of Mamma's funeral was like the hoods reunion! The Daddies made the arrangements and paid for everything. They had it in a beautiful church, and the sweet smell of the thousands of flowers filled the somber sanctuary. Her casket was pure white like she was washed of all her sins. Mamma was dressed in a white silk gown with a headdress of pearls like she was ready to step right into the pearly white gates of Heaven. And, the most perfect peaceful expression graced her face.

I was proud to say that this woman lying here was my mamma. The huge sanctuary was packed with so many people, some I knew and a lot I didn't. I saw some of the Aunties and Daddies. Mammy was there with a dark skin, short man. I saw some of the kids I remembered watching as they played on their porch with their own families.

One by one they all came up to me to give their condolences. I tried to keep a strong face, but inside I was dying. I was angry.

"How did I let this happen to me?"

"How did I let my life go by and never be a part of it or enjoy the good in it?"

"Why did I stay so long?"

"Everyone's life seemed to be perfect, but mine. I sat in that window and allowed everyone to have a life except me."

Unexpectedly a tear escaped from the corner of my eye, I wanted to catch it before anyone noticed my pain. I reached into my purse to get a Kleenex and felt a warm hand on my shoulder. I looked up and there he was. Henry the love of my life.

"How are you?" His heart said in a gentle voice.
"I'm fine." My eye's answered, but my heart was devastated.
He gave me that look like,
"Yea right!"

I gave him a look back that said,
"Don't look at me like that." I said. "I'm fine."

Still looking at me with that same look his heart said,
"Joyce we all watched you every day sitting in the window. We all know that you are not fine. You were not fine then and you sure as hell are not fine now that Mamma Jean is gone."

Henry could see the tears swelling up in my eyes. He leaned over, gave me a hug and for the first time in my life I felt safe. I was in the arms of the one who made me the keeper of his heart.

Henry took on my burdens as we hugged. I broke down and I cried, until I had no more tears to cry.

Henry whispered in my ear,
"I will never let you go."

I raised my head from his tear soaked powder blue shirt and his multiple shades of blue silk tie making the perfect combination for his midnight blue silk-tailored suit. I was embarrassed for breaking down.

Henry looked me in my eyes and said,
"See I told you, you were not okay."

27

I was amazed that he knew me so well after all of these years. I could not hide how I was feeling from him.

"Thanks," my heart replied, trying to dry his soaked shirt with my snotty Kleenex.

He leaned over to me as if to reassure me, "You're fine."

As I continued to clean his shirt, he grabbed my hand. "Just please stop, I can clean it later,"

We both laughed.
Without even thinking my heart said,
"I miss you and I love you," His heart replied,
"I love you too, and I promise to never leave you again."

Henry became my rock and stayed with me.

I quickly gazed my eyes on a fast approaching Mindy. He turned around right in the nick of time to become a barrier between me and her.
"She has her nerve to come to my mamma's funeral." I thought to myself.

The whole time she was sick, Mindy never bothered, not even once, to come and see about her. No one did. And now, she is here like this makes all the years of neglect okay.
Henry grabbed Mindy before she got too close. Mindy looked me right in the eyes and as our gaze met, our hearts made peace.
My heart spoke,
"Hey Mindy how are you? You look great! How many years has it been? And who is this little princess hiding behind you?"

My heart was like a loaded automatic pistol shooting questions at her before she answered the next. I didn't want to show how weak, I was right now, so I tried to keep light of our first encounter.

Henry reached down and picked up a beautiful chocolate little toddler. The girl was in a pastel pink dress, with a crisp ruffled collar, little white socks, and the smallest pair of pastel pink patent-leather shoes. I had never seen shoes so small. When she looked at you with her big brown eyes, she made your heart melt.

"And what is your name?" Henry asked her.

To both of our surprise, she answered in the most perfect English

"My name is Angela, and I am my mommy's princess."

We all laughed at her response. I could see in Henry's eyes the longing for a child. He was entranced by her presence.

"She must be a handful," Henry said, while placing Angela the princess back to her royal floor.

"Yeah, she is, you never know what is going to come out of her little mouth," said Mindy.

She reached around Henry, gave me a hug and said,

"How are you doing Joyce?"

I could feel her guilt for never coming back, but I understood our neighborhood wasn't some place that you would want to come back to.

"I'm okay," my heart sounded as I nodded my head.

"Well, I'm glad to hear that. I just wanted to come and speak. You take care."

Her words were assuring and genuine.

"You too," I replied. "And take care of that little princess," my heart said while looking down at little Angela.

Henry and I watched as they both walked away looking for a seat on a crowded pew.

"I would have never seen that coming?" Henry said, shaking his head from side to side.

"What?" I asked.

"Mindy with a baby, she just didn't seem like the motherly-type." He replied. "Also, if my mind serves me

right, you and Mindy were tighter than a rash on a baby's ass. So what was that all about?" He asked.

"I thought we were talking about the baby not the relationship between me and Mindy." I replied instead. "You know things change and so do people." "Yea, I guess." He murmured. "But I often wondered, what could have ever happened to cause y'alls friendship to change."

"Now you are just meddling, mind your business." I answered. "Like I said before, people change."

I lowered my head and remembered when Mindy was five or so. She snuck over to my house and climbed in through my window for the first time. She did it time and time again until I just stopped locking my window. She would crawl under my bed and cry herself to sleep. It happened so often that I began leaving a folded blanket and pillow under my bed. Mamma thought that I had an imaginary friend that lived under there, but it was just Mindy's and my little secret. She finally stopped crawling through my window.

Sometimes when she was feeling sad, she would tell me about how she would wake up with his private in her mouth. How he made her to suck it until the stuff came out. She said sometimes it was okay because he would put his finger down in her private and she said it felt like heaven.

I remembered Rubert, and the day he died, how lost she was. He had her head so screwed up, she didn't know whether to love him, hate him, miss him, cry or be angry for not killing him herself. The things he did to her kept her mind in constant turmoil. One minute she was happy, then sad, and then angry sometimes. It was hard to peg her. You didn't know whether to laugh, cry or go kick some ass with her. But I accepted Mindy at face value, and we, I thought were friends.

Henry could tell by the look on my face that the sadness of it all was getting me down.

He put his arm around me and said,

"I'm sorry I brought it up."

"I sometimes wish I could forget our childhood memories, because they are more like nightmares than memories." I replied. I needed to change the subject.

"How is Rodney?" I asked, forcing myself to smile.

"Oh, he is fine. You will never guess who he married?" He answered.

I looked at him with no intention of trying to guess. He could tell I was not in the mood to play the guessing game.

"Okay, okay, I'll tell you — Annie."

My mouth dropped open!
"What? That old hoe! She landed Rodney--- the pimp?"

"Wow, you really are surprised, now why is that?" He asked, folding his arms across his broad chest waiting for me to tell the gossip.
"No reason I guess. I thought he'd never marry. I didn't think pimps got married." I replied, laughing with my heart.

"Didn't you know Rodney ain't a pimp anymore." He said. "And Annie ain't that same old hoe. Things changed for them. I don't know if they won the lotto or what, but they came into a large sum of money and are trying to change this whole game."

He continued,
"Rodney always wanted to be the number one son. Since that's never going to happen, he just gets his rocks off by making everyone's life miserable. He has become the thorn in my side, but I'm not worried because I will always be the HNIC."

Henry had such a smirk on his face, as he glared in Rodney's direction. When Rodney looked over in our direction,

31

I could tell their feelings for each other were mutual. I looked over to catch them both in a stare down contest. Annie was sitting so close under Rodney, you'd think she was his security blanket or something. It was like she was afraid someone was going to take that sorry ass excuse for a man.

I looked at her with pity, you can take the hoe off the street, but she will never enjoy one good night of sleep. It was a shame because she had always been the prettiest one. Henry could tell that we both had been caught up by their presence and we both focused back on our peaceful conversation.

Henry continued
"Where was I?"

He quickly gathered his thoughts like nothing had happened.
"They had a son some years ago I guess when we were kids. He must be about twenty or so now. His name is Eric. Annie gave him away like a puppy in a litter without even blinking an eye."

I shook my head and my heart said,
"There you go again, meddling."
He knew I had a thing or two to say about that hateful ass Annie, but it was my mamma's day, so I kept my feelings to myself.

Henry pushed himself closer to me.
"So what are your plans later?"
I looked at him and he sensed my situation.
Then said,
"Have yourself packed, I'll be there to pick you up about nine or so."
He paused for a moment, looking me up and down.
Then he said,
"Please dress to impress! I want you to meet some of my friends and although you are pretty, your attire is not. You need to handle that!" He said, pointing his finger on my dated black basic dress with a velvet trim and lace front.

"Or do I need to get Mindy to give you some pointers on how it's done?"

"Hell No, fool I know how to dress." I answered sharply. "I maybe not as fine as Mindy, but I'll be passable." I told him.

He looked at me in all seriousness and said,
"Look woman I don't just need you to pass, I need you to look fine if you are going! I can't have my woman going around with me looking all tired and any kind of way."

His response shocked me!
My heart replied to that shock.
"Your woman? Whoever said that I was your woman?"

"I did just now. Haven't you been listening?" He said.

"Is that anyway to ask a woman to be with you?" My heart said.

"Yea, it is when two people feel the same way and have the connection like we do, even if one of them is too scared to admit it. So I will save us both some time and move this relationship along. If I left it up to you, you would still be sitting in the window for the next five years watching everyone's life go by. I am here. I came back to save you from yourself. I am the one you are going to begin living life with. I am the one who loves you. I have loved you since that scream. It shook the neighborhood and changed my heart. Together we made Beauty and somewhere out there, I pray she knows she was made out of love." He whispered.

I couldn't believe it! He knew all this time! I thought our secret was in the grave with Mamma. So many days sitting in the window I wanted to tell him about our beautiful secret and to my surprise he knew all the time.

He looked at me and said,

"Yeah, I knew! Sometimes I would sit in my bedroom window and look at you looking out and I sometimes thought to myself. Is she thinking about me the way I am thinking about her?"

"Then I would see that blank look in your eyes and sometimes it made me sad because I couldn't make it better for you. Well, now I can. I came back to save you. You are my heart and without you I am nothing. I love you Joyce please chose me again?"

It seemed as if the weight of life was lifted off of my shoulders and for once, I was given the okay to feel and to love.
Without hesitation, my heart responded,
"What took you so long?"

We grabbed each other and from that moment on, Henry and I were inseparable. Henry filled the space that Mindy had left so many years ago.
We never made it out that night. We started where we left off, but this time, it was on our terms, not the terms of the daddies.

• ———————————————————————————— •

Life with Henry was great! He had such a great sense of humor and he made sure I smiled every day. I loved Henry, and I knew Henry loved me! There wasn't anything he wouldn't do for me. He was my protector, my lover and most of all, my friend.
Henry moved me out of the old neighborhood to the other side of the city where the houses were big and the yards were well-kept. Our home was the biggest one in the neighborhood with the long driveway. The whole estate was encompassed by a large cast-iron fence. The front of the property was protected by a cast-iron gate that opened on its own as soon as the car got close. The driveway led up to a mansion with more bedrooms than I could count, and just as many bathrooms. It was

decorated perfectly for a king and I was his queen. In all of my dreams I never thought that I would go from a two bedroom shack with one bath, to a mansion so big our whole hood could almost fit inside of it.

Henry had a special room made just for me. It was made of all glass so I didn't have to stay in one place to look out of the window. The whole room was the window. The house was staffed with a cook, a gardener and maids. I even had my own driver, because I never learned how to drive. Henry, to my surprise, was the Pastor of the big church where Mamma's funeral was held. It was Henry, who had arranged and paid for mamma's lavish funeral.

The first thing we did was get married. I became the First Lady of the biggest church in the city. I never thought anyone would marry me with all the baggage I had. But it is true, God got somebody for everybody! You just have to keep your heart open to receive the blessing.

Mamma always told me in life there are many roads to travel, so make sure you have the necessary provisions to whether the curves and the strength to endure the journey.

Being first lady at the church was easy, all I did was sit on the front pew, smile and look pretty. At the end of each service everyone would march around me, kneel and kiss me on the hand like I was a queen. I smiled and nodded as each one walked by. Henry was so protective of me. After their parade was over, he would come down from the pulpit and escort me to a special room made just for me. I would stay there until he was done talking to the men about church business.

I never kept anything from Henry, but sometimes I wondered what he was keeping from me. Henry had a way of blocking me out of his thoughts. The things he wanted to keep secret, he kept secret.

Sometimes we get so caught up in life we never make accommodations. If ever the bottom drops out and you're left sitting there hanging out on a limb with no opinions--it's rough.

The bottom had already fallen out of my life once, and Henry picked me up. I thought if it ever happened to me again, I might not be so lucky this time. So, I had a cushion, a nest egg, just in case. If Henry had something to hide, I needed an escape route too.

We both wanted a son, but after trying, and trying again, I never got pregnant. We sure enjoyed trying, but still nothing happened.

Syn was conceived under so much pain and anger. I begin to believe my soul closed my womb, so that love could ever be taken from me again. I knew loosing Syn bothered Henry. It bothered me too, although we would never say anything about it.

Out of all the things in my life I regret, the one thing I regret most was never talking about Syn or even try to find her. We both wanted to bring up her name but the memories and the pain we both felt the day she was conceived, were too much to bear. The one small blessing we did have, had become the big elephant that wedged itself between us. All the prayers we prayed and tears we shed, we never could get over the loss of Syn.

Henry and I tried to fill our spare time with meaningless activities to keep our minds occupied. I found a love for reading, while Henry spent a lot of his time in his private study doing whatever he did in there. I was never allowed to go inside. I didn't mind because after all, he had a life before I ever got there. When we did leave the house, we visited the church members. At least, I thought they were our members. We went to their "high-siditty"houses. Ate their little sandwiches, and drank some nasty tasting wine. None of the ladies had much to say to me, so I just sat next to the window until Henry was ready to go. Like always they came over to me to show respect. They bowed and kissed my hand.

One night we went to a church gathering. Like always, no one really spoke. So I looked for a quiet place next to the window. This house was beautiful, different from the others and decorated to the nine. The oversized windows were covered with big purple and gold swag and jabot curtains with so many pleats you couldn't tell where one began and the other one ended. The winter white carpet was so plush that my shoes sank with each step. But your footprint quickly disappeared, as you glided across the floor.

The room was divided by a brass spiraling staircase that stood in the middle of a day room. It was the perfect place for a formal gathering. There was hired help serving the fifty or so

guest. You could tell that it was a very private affair, because the conversations were kept at a whisper and everyone was gathered in their small huddles of less than four. I knew I was out of my league and wandered around until I found a nice cozy sitting area with two wing back chairs surrounding an antique table. On the table sat the most beautiful figurines of a man and woman in African attire. A huge flower arrangement sat on the back side of the table with fragrant fresh cut flowers in rich shades of pastels. I sat there admiring them. They kind of reminded me of the wild flowers that manage to survive in the cracks of the sidewalk of our run-down hood.

As I reminisced about the past, a little girl came and sat in the empty chair next to me. My heart knew her innocence and I spoke.
"Hi, how are you?"
She looked up at me with tear-filled eyes and in a low voice and said,
"Mamma says it's time to go to bed and I don't want to go to bed yet," she began to cry.
My heart fell and responded,
"Oh, don't cry, when you go to sleep, that's when God has a chance to sprinkle beauty on you. Don't you want to be pretty?"

Her little face lit up and a small smile came over her petite chocolate brown face.
I looked at her again and realized that it was Mindy's little girl, Angela.
Surprised my heart said,
"Hi Angela, you don't remember me, but I met you when you were a very little girl. My name is Ms. Joyce and I knew your mamma when she was a little girl just like you."

She looked at me in amazement and replied.
"When you met me was I pretty?"
"Of course you were!" I answered.

She sat back in her chair soaking in the compliment, not even the slightest mention about me knowing her mother. She's a little Prima Donna just like her mother, I thought to myself.

A few minutes went by and she looked up and saw her mother Mindy standing behind my chair. Angela jumped up and began pulling on her mother's hand to get her attention.

"Mamma this lady said I was pretty. Am I pretty?" She asked.

Irritated of her child's disobedience Mindy replied, "Of course you are! You look just like your mamma. I have been looking for you all over this house little girl! Didn't I tell you to get to bed?"

She looked at her mother satisfied with her response that she was pretty and went upstairs to bed. I stood up and was face to face with Mindy.

At first I could tell she was little stunned.

"Mindy," I asked in a low voice.

"How are you? She replied,

"Better." I kept my answers short, so not to prolong the conversation.

I was so hurt from the way our lifelong friendship was so easily ended. Both of us were guilty and were to blame, but our pride was not going to let neither one of us break down and admit it.

Before the encounter got too awkward, I saw Henry out the corner of my eye. Henry being Henry came in to rescue me like always. But this time, I wished he hadn't, because there was so much my heart wanted to say to her. After all, she was my sister and the only living relative I had. I wanted so badly to tell her that I still had the pillow and blanket under the bed waiting for her, but Henry managed to wedge his thick stocky frame between us.

"Hey ladies!" Henry said, reaching out his big strong arms, catching us all in one big huddle and hugging us until it was hard to breath.

38

He looked to the ceiling as if to thank God for allowing him to be positioned between us.

"How lucky am I to be in the presence of the two most beautiful women in the world." Henry said.
We blushed!

He released Mindy and grabbed me around the waist and pulled me even closer.

"Oh Henry you still the same best ice cutter around!" I whispered.

After all these years, Mindy still was the most sarcastic woman ever. She looked at me, then back at Henry.

Mindy nudged him to get his attention.
Then asked,
"Henry, can I speak to you for a minute over here for a second?"

Henry released his Kung Fu grip from around my waist and followed Mindy without any resistance.

I sat back down and pretended to stare out of the dark window.

Mindy never could whisper.
She spoke to him peering over at me from time to time and said,
"Henry I thought the *Associates* made themselves clear about the code rules. No outsiders are invited to the meetings."

Henry looked back to see if I was paying attention. I kept my eyes on the window.

As soon as the coast was clear, he replied,
"You know that Joyce ain't going to tell no one! You know better than anyone that Joyce can't talk. Plus, she is my wife not an outsider, and where I go she goes. I can't

39

believe you Mindy! You guys were thick as thieves when y'all were coming up! I don't know what happened between you, but I sure do wish you both would squash this whole childish feud."

She looked at him unshaved by his reconciliation comments and stayed committed to her agenda.

Mindy replied,
"Right now the *Associates'* project is the most important piece of my future. I don't want to stand behind a styling chair for the rest of my life. I have a responsibility to my husband. May he rest in peace. I need to rebuild the beauty school in his honor. It's the least I can do, and the *Associates* are the ticket to my success. I am working on gaining their respect. They are the ones with the money and they are the ones who are going to take over this city now that the *Partners* have grown weak. If you play your cards right, you could hit the jackpot too. I've heard through the grapevine that the *Associates* have their eye on the church and want to go into business? Henry you can't be the king forever, and you had better pay attention on which way the wind is blowing. The old way of the *Partners* will soon be blown away to make room for the new---*the Associates*. Right now, I like the feel of new fresh air."

Henry was always his own man, not a follower and I could feel the tension in his voice.

He said,
"Look Mindy, when you came to the *Partners* about your plans for *Beautiful One School of Cosmetology*, I told you I would give you an answer. Now I think you are playing us in the middle, so you can get what you want? I don't like being played. I'm no one's punk, so don't throw the *Associates* in my face like a threat! What? Am I supposed to be scared and join up with them because they are the new kids on the block? Remember, I am part of the original. I am the block. If you really wanted to honor

your dead husband, the *Associates* should be the last
people you should want to climb into bed with. You
might end up being their hoe."

He murmured angrily.

"If you don't build your school on a firm foundation, it
will just crumble and fall. The *Partners* are still very much
alive and stronger than you think. The *Partners* don't need
the *Associates*, the *Associates* need the Partners. I can see
right through your manipulative plan, but please do me a
favor. Remember who I am, and I don't owe you
anything." He snapped at her.

He continued.

"The *Partners* control this city. Even if you get the
funding, we give the say so if the school ever opens." He
fired off.

Henry could feel their conversation was gaining attention from
the other guest and he softened his tone. As he calmed down,
he said.

"Look Mindy none of our lives were great growing up.
Truthfully, it was pretty bad, but we all manage to grow
up in that hell hole and become something. I know how
you lived! How you were treated like a dog that lived in
its own mess! So quit the spoiled kid act! Drop it! You
don't play that part well anymore."

"If I help you", he continued, "It's not because I am scared
of the *Associates* or looking to give in to satisfy your selfish
needs. I will help you because this community needs a
school, and as long as I am a man of God, I fear no man or
the *Associates*. As far as the Associates wanting to go into
business with me, I am not broke! I worked for everything
I have, so please don't think you or anybody else makes
rules or plans for me and mine!" He said, looking her
directly in the eyes.

Henry's face was solid and his words were unshakable.

"If you still want the *Associates* to fund your venture, you
are on your own. Do you even know the members that sit

on the board of the *Associates*? Your so called new friends or business partners? The ring leader might surprise you? You need to ask some serious questions like, why they are being so generous to you anyway? What are you going to owe them in exchange for their 500 hundred thousand dollar donation? Who asses are you going to have to kiss? What secrets are you going to have to tell to get what you want? Right now I think you should be more concern with what you've gotten yourself involved with and not my wife Joyce."

Mindy looked back at him and was speechless, she was so used to bullying people to get her way, but the way Henry was handling that ass, she knew who not to mess with --- and that one was Henry! His new found love for the Lord changed his past life and how he dealt with people.

Mindy's voice changed to a business tone, realizing that she had lost her leverage.

"So can I still expect an answer about the permits?" Mindy asked in a submissive tone.

Henry replied, noticing her surrender,

"Like I said before, who you chose as friends is up to you. You'll get a call next week sometime."

Henry turned his attention from Mindy, then walked up to me with a sexy swagger and tapped me on the shoulder saying,

"Babe you ready to go?"

I looked at him and could read the rage in his eyes.

"Yes love, whenever you are." I said, smiling.

He smiled at me and gave me a warm kiss on my forehead.

"You stay pure baby that's what I love the most about you. You know how to be a lady at all times."

He turned once more to see Mindy absorbing our affections.

You could see the envy all over her face. I made sure she saw me as I gave him another kiss.

I put on a sarcastic smile, the kind of smile that says, "I know you wish you were me heifer!"

Then I sashayed to the door and waited for Henry to say his goodbyes. We exited as a fortified team. I was so proud to say he was my man. Henry opened the car door and I got in.

Once we were both inside the car, Henry closed his car door and I thought I had entered into War World III! He was cursing, yelling and pounding on the steering wheel. I sat as still and as quiet as I could. I didn't want to become an innocent casualty caught in the crossfire, by this one-sided war.

I had never seen this side of Henry and I was afraid. It took about ten minutes or so before he calmed down. He looked at me and I felt the air in the car changed like a bad omen was hovering over us. "What's wrong babe?" I asked quietly.

He looked at me in a disturbed way and replied. "I think I've made a deal with the devil."

I let out a nervous chuckle to help ease the tension. "It can't be that bad. I know Mindy hasn't always made the best choices, but what on earth could she be involved in that is so bad? I asked.

Henry dropped his head, then said.
"There is so much you don't know. So many things I have hidden from you, but now I am against the wall. I think they are trying to frame me, and I don't know what to do Joyce! I have failed us."

Henry broke down into tears, then he laid his head in my lap. I stroked his head.
"Baby everything is going to be okay. I'm here for you! Just tell me what you want me to do?" My heart said in a nurturing voice.

Henry whispered,

"There is nothing I can do! There is nothing you can do! You don't understand. This is bigger than the both of us. If I tell you Joyce, you have to keep it secret forever. If you ever talk again or mention it to anybody, your life will be in danger. I don't care if it's your best friend. That person might be in involved, and your life will be in danger."

I didn't know what to say. I wanted to help, but I also didn't want to be involved. I just wanted to sit in my window and live in my fantasy land. I looked deep into his eyes and saw the seriousness. He needed me.

So, I said

"Babe you know you can tell me anything and your secret will be safe with me."

Henry sighed a gasp of relief.

"You just don't know what this means to me. I feel like I am living two separate lives, one with you, and the other life I have devoted to the *Partners*." He said.

I looked at him and said,

"*Partners*, who the hell is that?"

Henry looked at me puzzled. He knew I was totally clueless to the life that had been going on around me all of the time. Sometimes you have to shield yourself to keep from being caught up and swept away with all the chaos in your life, and my shield was my silence.

He knew to handle me with caution because my heart couldn't take much more.

"Let's just go home, where I know it is safe and I will tell you all about it." He said. "I hope you are well-rested because we might be up all night."

On the way home my mind raced with questions. I couldn't wait to get into the house. Whatever it was, I was ready because the suspense of Henry's secret was eating me

alive! His secret was the other part of Henry that I didn't know. I wanted to love all of him, not just the part he revealed to me.

The Henry, who spoke to Mindy is the Henry I had never met. It was like being married to a man with a split personality. He was only letting me see the best of him. If I was going to really love him til' death do us apart, I needed to know who I was married to. All the sides. The good or bad.

Henry took my hand and led me to his private office. Once inside, I knew Henry knew a different God from mine. He dimmed the light and we sat at a table with our arms resting on it holding hands facing each other. I felt like I was in a horror film, sitting in the dark waiting for the villain to pop out at the least expected moment.

Henry began to chant as if to drum up unwanted spirits.

"Humm dunn dunn dunn humm dunn dunn dunn," over and over.

His body swayed from side to side as he repeated the chant in an eerie tone so high-pitched that it burned your ears. His deep bass moans sent vibrations through the room and fluttered your heart. Shadows appeared to be coming from the walls, gliding, moving about, passing through one another as if to communicate the events taking place.

I kept my eyes locked on Henry, to keep me from feeling alone and scared. Then in one blink of an eye, his face lost all expression and his eyes rolled to the back of his head. Only the whites of his eyes showed. I knew Henry was gone. A strange female spirit came into him and changed his whole persona.

I was entranced, filled with a paralyzing trepidation. I wanted to run away and get out of there. I wanted to forget it ever happened. Whatever Henry was into, I wanted to be separated from it. But part of me was tired of always being in the dark. Not knowing my past, who I really was or what was going on was eating me up. So I decided, if I had to enter into the depths of Hell to find my true identity, I was willing and ready to go.

I cleared my head of any thoughts and freed myself from the once felt fear. I allowed the spirit to speak to me. She was

massive and seemed to fill all the space of the room, but was still small enough to sit in front of me. Her eyes were large, dark, empty holes, they showed like a picture screen. Her lips moved, but her face never had an expression. I couldn't say if she was pretty or not because she looked like someone from another world.

When she began speaking, her voice sang like a lullaby. I felt drunk with sleep as I drifted into a daze like a dream.

She spoke the history of generations past.

"I am Zota the princess of clarity. I am the doorway of the forgotten. I am the avenger of wrongs and the holder of secrets. I was awakened because of the death of the powerful voodoo priests Asela. She was killed by Mabel, also known as Big Mama, your grandmother. Mabel came to her in the quest for power. Asela told her that she needed to have a sacrifice. Mabel's was selfish and refused to give up anything of her own, so she killed Asela in cold blood and offered her still beating heart to the spirits. She left behind two children, Samuel and Barbra. Because of her cruel act there was a debt that needed to be paid. All of her generations will be cursed, until it is paid."

"Mabel was the daughter of a poor sharecropping family. She was loved, but nothing was ever good enough. She was never satisfied. Her father, desperate to please her, gave all the family had to make her happy. Mabel was still not satisfied and ran away to the big city to make a better life for her."

"When she arrived, she realized life wasn't as easy as she believed it to be. She was homeless living on the streets and begging for food. Until one day a stranger asked her to give him a wet tip. Mabel was unaware what it even meant, until the man pulled out his privates and urged her to put it in her mouth. In exchange, he gave her fifty dollars. She had never seen so much money. Before long she had a clientele. She gathered some girls, got an old

house and opened a gambling hall and hoe house. She
was happy until one day some of the men got out of hand
and raped her. This is when she realized no matter how
much money you have, as a women you are still weak and
vulnerable in the sight of a man."

"Mabel became pregnant from the rape and had a baby
named her Joyce, that's who you are named after. Joyce
was raised right along with the hoes. As soon as Joyce
was of age, she became pregnant with your father Rubert."

"Joyce hated Rubert. She turned to a life of heroin and by
the time she was twenty-five she was dead. Mabel was
forced to raise Rubert. He started calling her Big Mama.
She raised and trained him in the business."

"Mabel still was not happy and went to Asela, who was
working as a fortune teller to support herself and her two
small children Samuel and Barbra. When Mabel asked
Asela how could she obtain power, Asela told her she
would have to sacrifice something dear to her to the Grand
Master. If the Grand Master accepted her sacrifice, he
would grant her great power in exchange. Mabel became
angry with her response and killed Asela in cold blood.
She felt she had given up enough, and she was not willing
to give up anything else."

"After Mabel killed Asela, she realized Asela was more
than just a fortune teller. She was a powerful Voodoo
priestess. The spirits appeared and gave Mabel an
ultimatum in change for her life. She had to raise Samuel
and Barbra. Then all of the power that she wanted would
come from the powers given to the children. Samuel was
given the gift of reproduction and Barbra was given the
gift of persuasion. She agreed and raised all the children
together."

"Mabel made the children into her slaves. They all called
her Big Mama. When they were young, they did all the
chores in the house. Once the children were old enough,

they plotted an escape. Big Mama found out about their plans. She threatened to kill them, but they begged for their lives. They told her how she could have unlimited power of her own, if she would agree to let them go. They told her their powers were in their blood. She cut their wrists and drank their blood, but it didn't give her power. However, it did form a bond with them. Together they became the *Partners*, one could not survive without the other."

"Mabel realized there was more money to be made by using the powers of Samuel and Barbra. Samuel had a perfect plan to establish *"Loving Holms"* for girls and *"Boy's to Men"* for boys. Barbra went to the Mayor and used her powers to convince and persuade him to give her a two block radius of old abandon houses. Then she went to the group home and convince girls who were about to be eighteen to go with her. She told them she had training available for employment, and she would give them a place to stay. Rubert got some young boys hustling on the streets and taught them the pimping game. From that point on, they became 'the daddies or pimps' to the young girls."

"The boys did what they were told. Rubert saw how weak and defenseless the girls were and became their king. He controlled their every move like puppets on a string. He made them his own harem. He lay with them all, except Jean, who was the strong one. So instead, Rubert raped her to show off his power. She became pregnant with you."

"The other girls got pregnant too. However, because of all the sleeping around, no one knew who fathered whom. When Big Mama found out about these actions, she was outraged. She knew her only cure was passed down through her blood line. Big Mama became more evil and vengeful. She no longer cared about what happened to the young girls or the daddies. Rubert's cruelty became a relentless reign, which lasted until he died."

"Samuel and Big Mama's evil grew strong. Neither Barbra nor Rubert could contain them. One day Samuel sat alone in deep thought on how he could make lots of money. He created a set of counterfeit money making plates. When he saw how they worked, he realized he could create anything he thought about. He was convinced, if Big Mama had all the money she wanted that she would release them. Their partnership would end, and they would be free. Then, they could burn down the "*Loving Holms*" project and walk away free."

"When Rubert found out about Samuels plans, he took his granddaughter. He gave her to Big Mama as a slave and to protect his bloodline. He believed Big Mama had no idea who she was, but she did."

"For Samuel, burning down "*Loving Holms*" was a perfect plan. Neither he nor Big Mama cared about the lives that would be lost. His mind had become so clouded from Big Mama that he no longer valued life he just wanted to be free. Samuel gave the plates to Rubert, but before Rubert could deliver them to Big Mama they were stolen. Samuel didn't believe they were stolen. He believed that Rubert was being greedy and wanted them for himself."

"When Big Mama still refused to give Samuel and Barbra their freedom, Samuel became outraged and killed Rubert. Big Mama never knew who killed Rubert and was devastated. She didn't know who to trust, or who to believe? Big Mama was growing weak. She knew if Samuel was made head of the *Partners,* she might be the next one to be killed. So she made Henry the leader of the *Partners,* because his heart was so pure."

"Your and Henry's daughter Synthia, is the true heir of the "*Partners.*" Only she has the power to change the evil the *Partners* have created. She has the bloodline of Big Mama and the only living leader of the *Partners,* Henry."

SYLVIA HARDIE

"Barbra decided to get Samuel as far away from Big Mama and Rubert as possible. She used her powers her gift of persuasion and placed a thought in Big Mama's mind that Samuel and she were dead. Then she used her powers to change Samuels mind into new thoughts. They started a new life unable to be found by either Big Mama or Rubert."

"After Rubert was killed the plates were never found. The rumor was Sugar Cat stole them from Rubert. She was killed. Still the plates were never found. Barbra thought Rubert gave them to your mamma, and they were hidden in your house. Now that your momma is she's dead, the secret dies with her. She was the last to know the secret. Now, fifteen years have gone by and everyone is still looking for the plates, you have the secret buried in your mind, and it's time that the truth is told."

In one instant all kinds of memories went through my head. My whole life was playing back to me. It was like putting together an intricate puzzle. Now, I had all of the missing pieces. I looked at all the parts of my life as a whole. So many things that never made sense, now played like a movie with edited scenes.

It was all making sense now. I played it back in reverse to get a better understanding of it. I thought Sugar Cat left because she wanted more for herself. But she was killed. That explained why Annie went to live with Mindy. That's why they got so close, Annie didn't have anybody else.

When Rubert died Mindy was inconsolable, she had a secret and was too scared to tell. I remembered how Rodney used to look at Henry. There was so much anger and resentment he carried in his heart for Henry. Rodney felt the birthright of *the hood* should go to him, but Rodney had his own secrets. I remembered the night Annie and Rodney left. Annie had her baby, and Mindy's mamma gave it to one of the Daddies. He took it away. Rodney was waiting for her to have the baby, so they could leave.

The baby had been gone about two months or so, when they left. There was a full moon that night. However, the moon was different this night. It shined on the neighborhood like the sun on a bright summer day. No one was out that night, except Rodney. He was tinkering under the hood of his new used car he had just bought.

When he closed the hood of the car, I had a clear view of the car. It was all packed up like he was going on vacation or something. He went to his trunk and got out a shovel. He then walked over to his mamma's flower garden, carefully picked up the flowers and set them to the side. He began digging a deep hole. He almost disappeared into the ground, he dug so deep. After a while, he climbed out of the hole with a briefcase. He dusted it off, set it to the side, filled the hole back up and carefully placed his mamma's flowers right back so neatly you never would know there was just a hole there.

Then Rodney took the briefcase and threw it in the back of the car. Rodney looked around, with a paranoid look on his face, to see if anyone saw him. He looked straight into my window. I leaned back so he couldn't see me. I knew whatever was in that briefcase was something special, because he had a look on his face like he was the new lottery winner.

Rodney thought no one saw him but I did. I was in the window. He then drove over to Mindy's house and tapped on the window. Soon after, there came ole' fast-tailed Annie. They got into the car together and drove away. I don't think Annie knew about the briefcase. Once the memory was revealed to me, I blinked my eyes and Zota was gone. Henry was sitting in front of me again.

The room became bright again and the fear of life I once felt was gone. I looked deep into Henry's eyes and poured the whole story out to him just like it was on replay to me.

Henry jumped up in anger,
"Joyce, are you sure it was a briefcase?" He asked.

I was shocked by his response, making me question myself.
"Yes," I responded, by nodding my head up and down.
"Was it black with a gold trim?" He asked.

"Yes." I replied.

Henry sat down like he was Sherlock Holmes, and the world's greatest mystery had just been solved. He never once mentioned the events of the spirits or Zota. I wondered if Henry was even aware of the demons that live inside of him?

Henry's excitement was intense as he continued to ask me questions.

"Joyce, are you sure? Are you really sure?" He repeated over and over, as if I didn't understand the importance of my new revealed secret.

"Joyce the briefcase holds the greatest gift for any poor or rich man for that matter. In the briefcase, there were some steel plates for making counterfeit money. Many lives have been lost and sacrifices made over those plates. Sugar Cat and Rubert lost their lives for those plates. Your mamma and you were beaten over those plates, and Rubert had me..."

Henry's words became thick and his voice cracked as he bowed his head to shield me from the pain on his face.

"Rubert had me to rape you, my one true love. He deprived us of our youth, our innocence. Everything was taken from both of us. When the plates came up stolen, everyone was a suspect. He beat me every day out of frustration over the missing plates. And, the things he did to my mamma, she was never the same."

"Rodney sat back watching all the pain and destruction he had created, knowing he had the plates all along. When Rubert lost the plates, a hit was put on his life. He already knew his days were numbered, and soon after he was dead!"

I sat still, unable to understand how Henry was so unaware of the conversation I had with Zota. If Zota was inside of him, why he was acting like everything was so new to him?

Henry was right. He did live two separate lives. This man that I loved so and would give my life for, is just the host for demons and secret things that should be forgotten.

I began to have doubts about Henry's true intentions for me. Did he love me or were the spirits just using me to get the information that is trapped in my head? Do they think Big Mama's secrets are trapped in me too, because I carry her blood.

I felt faint and betrayed I didn't know what to think. I couldn't separate what was real from present to past truths. The weight of the truth was too heavy to bear and rendered me paralyzed. I never knew what was in the briefcase. I just knew it was something worth burying down so deep you needed to have a shovel to dig them out.

I was happy Henry knew who had the plates, but now that he knew he was just like the ones before him greedy and ready to kill for them.

Rodney knew it was just a matter of time before his secret was revealed. If he knew Henry was the holder of the secret, what would he be willing to do to keep them? Kill my Henry? Was Henry's life now in danger? I looked at Henry. I could see the turbine wheels of his mind turning the expression on his face. He looked like something evil and praying for peace wasn't what he was thinking. Revenge was what was on his mind.

I leaned over to hug Henry, but his body was hard and cold. This was nothing like the Henry that held me close on so many cold nights.

I looked into his eyes, my heart spoke

"Are you in danger? You're not going to confront Rodney, are you? If you do, who is going to protect you? Can't you just go to the *Partner*s, whoever they are, and tell them who's got the plates? That way our lives can go back to normal."

He looked at me like I was a dizzy blond that didn't get the joke. Henry stood up and stretched out his frame. His demeanor and his voice changed. It was like the devil with a sheep's cloak now removed.

He said intensely.

"You still don't get it Joyce! You have got to start seeing life for what and who it is. I am the *Partners!*"

His words filled the room and took my breath.
"This power was given to me. It is my birthright after Rubert was killed. The torch was passed to me. I am the head of the *Partners*. I am the one who decides who lives or dies. I decide what business will succeed or fail. Who will win the elected positions and who will lose. I run this city."

I looked at him. Zota was right. Big Mama had sacrificed her soul and made a pack with the devil. Henry was her partner.

In desperation, my heart spoke,
"But, you are a man of God." I remembered why Big Mama gave him the birthright because he had a pure heart.

Henry's demeanor changed.
He now said in a humble tone,
"With the help of the Lord."

His head hung now, more humbled like he had to remind himself, who was the true owner of his soul.

He continued,
"God is the one who keeps the balance, and who keeps my heart in the right place."

The way he said it was like it was rehearsed. It seemed like he had said this many times before. My heart dropped with unbelief.

How could it be? How? All of the horrors, all of the disappointments and all of the oppression that the *Partners* stood for, he also stood for the same. My man, the love of my life, was this devil!
Henry was right. Life was beginning to be too real for me! How could I just sit quietly in my own silence living in a world

of fairy tales and rainbows when right before my eyes stood the Alpha of all Hell's secret.

I looked at him still confused. My eyes asked him with a timid eyebrow raised,
"If you are head of *the Partners,* why are you so worried about what Rodney will do?"

He looked at me in fear.
Then he said,
"I cannot let the demons take full control of me, I have to fight every day just to keep the dark side of me from taking over. As long as I have a divided spirit, I am too weak to withstand Annie, the *Associates,* and the spirit who made the plates in the first place. Those same spirits now possess the Mayor, Chief of Police and many business owners. They are all corrupt and evil. I have managed to keep the peace in the city by putting them in office. In exchange, they agreed not to kill our daddies and Mammy. Because what they really want, is the money making plates."

He continued,
"They are hard-core killers. They are the ones who killed Sugar Cat and Rubert. They are known as the *Associates.* If they think I have had those plates all of this time, I would hate to think of what they would do to me. What I don't understand is, if Rodney has the plates, and he is a part of the *Associates,* why is Rodney accusing me of having them? Unless, the *Associates* don't know Rodney has been hiding the plates all this time. Then he knows he is a dead man walking. So he is trying to frame me. This way it will take the heat off of him."

Henry took a deep breath and kept talking.
"If the *Associates* think, I have been hiding the plates all of this time. It would be considered as the ultimate betrayal and is punishable by death. Rodney knows this that's why he is trying to frame me. He knew all the time the power the plates had! Rodney's selfish-ass who never

cared about anyone but himself. He knew by taking those plates the whole hood would be in danger. All the lives that were lost, and the people who were hurt over those plates! I wish Rubert had never brought such an evil to our community." He sighed.

"Now, Annie is the ring leader of this whole lie." I whispered to myself, "That evil heifer!"

He ignored me and continued,
"Rodney was never very smart to plan such a scheme, but Annie was always smart and witty. She said that she would do anything to get out of the *hood*. Now it is all making sense! Rubert told Sugar Cat about the plates. Before she could get them, Rodney stole the plates and hid them in the garden. He knew all the time someone would have to pay. They sat back and let Sugar Cat die, then Rubert, and now me. If I'm dead, then the birthright is passed to him, and they win. They will have it all the plates and all the power. I can't let that happen! I can't let Rodney and Annie run their course of destruction. I, with God's help, will keep the balance. I am the Pastor of the largest church in the city. I try to make it right for everyone who grew up in the *hood* by giving them whatever their dreams were. With funding from the *Partners,* I was able to fund the church, in return I used it to launder dirty money for the *Partners*."

"Now Mindy wants a beauty school. She is asking the *Partners* for the funding. In exchange she will have to do something to benefit the organization, no matter how wrong it is. That's how this whole thing works. It's pure evil. It's the devil."

"Rodney wants to have power and rule over everything, and he is willing to sacrifice his own brother. Framing me is the plan. He can no longer hide it. They need a scapegoat to explain where the money is coming from. They think they are going to use the church. I'm not going to make it that easy. They are going to have to fight me

one on one, face to face." Henry said in a firm and hollow voice.

I told him,

"Think Henry. Think. What is your next plan?"

I sat there watching Henry speak gibberish as he held his own one-sided conversation with himself. I wished I could help him, but right now my input wouldn't be enough. Henry was fighting for his life! If Rodney and Annie get away with their plans, my Henry will be dead, and I can't live without him.

Henry looked over at me deep in thought. He could tell that I was affected. He calmed his tone and wrapped his tender arms around me. Like always, he changed back into the man I knew him to be. Or should I say the man I wanted him to be.

Henry turned out to be the best actor ever. True, the deceit and betrayal Rodney and Annie had done over the years was unbelievable, but Henry's role in it all was unforgivable. Henry knew better, he was a man of God for Christ sake!

Where is that faith he preached about every Sunday, or his favorite quote I'm leaving it all in God's hands? Henry had not changed. He just figured out how to play the hustle game.

Why didn't I question more? I saw all of the signs! The big house, the fabulous cars, and more money than any Pastor would ever have. The church with no mortgage, the way the members would parade around us, kneel and kiss our hands like we were royalty.

Then, like a pile of bricks being dropped from the sky, it hit me. Everything he told me was true. He was the king of this city. He ruled it all, and all of the power did belong to him. And with one call Rodney and Annie would be dead.

I knew that there was more to this story, but I was not going to sit around to watch how it all ended. This was not my war. Henry was, who he was, and that was never going to change.

Like he said,

"Anytime you take a gift from the *Partners* you have to sacrifice something."

I was not willing to sacrifice my soul for love and power. I knew why he was telling me all this. I was being tested to see if I accepted all that the *Partners* had given me. What did they have to give, the so called good life in exchange for protection money and power?

He wanted to know if he could trust me. What he didn't know was, I was going to fail my test. The question was, would I ever tell a soul what I knew? The answer was no. I would never say a word. I had already lost the most precious beauty, my daughter Syn. I had sacrificed enough! I was not willing to give up anything more.

I immediately realized, this beautiful life had been just a façade. The truth felt like a black cloud, so thick it choked me with every breath. I gave Henry the missing pieces of the puzzle to the mystery many of generations'. He knew the location of the missing plates and that was enough. I wanted out, even if it meant losing my Henry. I was going to put my trust in something real, something good. God was going to be my protection. He was bigger than the *Partners*.

I turned from Henry, went into my bedroom and gathered a few clothes. It was like walking in a daze.

I could hear Henry yelling,
> "Put that bag down before I give you another ass whoopin', but this time you might not make it through with your life."

I walked right past him, he knew I was finished. If he had to kill me, that was fine. I really didn't care. I didn't have much more to live for. Life had not been that great to me anyway. I went out those big massive doors for the last time never wanting to return to that life again.

I had the driver take me back to *the hood*, the place were all my hurt and pain began. I went back to the house of hell and devastation, where I sat in my window in peace. Because, I

knew that the demon that once dwelt here, now lived in a massive house and was the Pastor of the biggest church in the city.

I sat there in that window year in and year out playing my life with Henry over and over again in my mind. I knew who I was. Yet, I still sat longing and wishing my sweet baby girl was in my arms. Then one day, everything changed and life for me would never be the same.

SYLVIA HARDIE

The Beautiful One

⁀Mindy

"Hey baby, how is you? He said.

"Fine love just been sitting here waiting on you to
come, so I can place some of this good loving on
you." She said.

"Well, before you get to placing something on me.
Can you place some food on the table? A brother
needs energy for all that?" He asked.

"Sure, baby anything for you." She answered.

I could hear mamma and daddy in the front room. She
always made me go to bed early when she knew he
was coming over.
I prayed to God,
"Please let him stay in Mamma's bed instead of getting in
mine."

I cringe at the thought of him pushing me in my back to
wake up me up. All for the single purpose of putting his thing
in my mouth, and his slime being my meal for the night. I gag.
It reminds me about how hungry I really am.
"Please God, tonight make it stop."

I can still remember the first time he did it. I was about eight.
He told Mamma to go out and get him something to eat. While
she was gone, he told me that he was going to give me my
dinner early.

His commanding voice spoke with promise. I quivered with fear, and with one hard gulp, I swallowed. I looked down at his shoes. They were shining so bright, I could see my reflection. I hated what I saw. I got up and went to my bed.

As I tried to fall asleep, I kept repeating to myself,
    "It is just a dream!"

Just a dream I wanted to believe. What had just happened wasn't real! I told myself it was the type of dream that you still feel while you are still awake. I never told Mamma, but sometimes when we were alone, the way she looked at me. I could tell she knew something happened. But we never spoke of it.

When Daddy comes over, she sends me to bed early, and she doesn't leave me alone with him. But the second she falls asleep, he comes in my room and shoves that big snake down my throat. I swallow. He returns back into Mamma's room.

Sometimes I climb out the window and go over to Joyce's house. She always keeps her window opened for me. I get under her bed and go to sleep. Joyce always keeps a pillow and blanket down there for me.

Joyce is my best friend. I guess I like her mainly because she don't talk anymore, so I never had to worry about any of my darkest secrets ever being told.

She had stopped talking a few years ago. It was on the day our Daddies came over and beat her and Mamma Jean. I guess they beat them for having a heart and caring about other people. After they beat Joyce, they took more than her fight for life. They took her beauty secret, and she hasn't spoken since.

Mamma Jean, Joyce's mamma, was sent from heaven just to watch over us children. She was sent to make sure our lives were filled with just a small glimmer of hope. She made sure we were cleaned and feed. She didn't care who your mamma was, if you were in her presence, you were one of her own. She had eyes of such love and compassion, you knew one day everything was going to be alright.

She was the one who made sure everything was good for "the social show". This is what we called the every 6 months visit from the social worker. None of us received aid, but since we had home learning classes and never went to a school, a social worker came to check on things. Man, did they put on a show. The fake teacher hired to come in, called our way of learing "private special education". We laughed hearing it for the first time. It was special alright. There were no other children who learned what we had learned.

The truth is our only real learning came from Mamma Jean. The daddies insisted that we learned reading and counting. They wanted no excuse for a shortage of money when we got old enough to join their pimpin and hoeing game.

I was always so envious of Joyce and her mamma's relationship. Why didn't God give me a loving, caring mamma like Mamma Jean? All of the other mammas respected her. She was the oldest of all of the mammas, and she tried to live an example of what was right. Even though there was nothing right about any of our lives!

We live in a neighborhood of two blocks that was enclosed by a tall, concrete fence so high you couldn't see outside of it. There was only one entrance into our hood. Although there were no physical barriers keeping you from walking out, it was fear itself that kept us locked up like caged dogs. If you asked me it was more like a prison camp for the unwanted. The only company we had was from our no good Daddies and the men that came in at night with their fancy cars and tailored suits.

Our block came alive at night, and it was one big perverted party. It was like grown folks, Halloween. They were always excited about the degrading horrors that awaited them. The men went from house to house to fill their bags with treats. Then, when the sun came out, our neighborhood went back to normal, sad and depressing.

Mamma Jean was the one who had a way of making our days joyful, until the awful day Joyce's little sister was snatched up by a big long car in broad daylight. When they took Lil' Syn, Mamma Jean's spirit flew away with her. After Lil' Syn was taken neither of them were ever the same.

64

Mamma Jean was crippled and Joyce tried to take care of her the best she could. None of the mammas ever went over to help, because they were evil and just didn't care. Joyce on the other hand still had a heart. Although she no longer talked like regular folks do, she and I had our way of communicating with each other without ever speaking a word? If you sat quietly next to Joyce, you could feel her love and her heart could speak to you and your soul felt at rest.

The aroma from the kitchen ran up my nose and invaded my thoughts. The scent lingered over my bed as if to tease me saying,

"Come and get it! Come and get it!"

But I knew if I came out of my room, the hell that would follow wouldn't be worth my effort. My stomach growled like a roaring lion ready to strike the first sign of prey. However, my small stature was no match for my drunken mamma and my two-faced daddy. The fact of the matter was that my mamma didn't give a damn about me, nor being someone's mamma. She cared about two things her drink and her man, and anything else was of no concern to her.

Mamma was weak and all the fight in her was gone. I used to think that if you carried the title of "Mamma," you loved and took care of your child, but not all women who give birth to a child are mammas. And my mamma needed her ass whooped for carrying a title she definitely didn't deserve.

The other Aunties were nothing like that. They might not have had the greatest life, but they did care about their children. They did the best they could with what they had.

But my mamma didn't care if I ate, had clean clothes or if my hair got combed. She never taught me anything. She barely even talked to me. I believed she blamed me for her situation. What she failed to realize was, we were both in the same situation.

Mamma's uncaring treatment for me filled my heart with anger and hate, and today I was to my limits. I was so hungry!

I told mamma I was hungry earlier and she acted like she didn't hear me. I only had a small bowl of oatmeal for breakfast and that was hours ago.

Mamma said,

"I don't have no food for you, so stop beggin."

She told me that,

"Don't nobody want no nagging', beggin', desperate
woman, just take what you get and be happy."

I knew she quoted that sentence right out of the pages of
my daddy's, "how to treat a hoe manual," called *Pimps up, Hoe's
down*. I know he must be the author, because he sure kept us
face down.

I looked into my mamma's eyes, they were yellow and
tired. The yellow was interrupted by the blood veins that
stretched across her dilated pupils. Mamma's face sagged from
lack of sleep, and her body was jittery from a life of unrest and
constant abuse. I was always amazed how she stumbled about
with one hand clinked to her plastic cup full of Gin, and her
two-stained fingers clamped on a cigarette. She never spilled a
drop of Gin or let her cigarette ever go out.

Watching her was a real circus act. Mamma was a real life
juggler. Not one day went by without her having a cigarette in
one hand and a drink of Gin in the other hand.

Mamma looked back at me in disgust, as if my presence
alone was the cause of her misery. She sucked on her one good
tooth and said,

"Now take your raggedy, nasty ass to bed. Ain't nothing
for you here."

She caught my eye as I looked over to our dirty roach
infested table and saw a piece of a slice of bread. She had some
pity and handed it to me then sent me to bed. The bread was
hard and dry. I pretended that my bread was crumpets and my
cup of water was tea, like I read in a fairy tale book. I was the
queen sitting on my throne enjoying my snack. But in reality,
my stomach still growled from hunger.

So many days, I would cry thinking to myself,

"How could she be that cold and heartless. She was eating
and enjoying herself, knowing her child lay there starving,
with the smell of fried chicken and home fries taunting
and teasing her?"

The aroma became my lullaby, as I drifted in and out of sleep.

I still wonder sometimes, why God allows mammas to
hurt their babies. Why don't they realize, we are the beautiful
ones?

My mamma was a cold piece of crap. But she was only a
little worse than all the other mamma's that live in our ten
house *hood*. All of them were pretty bad, except for Joyce's
mamma.

Joyce's mamma was just like the mammas you saw on
television. She cooked, cleaned and talked nice to everyone.
She looked after all the children, like a mamma hen. You
couldn't do nothing wrong, 'cause she saw everything. That's
how she got the name, Mamma Jean. Everyone else's mamma
we called them Auntie, but Mamma Jean was the true definition
of a mamma.

The *hood* had a way of finding your weakness. Once that
weakness was found, it was used against you to break your
spirit. The daddies knew that children were Mamma Jean's
weakness. I think that's why they took little Syn.

Mamma Jean's was the only house with two kids. We
were all kind of jealous, because Joyce had someone to play
with and to love. Joyce was much older than Syn, but it was
like having your own baby doll, and we never had any of those.

Lil Syn is what we called her. She was a happy child. One
day while she was outside playing in the yard, a black car came
out of nowhere, put her in it, and we never saw Lil' Syn again.

Mamma Jean had a bad leg from the beatings the daddies
had put on her a year before. But when they put that baby in
the car, she mustered up all the strength she had and made that
leg run like a track star! She ran out the house and chased that
car, until all of her will ran out. She collapsed in the middle of

the street! You could hear her moaning, screaming and crying. It was like they had taken a piece of her, and it was gone forever.

I looked out of my window and saw the whole thing. All of the Aunties did! You couldn't help but to feel pity on her. I don't care how hateful or cold you were. The sound of her cries broke your heart. You felt the hurt just the same as she felt it. We all were paralyzed from disbelief.

Mamma Jean laid there in the middle of the street for a long while, as if time stopped. All the other aunties stayed in their houses. No one came to help her. I still remember that day as if it just happened. I was twelve, but it still seems like it was yesterday. Mamma Jean and Joyce never talked about Lil' Syn. No one did. It was like the five years she had lived in *the hood*, never existed at all.

One thing about me and Joyce is, we had secrets that were so bad back then we just made up new life stories. It took us less work to live make believe lives. We lived our lives by the recreated rendition of what we thought a normal life would be like. It was one of the only things that helped us and kept us from losing it all.

All the aunties were jealous of Mamma Jean. They thought, she felt, she was special because she was allowed to have two children, when everybody else only had one. I knew better, because I was there. If they only knew the secret, they would have understood the real meaning of love.

I still remember the day that changed everything for Joyce. Before that, I always wondered about the things that can make people change. I thought about the things that made people do what they do to you. Did they ever change? How did they change? Did their change come quickly? Cause I know, when they do what they do to you, your change can happen in one instant.

I know for a fact this is true, because I was there that day. We were playing and talking one minute. Then minutes later, Joyce was changed forever. Whatever happened to her was so bad, it stole her soul, and it also took her voice, which was her only means of expressing her pain.

On this particular day, all the Aunties were more stressed than ever. Us kids knew the drill. We stayed quiet and out of the way. It seemed like the daddies came all at once. They were in and out of each house like they were doing a shake down. From what I can remember, it was something about some plates. I couldn't understand what they were talking about. I remember thinking if they were hungry, we had plenty of plates in the cabinet, just no food to put on them.

Joyce and I were playing outside. We could hear some loud yelling coming from Mamma Jean's house! I guess it was her turn to get the plates, but she just kept repeating,
"IT'S NOT ME! IT'S NOT ME!"

With every answer of denial, you could hear the fist of one of the daddies as they sent another blow to her face. The more she talked, the more the beaten continued.

I looked at Joyce, and she looked back at me. When you're small you don't understand what grown folks are doing. You don't know anything about life. You just do what you're told and that is what we were taught.

"Stay out of grown folks business."

I was seven and Joyce was twelve. There was nothing we could do. No amount of crying, beggin' or fighting for Mamma Jean would help. There was no one to call for help. We were helpless. The only thing we knew to do was to keep playing and keep our heads down.

After all of the commotion was over, the two men came out of the house. They walked right up to Joyce. In one quick swoop, they had grabbed her frail arm and took her around to the back of the house.

I didn't know what to do, so I just kept playing in the dirt. I saw Rodney run up into Mamma Jean's house and run back out with a black briefcase. Then, strangely the daddies got Henry from across the street. He was pulling and fighting

trying to get away, but he was no match for the daddies. They took him to the back where Joyce was.

I waited for a little while, suddenly I heard the most horrifying scream from Joyce. It was the last sound I ever heard come out of Joyce's mouth. That one scream sealed her voice and left her in silence.

The Daddies walked from the back of the house, got in their car and drove away. I waited, hoping Joyce would come back so we could finish playing, but Joyce never came. I was scared for the first time in my life, because I thought Joyce was dead.

I got up and went to find her. There she lay in a ball shivering in the hard, hot dirt. She was bloody and naked. The look on her face was like a blank page. Once I saw she was alive, I ran to check on Mamma Jean inside the house.

I first looked for her in the bedroom. It looked like a tornado had hit that room, but she wasn't there. I yelled out and searched all over the small two bedroom house for her.

Finally, I heard a whimper coming from behind the couch. It was Mamma Jean in the same state as Joyce. I didn't know what to do! So I put a blanket on both of them, went home, got in my bed and said a prayer for them both.

Mamma Jean's house was silent for about a year. No one ever went over there, and you never saw them come outside.

Then one spring day, Mamma Jean come out of her house and sat in her rocking chair holding a baby.

Jealousy and rumors flew around the houses like the garbage flying in the street, during a wind storm. The Aunties were like the mean witches of the west. They jealously said,

"Oh, she thinks she better than us cause' she got that new baby!" "What makes her so special?"

The more they talked, the more Mamma Jean bragged on her new baby. As if she wanted to piss them off even worst.

70

But I knew better, and if the aunties had only looked a little closer they would have seen what I saw. That baby looked just like Joyce and that Henry from across the street. Mamma Jean named the baby Little Syn. I had never seen a baby more beautiful and happy. She put a smile on your face just to hear her laughter.

As little Syn grew, so did the distance between the Aunties and Mamma Jean. Mamma Jean didn't care she just stayed the same. She watched over all of us, as if we were all her own.

Joyce on the other hand was like a zombie most of the time. She would just sit in front of the window looking out in a trance. I never saw Joyce pick up little Syn or treat her like she was her own. I guess she had made up and lived in her own reality to protect her secret. But to me, Lil' Syn was Joyce's best kept beauty secret. As far as Joyce was concerned, that baby did belong to her mamma, and she had just gotten herself a new little sister. I guess if she thought about it that way, the truth didn't hurt as much.

Many years went by, things between me and Joyce changed in some ways, but remained the same in others. We had a bond that was special. I could look at Joyce and know what she was saying without her ever speaking a word. Our pain spoke the same language, and our hearts felt the same pain. It was strange because I don't' ever think Joyce even realized she didn't talk. In her reality, life was a fantasy world where she felt she was normal.

We all lived anything but normal lives. The truth was, we were the product of heartless pimps and an evil madam, who were only aroused by the sight of the all mighty dollar.

I know for sure Rubert was the ringleader of his four foster sons: James, Charles, Steve and Earl. They were raised by a hustling dope slangin' hoe-havin' heartless foster mother called Mammy. She was Rubert's wife. But Rubert did what he wanted. He was everybody's daddy, and his word was law. Everyone was scared of him. I think even Mammy.

Mammy hated my mother. Hell, Mammy hated all the aunties. She looked at them with disgust in her eyes. I guess she hated them for having affairs with Rubert. What she didn't understand is, no one had any control over Rubert's actions. He did as he pleased. Even the daddies knew not to interfere in Rubert's affairs.

No one truly knew who their father was, so we all assumed Rubert was daddy to us all. He would come by our house on a regular basis, which is why I believed he was my daddy. I think my mamma had it the hardest and was abused the most, all because of me and her love for Rubert.

I'll never know why Rubert and Mamma had such a connection. He was cruel and heartless. It seemed like the worst he treated her, the more she loved him. I was caught in the middle. A real love triangle of dysfunctional feelings.

Mammy hated the sight of me, because the Aunties said I looked like Rubert spit me out. I think they only said it to taunt her and to make her feel bad. That's what they always they did to people. I personally never could see the resemblance.

Nevertheless, Mammy and Rubert always treated our mammas like female dogs. However, what they did to the boys, they brought into the program was a shame.

They were beaten, molested and forced to grovel like slaves. It stripped away their manhood. Their heads were so screwed up. They didn't know the difference between right and left or right from wrong. They were talked to like dogs and trained to become killers. They were put on ready to strike and attack on command. Between all four of the boys, only one was different-- Charles. He was bigger and stronger than the other boys. His spirit wasn't easily conformed to the life, he was expected to live. His mind was sharp and his demeanor gentle, even Rubert dared to challenge him. So Charles was like a median. I believe it was he, that kept us alive.

The other three boys: Earl, James and Steve were more like the three Stooges, going in circles and getting nowhere. None of them could come up with a complete thought, nor were they bright enough to come up with the moneymaking business

that encompassed our ten house radius. It was Rubert and that heartless heifer that did it.

These people ate, slept and thought of money and lots of money. More was never good enough. They would get the girls from the state right after their eighteenth birthday. Then pass them around to those no good boys of theirs. Mammy knew once the girls turned eighteen they had no place to go.

All of the state support stopped. They were left with nothing and nobody. She promised the girls hope. All they had to do was enter into her nonprofit program called *Loving Holms... a place to be free.* The girls jumped at the idea, mainly because most of them were homeless living on the streets.

The Mayor had given Mammy two city plots and on the plots were ten little shack like shanties. The city built a brick wall fence to keep us inside and separated from the city. Then, they gave her grant money to clean up the area and make it livable. Once the project was complete she was given awards for investing in an impoverished part of the city and for helping young girls change their lives.

Then Rubert and Mammy started another program for the boys called *Building Boys to Men.* The program recruited foster boys during the summer. They were promised free training and pay. The program was designed to teach you the skills like Carpentry, teaching the boys how to refurbish the condemned houses. Rubert and Mammy didn't put in all the money that was allocated to improve each house. Instead, they pocketed most of it, leaving just enough so the houses could pass code.

What they didn't tell the boys was they were going to be working from sun up to sundown, and the pay wasn't enough to buy lunch.

Once in their program, you swore total allegiance to the *Partners* and failure to do so would be detrimental to your life. The boys feared Rubert and Mammy. They did what they were told.

When the houses were complete, the girls were so excited. Mammy had promised them housing and job training, so one day they could be independent. They truly believed they

would own their own home and be free to choose their own destiny. This was a dream come true, after living a life of foster homes, group homes and homelessness.

What Mammy didn't tell them is the houses would become their jail cell, and their sentence was life. Those sweet talking boys did as instructed and gave them one child each.

The children were used as leverage to control the girls. Every time they thought about leaving or didn't make their quota the children's lives were threatened. The job training turned out to be hoeing and the hopes for independence came at death.

The ten houses sat right behind an old condemned dry cleaner, and a high brick wall surrounded the two blocks. There was only one way in, between the cleaners and the wall. Our *hood* was separated from the rest of the world.

The police and social services must have been in Mammy's back pocket, because they never really checked on the living conditions of the families. At night the men ran in and out of our houses, like wolf packs in heat. They did anything and everything they wanted to our mammas.

Life happened to the young former foster girls so fast, they didn't know what hit them. They went from an unbelievable dream of happiness to a life filled with bondage and despair.

Mammy's four foster boys became known as our daddies, and they were trained to be the coldest pimps alive. A nice word never came out of their mouths, and they treated us like street mutts in a kennel.

At the end of every week,
    "A heifer better have their money!"

If not, everyone in the house was going to work to settle the debt. They left just enough money to buy a little food to keep you this side of starvation. You wore what they brought, and the furniture was donated by a second hand store. I believed the worst projects in the city were better than how we lived. In addition to the roaches and the bed bugs that came out of the used furniture and donated clothes, your body stayed riddled with sores and whelps. We had no money to buy soap,

toothpaste or anything nice. I woke up each day hungry, filthy and unwanted. Our mammas did sometimes steal a couple of dollars from their johns. They would get what they could and made out best with what they had.

One thing I could say for Mammy is she was a genius. Out of the despair and hopelessness of others, she was able to profit and grow a business. She won awards and recognitions for cleaning up the city. Yet, people never knew that this cleanup was really a filthy plan of corruption, built on the blood and tears of women and children.

I met Mammy one time in the middle of the day, when I was small. She was a medium height woman, stout and strong, with a pure white afro. Her face carried a serious expression upon her pitch-black skin. Her eyes were marble green and clear. You could see straight through to her non-existing soul.

One lone stare was capturing. She walked with an ivory cane. It was engraved with words going down one side and numbers going up the other. If I believed in anything, I believed with my whole heart that she was the devil. She plagued our hood with destruction. When she talked the words slurred together like a song with no melody. She smoked a pipe of strange herbs. Her frame was draped in a long black house dress.

When she entered our house the air felt cold and void. She had a smell of stale pork grease and rotten eggs that hovered over her. When she passed by me, her presence was haunting. I pressed my back to the wall for a little comfort. She looked down at me, and I felt my body shake in fear. I quickly looked away, but her haunted stare had impressed a permanent picture in my mind.

She had come there looking for Rubert. I don't know why she came there looking for him. He never stayed at our house for more than a few hours at a time. Plus, he rarely came by during the day.

My mother bowed before her as if to give her respect, and she kissed her extended hand like she was the Great Holy Mother. All I knew was Mammy was the creator of our hellhole, and Rubert was our Master. The whole ordeal was eerie. I will never forget meeting Mammy. I never knew where she

lived, but I knew that it wasn't far because she knew everything that happened in our *hood*.

I believe if Mammy hadn't come into our mammas' lives, they would have found some way of making it on their own. They had an undying spirit for survival and dreams for a better future. I knew I wanted something better too. I knew as soon as I got my break, I was going to take it and never look back on this hell that was my childhood.

My whole life changed the day Annie came to live with us. I never asked why she came, but I was grateful she did. Annie lived two houses from me, and she was older and more mature. She often laughed at me and Joyce, and she never talked to us.

We were nobodies to her. Between Joyce not talking and acting weird, and me always smelling of piss, crap or whatever other disgusting smell that came with living in filth. How could you blame her, who would want to come around. But we admired her with the admiration you have for a big sister, who had all the answers, but never any time to give them to you. We wanted to be like her, dress like her, and look like her. Most of all, I wanted to smell like her.

To Annie we were worthless trash, and we knew it was true. The day she came to live with us, she was bloody like Joyce was on that horrible day. However, Annie was different because she still had a fighting spirit. Her spirit gave me hope for a better day.

After some time, I believe she began to realize she was no better than me and Joyce. She slowly opened her heart to me and taught me what she knew about the world. She showed me how to love myself, to clean myself and to wipe my butt after I used the bathroom. She taught me how to keep my panties from sticking together in the seat. She showed me how to keep my feet from itching at night. She showed me how to clean, cook, wash clothes, and how to mend my clothes when they got holes in them.

My mamma never taught me anything. Really by the looks of her things, I don't think she knew herself. I mean after all she had raised herself. She had spent her entire life in and out of foster homes and group homes. I gathered that no one there ever took the time to teach her anything.

Annie was the first person to tell me I was beautiful. After I washed my face, I almost could see the beauty she saw in me. Every day she had a regiment, which included: clean the room, take a bath, get dressed, fix some breakfast, iron your clothes and read something.

Read "ANYTHING", she would say.
"This is how you stay enlightened."

I never understood what 'enlightened' meant, but if Annie said it. I did it. She was the closest thing I knew as a mother. I followed her around like a lost puppy, waiting to catch any scraps she threw down.

During the time Annie lived with us, her stomach got bigger and her feet would swell from time to time. Life was so strange because no one said anything. I guess I was the only one who noticed, or maybe I wasn't. People in our *hood* believed, if you ignore something long enough, it will eventually go away. In this case, one day it did. Annie didn't have a stomach anymore. She never mentioned it, and neither did I.

I just loved her, and I believed she loved me back. For the first time in my life, I believed I understood what love was. Then one night she climbed out of my bedroom window to be with Rodney in his old raggedy Buick, and she never came back. When she left me, I felt sick. It was like I was in the bottom of a pit, left to rot alone. Once again, my faith in life was lost.

I never forgot all Annie taught me. The time with her was one of the best years in my life. But the night she left, I cursed her and vowed I would never forgive her. That curse, I would learn to deal with for years to come.

While growing up, Joyce had a mad crush on Henry. He lived right across the street from Joyce and was the eldest male child of *the Hood*. Growing up, Henry was a short fat kid who bullied everyone. He was a minor pimp or a pimp in training,

77

either way you put it---it was all bad. His daddy did everything in his power to teach him the ropes. I guess even pimps need to have someone to pass their legacy down to when they die. Henry was the appointed one.

He called us everything he could think of to degrade us. I remember one time when Joyce and I were outside playing runway model, prancing up and down the sidewalk minding our own business. Henry came up behind me and tripped me.

I fell flat on my face.
He put his foot on my back and said,

> "Get use to that position heifer, that way no man can see your face while he does his business."

I knew hoeing was my fate, but there is something about hearing someone reminding you of your doomsday. It drains all of your energy and all the fight from you.

Joyce, on the other hand, saw a loving spirit in Henry. She believed that one day he was going to love her like a real man is supposed to love a woman. There was no point arguing with Joyce. For one, it would be a one-sided conversation. Joyce's mind was so screwed up that reality and fantasy crashed together. She didn't know the real world from her fantasy world.

The truth is, she had eyes only for him. I left it alone because even Joyce deserved to have a ray of hope. She too needed to escape this place. So, if she wanted to do it with Henry, who was I to take that dream from her? After all, she spent most of her days sitting in her front room window staring into space, living in a world of silence.

One day, when I was about fourteen and Joyce was seventeen, she came racing outside. She made a straight path for Henry's house across the street. She had a weird look in her eyes, like she was in heat and the only one that could put out her fire was Henry. Before she could arrive, I made a b-line to stop her in her tracks. I knew Henry. I didn't want her to be hurt by him. I looked her straight in her face, and my heart spoke to hers.

It said,
"Joyce, what the hell do you think you're doing?"
She looked back at me with a look that said,
"Get out of my way!"

I shrugged my shoulder, letting her know her threatening look was no match for me.

My heart spoke to her again saying,
"Fine Joyce, but don't come crying to me when Henry
hurts you."
Her heart answered,
"I don't need you to protect me anymore. Now move out
of my way."

I stepped aside, allowing her to continue on her path right up to Henry. He watched her as she approached. I was surprised. They seemed to have a connection like Joyce and I had. They communicated the same way she and I did. Standing there in disbelief I thought to myself, maybe I was wrong about Henry. Maybe he was going to be the one to love her. If so, he would have the woman of his dreams someone sweet and kind, who never said a word.

From that day forward, I began to understand what happened to Joyce on the terrible day when she was 10. The Joyce I knew died. All that was left of her was her heart. She kept it under lock and key buried and hidden so deep inside. The old Joyce was in a voided place, imbedded so deep within her soul that she couldn't even reach it. The only way you could communicate with Joyce was if you had a pure heart, a true feeling heart that had good intentions and love for mankind.

I understood Joyce, and my mind was at rest. I knew Joyce was going to be okay. She didn't need me to be her protector anymore. I knew I could leave this place in good conscience. No one could hurt Joyce anymore. She could make it on her own.

Life without Annie had left a hole in my chest. No matter what I did, I couldn't fill it. I kept up my reading and did my modeling thing, but without her it wasn't the same. Life in *the hood* was changing and everybody seemed to be on edge.

Rubert hardly came by. When he did come by, it was like he was sneaking around. He was afraid of something or someone. If he spoke to me at all, it was to ask me if the coast was clear outside. I don't know what Rubert did, but I did know he was changing too.

One day as I was in my room, I heard Rubert and Mamma talking. This time their conversation wasn't about sexing or eating. It was more like the conversation of a confession from a man on death row the day before his execution.

I pressed my ear to the door. I wanted to hear what this heartless man had to say to my mamma. Rubert's voice was different, humble and soft, unlike the hard, crafty, hateful tone I had grown to know.

> "Sandy" he said, that was my mamma's name, "I know life for you and the girls has been hell, and I know I am the cause. I could never undo all the wrong that I have done in this life. I would need two lifetimes to undo all the hurt and pain I have caused for so many. When I was young I had so many dreams for success I just needed to make it out of the hell hole I was born in. My mother was a drug addict and Heroin was her love and her life. I was just a liability to her. She didn't know how to love, to feel, to live. She took her last hit from her true love heroin. They were together for eternity. As I saw her dead body lying on the floor, I knew the love she had for her lover was more than she ever had for me and now both of us were at peace, she was only 25. She was an empty shell of a woman, who was never given a chance."

He went on talking.

> "I was sent to live with my grandmother Mabel Holms, I called her Big Mama. She wasn't loving or kind. She didn't bake cookies or knit you sweaters for your birthday.

Big Mama was a cigar smoking, gun toting woman, who hated kids. She ran a gambling joint outside of town, and people came from miles around to lose their hard earned money to Big Mama. But her real moneymaker was hustling hoes. She had about ten girls and they were under Big Mama's control. She taught them how to make her money. The men would wait in line to get a chance with one of Big Mama's girls. The girls learned from the best, because Big Mama could hustle the drawers off of a man. Before he knew it, he was standing there butt ass naked. That's just how she was. She cared about one thing and that was making money. That's all she taught us. That's all we learned. "

He kept talking.

"Big Mama didn't care much for kids, so we managed to stay out of her way and do our jobs. We were making drinks for the customers, dealing the cards, counting out the chips, keeping the place clean, and stealing as much as we could. At the end of each night, she would make us tally up all we had gotten. If you didn't make your share, she would beat you to unconsciousness. Big Mama would ask you one time to do something. If you didn't do it right away, she came down on you so hard with the beatings. You would have to lay there for hours just to get enough strength to get up."

He explained.

"In the house there were three of us. Barbra, Samuel and me. Barb and Sam were sister and brother. Sam was the oldest, but Barb was his protector. She protected him against Big Mama. Big Mama really hated boys, especially a weak fat boy like Sam. He was short and chunky. He had a look like he was always thinking about something, lost looking in space. Sam never talked much. He looked like an old man. His skin was thick and tight over his fat face, like stretched leather smooth and rich. He walked slowly but steady hunched over. He was too fat or too lazy to move any faster. It pissed Big Mama off."

81

She said,
> "He was a fat, lazy, good for nothing fag. His mamma
> took her life, so she would not have to look at his old
> face."

He told her.

> "Big Mama's words were cold and mean. She'd come
> after him with a vengeance. But, Sam was special. He
> had a gift. He could create whatever idea came to his
> mind. He was a master duplicator, but Big Mama couldn't
> see it past his appearance. Every time she had to see his
> fat face, it boiled her blood. She would beat him just
> because he was fat. Then beat him for eating. She'd beat
> him because he was lazy, and sometimes she would beat
> him just because."

> "With all of the beatings, Sam never said a word and he
> never cried or talked back. He just took it like it was the
> life burden placed on him. The more Big Mama tried to
> break him, the quieter and withdrawn he became. Sam
> was different. He was a creator, and Big Mama was a
> destroyer. He liked to do hair and make-up and nails. He
> could make clothes out of rags. He could put an outfit
> together that made you look like a superstar. He was
> smart and had talent. Big Mama didn't see it. All she saw
> in Sam was weakness."

> "Barb on the other hand was the brains of the two. One
> wasn't complete without the other. Barbra was a stout,
> dark woman with eyes so green, if you looked deep in
> them you could see your future. They said that her
> mamma was a Voodoo Witch. Barb was called a Voodoo
> Princess, because Barb looked just like her mother, dark
> with green-colored eyes. They said that their mother was
> from Cuba. She escaped one night with just her and her
> two babies. They crossed the sea on a man-made raft. She
> worked as a psychic and was said to have connections to
> the devil himself. One day she gave the wrong person a

good reading. They killed her in cold blood. She became their sacrifice for their gain."

"Big Mama stayed clear of Barb. She believed Barb could put a spell on her. I knew Barb. She was nothing like that. Barbra's heart was pure. She had so much love in her, but she never let Big Mama know her love. She acted just as cold as Big Mama did, so she'd think she was just as evil. That was just to keep Big Mama off her back."

"Barbara was Sam's protector and she took care of him like she was his mother, so he called her Mammy. Each day Big Mama got more hateful. Her treatment of Sam got worst. You could tell that Sam's spirit was weakening and his gift was dying inside of him."

"We came up with a plan to get us out of there. I was the muscle, Barbra was the voice, and Sam was the brains. We had it all mapped out. We were going to make Big Mama a drink. Sam had made some concoction that would put her to sleep. Then, we were going to steal the night's winnings and make our getaway. We thought our end was near. "

"One night, while we were planning our escape, Big Mama heard of our plans. She stormed through the door, so fast it blew out the candle we were using to see our plans. Big Mama stood tall over us, as we crouched down on the floor. When she spoke, her voice was sharp, and each word she spoke was said like a promise that sent a fear we all knew."

Big Mama said,

"How dare you ungrateful bastards plot against me? I know that you have been stealing from me. Yet I still fed you and put a roof over your heads. Did you think you could drug me then walk out of here alive? You belong to me, and as long as the air flows through your sorry worthless bodies, you will do what I say. I was treating

you like children, but since you want to be grown and do grown things, from now on we are Partners. Together we will take over this town. I have plans for you all."

She took a knife and cut our wrist and took our blood and mixed it in a bowl with some of her own and drank it.

"Your destinies are already spoken. Your futures are set. My word is bond. If any one of you ever try and break our partnership, I will hunt you like the traitor dogs you are, cut your bodies up with my bare hands and leave pieces of you all over the city. We all sat there too scared to move. I knew then our days were numbered. Big Mama was right. She did have plans for us and these would change us forever."

"Her plans for me were to steal and kill, whoever got in her way. She taught me the pimping game. She showed me how to keep a hoe in check. Barbra was more refined. She showed her how to start the non-profit *Loving Holms*. She taught Barbra how to sweet talk a man into giving her whatever she wanted. Barbra went to the Mayor with Big Mama's plans and presented it flawlessly. I think Barbra thought deep down that she could make a difference in the lives of young girls. She wanted to help these girls who had gotten lost in the system, because she was one herself. But Big Mama's plan was more evil and sinister, than you could even imagine."

"Big Mama's name was so bad in the streets. No one would deal with her. So, Barb became the face of the organization. She had the task of finding the young girls. I had the task of collecting the money and keeping them in check. All of the money went to Big Mama. She taught us the pimping and hoeing game. Samuel had the job of recruiting the boys. You know them as the Daddies. Together, he and Big Mama created an underground society called the Partners. Some of the members include the police, judges, politicians, even the Mayor."

"The Partnership is strong and is very much alive today. Barb, Samuel and I were just little puppets in her play of total destruction. Every order that was given came from Big Mama. Big Mama was pleased with what we were doing and the way things were going. But we were not pleased, because we still didn't have our freedom."

"Then Sam used his creative talent and made moneymaking plates. He thought if we could make enough money we could buy our freedom. I put the word on the streets that I heard about some counterfeit money being passed out on the street. Big Mama wanted those money making plates. I told her word on the streets was some man in Mexico had them."

She said,
    "If I had those plates I would have all the power I ever wanted."

Rupert said,
    "I agreed to deliver them to her in exchange for Barbra, Samuel and my freedom. Big Mama gave me three days to get them and deliver them to her. She told me if I failed, she would have us all killed. I told Sam and Barb. We all knew it was the only way we would ever have normal lives."

    "I had them. I hid them in a safe place, until the meeting with Big Mama. But on the day, I was supposed to deliver them, they came up missing. Someone stole them. I don't have the plates and Big Mama's words are bond. Now Barb, Sam and my lives are in danger. I am being framed and I don't know by whom. It was my responsibility to deliver the plates to Big Mama. I told her to take my life and to spare Barb and Sam. I asked her to let me be the sacrifice."

She never responded.

He continued,

"I don't have many days left on this earth. There is no way for me to make things right. I just want you to know it wasn't personal. I did love you. I'm just a shell of a man, who never had a chance. I have been taking orders. I have been doing what I was told all my life. My only hope is that my children will be better than I could ever be. Maybe they will make a real difference in this world."

I stood there motionless unable to comprehend all that Rubert had said. I wanted to feel sorry for him, but my heart wouldn't allow me to, because I believe no matter what happens to you in life, we all have choices. He was an adult. He could have run away. He did not have to stay and do all of those things. Rubert may not have had a whole lot of choices, but the main choice was between right and wrong. What Rubert had done to me, he did when Big Mama wasn't around. It was him that did that wrong. No one made him do it. So, I felt nothing for him.

I kept my ear pressed to the door still listening. Waiting for a response from Mamma, but she never said a word. Then I heard the door shut. That was the last time we heard or saw Rubert.

I saw Mamma cry for the first time in my life. I never believed she had any feelings, and I couldn't believe she even had a soul. It made me angry. She never cried for me. Yet, she shed tears for this man who treated her like the no good heifer she was.
Like they say, "Things you don't understand, you can't explain."

Three days later, Rubert was found dead in the back of Annie's old house.

After Rubert was killed, it was like a huge weight was removed from me. A veil was lifted, but there was still an unknown haunting feeling with everyone. Before, the fear came from the presence of Rubert, but now with Rubert gone, the fear

was still there. You just couldn't put your hands on it. You didn't know what was coming.

Everyone stayed in their house scared to go outside because they didn't know who would be next. The men at night came by less frequently. Even the Daddies' presence was gone. It was like the day before Dooms Day, and everyone was waiting for the bomb to drop. The suspense alone is devastating. The pressure for me was more than I could take. I felt so alone with Annie gone and Joyce in a private love affair fantasy world with Henry in her mind. I knew it was time for me to find my own way. If Annie could leave, so could I. I was not going to live the rest of my life afraid anymore. I was going to leave this place and never look back.

The day I decided to leave. I just left. I realized that no prison is strong enough to hold me, because my mind was always free. The only thing holding you back was me. I realized that even if there are bars on your windows, obstacles in your way, your mind is free to dream and hope for something better. No one has control of it but you. I realized I had control. Fear had become my prison, fear of Mamma, fear of Mammy, fear of Rubert and fear of the Daddies. I realized that fear is just a thought, you can't touch it, hold it and you can't even see it. Fear is just you not willing to venture into the unknown. For me, the unknown was what existed beyond the brick wall, beyond our ten blocks. For me freedom was calling.

For me, this prison of fear had become too much of a friend. But no more! I wanted more for me. I deserved to be free. So one day, I started walking. I walked right down the middle of the street in broad daylight. I didn't care who saw me or who was around. As I got closer to Joyce's house, I could see her watching me through the window and our eyes met.

"Where are you going?" her heart spoke.
"I am no longer afraid. I am walking to my freedom." My heart replied.

"Keep your eyes on the prize and never look back. I'm glad you are finally free like me." Joyce's heart replied.

Tears ran down my face, because she understood me. I knew one day our lives would get better. I knew one day we'd meet again.

I left. I had neither plans nor any money, but what I did have was worth more than gold. I was free. I had freedom. I had the will to change my life. I was on my own path. The only problem with the path was there was no plan for the path.

With no plan and no path, I wound end up walking aimlessly around with no direction. I would find myself in the same situation just a different location. As I approached the end of the block, my world all of a sudden became enormous. I didn't know what I was going to do, but my possibilities were endless. Then, I cleared the brick wall.

.   .

Suddenly, my eyes were opened. I saw the most beautiful city before me. The buildings were tall with glass windows that seemed to glow against the suns glazes. The streets were clean and each block was riddled with specialty stores and shops. I walked up and down each street, looking in each window. I admired the beautiful clothes, the knickknacks and the fabulous furniture. I had never seen things like this before.

I told myself that one day I would have the biggest house, a mansion. My mansion was going to be decorated with the best furniture money could buy. My closet would be full of those lovely clothes. Those fancy knick -knacks would be enhancing the decorum of my rooms. My daydreams engulfed my whole day. Before I knew it, night had fallen. Most of the stores were closing. The street lights came on, and my heart grew heavy with fear.

We were never allowed outside, when the street lights came on. It was our mamma's time to make our daddies' some money. I walked up and down the sidewalk. My legs quivered. Each step I took, I became unsure.

I just kept telling myself,
> "Just keep moving. No one can stop you, if you just keep moving."

Behind me, I could hear a car driving slowly. The rocks on the concrete cracked from the slow rolling tires. My heart began to race. I walked faster. The car moved faster. The only thought going through my mind was, "it's the Daddies." They were looking for me. Now that they have found me, my life would be over. The punishment for breaking the rules was Death.

Up ahead I saw a light coming from an old brick building. The neon sign flickered. Most of the lights were out, but I could make out the words, *Beautiful One School of Beauty and Salon*. My eyes lit up. I always wanted to be the beautiful one! "This place must be a sign," I thought. I walked faster and this time with a purpose. Then I thought again about the following car.

I told myself,
> "RUN!"

Just as I got to the driveway of the building, I could hear the car turn and drive away. The deepest breath of relief came from me, and I went straight to the building.

When I got there, I looked in the window. I saw women laughing and admiring themselves in the mirrors. These women were so happy with life. They were so sure of themselves. They were beautiful. For them, life was exactly what it was supposed to be--perfect.

The salon was old and outdated. There were cracks in the ceiling and rips in the floors, everything was cheap. The salon had ten stations. There were five on one side and five on the other. In between them sat an older looking gentleman gazing over them like a master insuring all the services were done to perfection. His eyes were cold and his expression was solid.

You could tell that he was the one running things. He never said a word. The women seemed to ignore his presence, as they were invested in their craft. The decor was modest and

the lights were dim, but what made the place come alive was the festive ambiance the beautiful feeling.

I fantasized about seeing myself standing behind one of those salon chairs making women beautiful and engaging in conversations. The longer I gazed through that big picture glass window, the more of my future I could see. This was the place!

Doing hair and helping women to become beautiful was my path. Someone had helped me to see some beauty in myself, and now I would help others. Beauty was my Destiny. I now had a plan. This building was my path to fulfill that plan.

I would let all of my past doubts of being ugly, dirty and unwanted go. Then I walked through those doors, never to see my old self again.

Life wasn't like I thought it would be. I left my two-block prison and traded it for a life as a servant. I worked in the salon during the day. Then I was a bed-warmer for old man Mr. Roberts at night. Mr. Roberts was the name of the man who ran the *Beautiful One Salon and Spa* down stairs and the *Beautiful One Beauty School* upstairs. He took me in that night and offered me room and board in his home. In exchange, I was his maid, cook, and whatever else he needed. I told him that I wanted to be a stylist. He gave me a job working in the salon. He said all my earnings would go towards my tuition for his school upstairs. Day after day I worked, so I could make enough money for a chance to attend *Beautiful One Beauty School*.

My duties were to clean the salon and greet the clients. I made extra money from being the shampoo girl. I learned how to give the best shampoos in town. I would massage the ladies into a peaceful haven, and they always gave good tips. All the money I made went towards the payment for my tuition to become a Cosmetologist. I learned that word. I would be a Cosmetologist. I loved that word. It gave me something to look forward to in life. It gave me power. I wanted so much to go upstairs and join the elite Cosmetology society, but I was patient, knowing my day would come soon.

Life with Mr. Roberts was much different than life at home. But it was totally the same. Mr. Roberts was much like my daddy.

I did whatever he asked, always answering,
    "Yes, sir."

    Once again, I was a puppet with no rights, no say and no control.

    Mr. Roberts lived in a mansion on the other side of town. It was full of rooms. I never saw many of the rooms, they were always locked. I was forbidden to enter into them. I always wondered what lay beyond those doors. At night sometimes, I could hear noises like a factory. I assumed they came from in the rooms; however, I never looked. I just did what I was told and never asked any questions.

    If I wasn't in the bed with Mr. Roberts, then I was in my small room right behind the kitchen. The room was very simple, with just a bed and a basket to keep my few belongings in. The room had no windows. When the lights were off, I was in total darkness. On my twin size bed, I had a fitted sheet and a thin blanket. Mr. Roberts didn't believe in giving you nothing for free.

He said,
    "Everything he had, he had to work for. So, if I wanted what he had, I was going to have to work just as hard."

    The house was huge with plenty of potential. But old man Roberts was so cheap he wouldn't even turn on the heat on the coldest winter days. Although Mr. Roberts had the salon and the school, I never could figure out where all his money came from. He didn't have any family that came by. Nor did he ever mention anything about his past. The only time we were at the house was at night. Between the salon and the school, it took up much of our time. When he was working, so was I. He would go into his office and leave the door cracked just enough to hear what was going on in the salon. I would always keep myself busy working. There were also times that I pretended to look busy, when I really was not doing anything at all. The salon worked like a well-oiled machine. The girls who worked there did their job without drama or backtalk. The atmosphere

91

was pleasant and the clients were plenty. I wasn't allowed to interact with clients, except when greeting and while giving the shampoos.

Mr. Roberts said that,
"I was just there to do a job, not to make friends."

Mr. Roberts lived a very secluded life and didn't talk much. He was short and plump with a rich chocolate color. His face was round and the expression on his face was always like someone always deep in thought. The few strands of hair left on his head were gray and each one laid down in a uniform order. Mr. Roberts was a great dresser. He was always sharp. Every time he walked out of the house, he was dressed to the tee. If he saw something he liked in a magazine, it wasn't long before he was wearing it. The odd thing was that Mr. Roberts never went shopping, yet he was always in the latest fashion.

I admired Mr. Roberts in many ways. I was only fifteen, and Mr. Roberts was much older. In public, I called him Mr. Roberts, but in private he was Big Daddy! He got off on dressing me up in school girl clothes. He made me wear no panties, so he could peek under my skirt.

He would say,
"His snake was my pacifier. So, suck on it before you go to sleep."

One good thing about Mr. Roberts was, he never wanted that kind of sex, because his thing never got hard like my Daddy's did. He just talked about it. Most of the time I think he just wanted someone to be near him, because nothing else happened, so laying with Mr. Roberts really wasn't so bad--- I guess. He never married nor had any children.

In some ways, I think he felt like I was the daughter he never had. He acted like my protector. He was like a father in a way. But his perverted mind and deep secrets kept us from a definite relationship. He never put his hands on me and I respected him for that. Yet, we had a strange relationship. I didn't love him or take care of him like I would do my man.

Nor could I go to him for advice like you would a parent. To me, he was just plain ole Mr. Roberts.

One thing was for sure, I owed Mr. Roberts my life and I knew it. If he had not taken me in that night, I might have ended up on the streets with a pimp. I had nowhere to lay my head that night. I had nothing to eat. A pimp would have spotted me miles away. They would have grabbed me up, and put me in a line up to see how many privates I could suck just so I could eat. I would have ended up in the same lifestyle that I had run away from. Thinking about this made me, so thankful for Mr. Roberts.

Three years went by. I had finally earned enough money to go upstairs to Mr. Roberts's beauty school. For three years I had cleaned, shampooed and greeted the clients, until my tuition for the *Beautiful One School of Beauty* was paid in full. I had envisioned walking up those stairs every day. Now it was finally happening. This was going to be the turning point of my life. My first day of beauty school was the day I had waited for my whole life. It was the change that shook my soul and raddled my cage.

I came early, sat in the very front of the room and waited for my instructor to arrive. I wanted to talk to her before everyone else arrived. I sat there patiently waiting with my hands folded in front of me. I was squeezing my hands so tight, because I didn't want anyone to see them shaking with nerves. I heard the door open. I excitedly turned around to meet my instructor. To my shock, I almost fainted as I saw the one who walked in. It was her. I was suddenly a little girl in my Mamma's house, it was Mammy.

The day Mammy came to visit was a day I would never forget, and she was one I would never forget. It was her. My heart dropped. Question upon question rolled through my mind like the last lap in a roller derby race. All kinds of thoughts and memories flashed before me, so fast I got dizzy. How? When? Where? Who? I was confused. I didn't know what to do. All this time, I thought I was free and I had run right back to Mammy. I sat frozen.

She came in, placed her things on her desk, laid down her cane, and took her seat. I watched her every move, thinking that I would run out as fast as I could. But, I legs wouldn't move. Then, she looked right at me. Fear ran through me and terror took over me. My heart began to beat 500 hundred beats per second. I could feel the sweat falling from my face and falling. I shook all over.

Suddenly to my surprise, her piercing eyes lit up.
She smiled and welcomed me.
    I thought,
    "What the Hell?"

Her voice was slow but steady. Her words seemed to glide into a sweet song. This was not the same Mammy that I remember some years before. This woman, who sat before me today, had a peaceful spirit. She seemed to have no intentions of doing me any harm.
    Then she spoke,
    "Hi Mindy. How are you? My name is Ms. Barbra. It is a pleasure to have you in my class." She said, with her hand extended.

She sat there waiting for a response with her hand extended waiting to shake mine. I was confused, but I quickly jumped out of my seat and shook her hand. I stood there frozen still watching her.

    I was still holding her hand when she asked,
    "Are you ok?" I released her hand and responded,
    "It's a pleasure to meet you too."
    I made my way back to my seat.

As I sat down, I thought,
    "Everything seemed right except her name. Ms. Barbra?"

I sat there thinking and said,
    "Hell no! That's her! Her name is Mammy! I would know her anywhere."

Like a ton of bricks it hit me! The day that Rubert came to the house and told momma his life story, he said Barbra, Samuel and he were raised by Big Mama. It all made sense. Mammy is Barbra and here she was sitting right in front of me. I figured she must be working on some new scheme to trick girls.

Soon the other ladies arrived. Some were new like me and others were close to completion.

I watched this Ms. Barbra closely all day, but there was nothing out of the ordinary. In fact, she played the role of a caring and attentive teacher.

There were twelve of us. Mammy playing the Ms. Barbra role took care to help us individually. She gave us her undivided attention from the time she walked in each day, to the time she left each night. I wanted to believe in her. There was nothing in anything she did which proved to be different from the loving teacher, she showed us from day one.

She was mother like, nurturing and always helping all of us. They all grew to love her. I grew to love her. I trusted it and it was true, she had changed. She embarrassed me and the other women there. She was the mother I never had, and she gave me the love I always longed for. Her peaceful spirit and kind words of encouragement greeted me each day. Her love and passion for Cosmetology prepared me. She had changed my disbelief. With each new day, she gave me all she had.

With each day, I left wanting more. I began to take pride in myself and beauty wasn't just something I saw from the outside. I now understood that real beauty begins on the inside first.

I sat one evening and thought about it all. I guess when Rubert died, it freed us all. Mammy, now called Barbra was able to start a new life on her own terms. No longer the owner of the *Loving Holms* organization, now she was helping girls turn their lives around for real.

She was giving them a skill they could be proud of, one which would help them provide for their families with pride and dignity. She was trying to do work to undo all the damage she had done to so many. All the wrong she had done to my ole trifling momma, was now being made up to me. Life is like day

and night. It's funny how life can be so dark. Then the sun comes out and erases all darkness. When light comes into your life, you never have to live in darkness again.

Barbra made her choice. She had changed. She would do good for others, while she was still alive to give back some of what she had taken away. Rubert on the other hand never gave to anyone. He made the choice to do what he did. He never had the chance to change. A peace came over me. I was not longer afraid of anything, and my nerves were at ease.

The program was one year. It came and went like a wind storm. Time passed for me so fast. Everything I knew in my life had changed. It all turned around and was rearranged into perfect pieces back in their proper order.

By the time school was over, I walked out of there nineteen, full of life and with limitless potential. I had fulfilled my dreams. I had stuck to my plans. Now I had a direction and a purpose. I was no longer the Mindy that accepted anything dirty. I was no longer abused, unwanted and scared. I was now Ms. Mindy. I was ready to take on the world and its challenges.

I began to work with Mr. Roberts, as a stylist and the manager of the salon. Mr. Roberts trusted me. He now saw me as a woman, instead of a school girl. We got married. I loved him for all he had done. I even got that limp snake of his to work. It didn't happen often, but it was enough to keep our marriage alive.

Ten years went by. During that time we had one child, I named her Angela. She was the apple of his eye and the heart of my soul. She brought so much laughter to our home and joy into our lives.

I watched Ms. Barbra get older, as the years went by. I began to teach at the beauty school during the day. I ran the salon at night. Many days Mr. Roberts was too tired to leave the house. He and Angela would keep each other company. I decorated the house with the finest furniture money could buy.

I made sure every closet in my house was full of the most beautiful clothes and shoes. The salon and the school flourished, and we made a lot of money. I was very happy.

Then one day Mr. Roberts asked me to drive him over to the school. Ms. Barbra was there. He said there was a disturbance and he needed to check it out. When we pulled up, I could see the lights in the school upstairs were still on. My husband got out and directed Angela and I to stay in the car. He leaned over and kissed Angela on the forehead.

She wrapped her little arms around his neck.

He whispered,

"Daddy loves you."

Hearing those words coming from a man to a daughter were words I never heard as a child.

"Love you too daddy." Angela responded with a smile on her face.

He then turned, leaned over to me and gave me the most loving kiss we ever had. Mr. Roberts was not one for emotions, so this took me by surprise.

"Babe, are you ok?" He asked. His expression was more serious than ever.

"Yea, I'm fine." I told him.

He turned and walked into the building.

Soon after he left, a car drove up. Three men got out and walked inside. For some strange reason, they looked familiar. More than ten years had passed, yet I could swear the men looked like Rodney, Steve and James, but it was too dark to really tell.

They entered the building. They only stayed for about ten minutes or so, then came back out and drove away. I waited for Mr. Roberts and Ms. Barbra to come out. Suddenly, there a loud explosion and light rang across the sky. The pressure of the explosion was so strong that it shook the street and blew out some of the windows of the car. I shielded my face from the heat and the glass. I could hear Angela in the back screaming to the top of her lungs.

"What had happened?" I thought.

I was dazed and confused. I needed to get to Angela to make sure she was okay, but I needed to go to check for Mr. Roberts and Ms. Barbra!

I tried to open the car door, but something had sealed it tight. I moved the glass and climbed over the seat to Angela. I grabbed Angela and held her tight, until the flames had died down.

I looked up toward the salon and I began weep. Once again the ones who had loved me were gone, and once again, I was alone. I grabbed Angela and held her tight.

Then I waited and waited for a fire truck, the police or an aid car to show up, but they never did. I didn't know what to do. I didn't know where to turn. So I called the only one I knew who could help me, I called Henry.

Henry came and took us home. He knew all about the explosion. He cleaned us up and promised to give us protection. He said that the hit was one from the *Partners*. He said it happened, because Mammy and Samuel did not keep their part of the deal. Big Mama had ordered the hit.

I paused in confusion. I told him I knew Ms. Barbra was Mammy.

"But, why did they have to kill my husband?" I asked.

What he told me, gave me the shock of my life. Big Mama ordered the hit on Mammy and Samuel. They found Mammy at the Beauty School. But, they had also found Samuel there. My Mr. Roberts was Samuel Roberts. I never knew I was married to Barbra's brother Sam. They had stayed together until death.

Life without Mr. Roberts and Ms. Barbra was unbearable. For a while, I didn't want to live myself. It was all I could do just to get myself out of the bed each day to care for Angela.

Depression fell on me so hard it took all my strength and my breath away at times. It was a noose around my neck choking the life out of me.

My beautiful black hair turned gray in the front. It reminded me of the gray hairs of Mr. Roberts. I missed him so much. I also missed the woman, who was like a mother to me, Ms. Barbra.

I thought I had life all figured out. I thought I had it all figured out. I was finally going to have it all. I had built this great new life full of love and forgiveness, only to have it snatched away from me in one instance. Part of me wanted revenge, but the other side of me knew it wasn't worth it. I realized that no matter how much good Mammy and Samuel did or tried to do, in the end they had caused so much pain to so many.

My mind could never wrap around Mr. Roberts. How had he ended up in my life? How had he become my savior, my husband, my love? Why did he have to die? He was a good man, and he didn't do anything to anybody, or so I thought.

Months and months went by. I still couldn't make it through the day without thinking about Mr. Roberts and Ms. Barbra. They had worked so hard in the end to help young girls like myself. They wanted us to have a chance for success, instead of clouded dreams of the devastation and past despair like the life I came from. They gave girls like me an opportunity for something real. They helped to give use a life full of possibilities and a reason to be proud.

The longer I thought about them, the more I realized I needed to keep their dreams alive. I didn't want their lives to be in vain. So, I decided I was going to rebuild the beauty salon and school and name it *Beautiful One*, because to me they were the beautiful ones.

I needed to know more about Big Mama and the *Partners*. What was their mission now that Big Momma was the only original living member left of the original *Partners*? Why was she was so pissed off that she needed to take the lives of these two people in their elderly years. They were no longer a treat, so why? I had so many unanswered questions. There was only one that I knew who could have the answers. That was Henry. He knew it was a hit that killed my husband and Ms. Barbra that night. He knew who ordered the hit. And, I knew he had

even more answers. He was going to be the key to unlock all of my unanswered questions.

I called on Henry once again. I asked to speak with him in private. He agreed as long as our conversation was kept a secret. What I was told would bond me to the *Partners* for life. If I broke the bond, the punishment would be death. I agreed.

We met in a back undisclosed room of his church. We sat face to face. I marked my promise to the *Partners* with blood. It was taken from a cut to my arm. Henry was always a big man, but when he spoke of the *Partners,* his frame expanded more and his tone changed. A possession came over him. As he began to speak, he almost seemed to go into a trance.

As he began to speak, he almost seemed to go into a trance. He started to sway from side to side. All of a sudden, another presence entered the room, and I knew Henry was gone. Only the presence and I were left in this conversation.

This spirit came as a woman with blackened eyes. You could see the future or the past in them. My heart dropped as she began to speak.

She said,

"I am Zota the spirits of the past, present and future. I am here to answer the secrets of your husband Mr. Roberts. His first name was Samuel. He and Barbra were the children of a powerful Voodoo Priestess Asela. She worked as a fortune teller. One day Mabel Holms, also known as Big Mama, asked for a reading. Asela knew her heart was pure evil. She knew Mabel was selfish and vengeful. Asela told her that her evil ways would end her life one day, if she was not willing to change."

"Mabel didn't care to hear what Asela had to say. Mabel just wanted to know how she could have power over men and money. Asela told her that in order to have total power, she would have to offer something more precious than gold. She would have to offer her soul. In exchange, Satan himself will grant her the desires of your heart. Mabel became outraged with Asela and called on the great

master himself. Asela laughed in her face and told her that she had no power."

"Mabel full of anger pulled out a knife and killed Asela in cold blood. As Asela laid dead on the ground, Mabel cut out her heart while it was still was beating. With her blood filled hands, she held up the heart calling on the spirits with no response. Then, she called on the great master and demanded he grant her request. Angered the great evil master sent me. I, Zota, appeared to Mabel. I told her that the one who she killed was a powerful Voodoo Priestess. I told Mabel that her killing of Asela had now cursed both her and her generations to come. The only way to remove the curse is to give a greater sacrifice to the Great Master."

"Mabel was afraid because she didn't realize the consequences of her actions, until it was too late. She pleaded for mercy and was willing to give up her own soul. However, it was too late. She was given a certain amount of time to gather her sacrifice."

"Asela had two small children, Samuel and Barbra. They were one day going to become a great and powerful Voodoo Priest and Priestess just like their mother. However, since Mabel had killed their mother, she had caused them their birthright. Instead of ultimate power, they would each be given a gift. Mabel would now be responsible for them, and through their gifts she would have power. But, she would never have power."

"Mabel agreed, but she hated children. She treated them worse than slaves. Samuel and Barbra grew up and tried to escape from her. When she learned of their plans, she made an ultimate pact and drank their blood thinking it would give her their power. Instead, her act bonded them together. They became *the Partners,* because each of them shared parts of one another. Their lives became intertwined and one could not live without the other."

"Over time, Samuel became full of anger from the years of abuse and bondage he suffered from Mabel. His heart turned cold and evil. He distanced himself from everyone, even Barbra. He was the mastermind behind *Loving Holms*. He made the money making plates. He was the one who killed Rubert. He was out of control, and his powers were growing stronger and stronger."

"Barbra could no longer stand back and allow Samuel's anger to hurt anyone else. She used her powers to change his mindset. His love for you and Angela changed his heart. She then used her powers to change Mabel's mind. She made her believe that Samuel and Barbra were dead. They changed their identity and started new lives at *the Beautiful One Salon*."

"For years they lived in the shadows of Mabel, until Rodney found out the truth of their existence. He killed them both. He did not realize that Mabel, Samuel and Barbra were are all connected."

"Now the only living descendent of Asela is Angela, your daughter. She will one day take her place as a powerful Voodoo priestess looking for revenge on the living descendent of Mabel Holms. Samuel was evil, but he did change. Angela will have to change too, if she wants to ever have a normal life. It is going to be your responsibility to steer her in the right direction. Do you have revenge in your heart for the death of Samuel, or are you willing to forgive with love in your heart? It's your choice."

I looked at Zota in wonder of what was just revealed to me.

Then she began to fade.
Before she faded, she spoke a word of promise,
"The words I have spoken to you are the secret you must keep till death. You must never tell a soul of this conversation, not Angela or even Henry."

As she faded to darkness, Henry's stature reappeared.

"Big Mama was the devil, and our neighborhood was hell. Our daddies and mammas lives were free of choices. They had no choice. Big Mama made all the rules and made all the decisions." He said.

Immediately, Henry began his story.

He said.

"They were all evil. One day, Big Mama sensed Barbra, Samuel and Rubert were scheming and plotting something that had to do with her. They knew Big Mama wanted money. Samuel took some steel and chiseled out an engraving plate for making money counterfeit money. He made three steel plates to make money. He made a twenty, a fifty and a hundred dollar plate. They told Big Mama the plates were with a man in Mexico. They told her they would kill him, and then bring her the plates, if she agreed to free them from the *Partners*. She agreed. "

"Rubert went to Samuel to pick up the plates. He was going to deliver them to Big Mama, but by the next morning the plates were gone. Rubert was framed for stealing the plates. Big Mama knew it, but she put out a hit on his life anyway. The day Rubert was killed the power of the *Partners* were weakened. His death was done unjustly. There are rules which have to be followed, even when you're dealing with the devil. "

"When Big Mama realized her power was weakening, she sought out to find Barbra and Samuel. There was some force which protected them. It was a power greater than Big Mama. Samuel and Barbra had changed their lives for good. Big Mama couldn't touch them, until you came along. You had Angela."

"Angela is the seed of Samuel, and she didn't have the protection. A hit was put out on her life. Barbra and

Samuel sacrificed themselves for your and Angela's protection. They became the sacrifices for the both of you."

"The plates were never found. So much blood has been shed, because of their existence. If I ever got my hands on those plates, I would destroy them myself. Big Mama's life is soon approaching its end. But, it's the daddies that still hold true to the bond of the *Partners*. Their bond holds me bound. Big Mama has something of mine dearer to me than my own heart. As long as I do her bidding, that precious item is protected."

Tears began to swell up in Henry's eyes. He came out of his trance like state.

I now had all of my questions answered. I could now have peace. I knew more than ever that I needed to be strong. I needed to carry on the legacy of those, who sacrificed their lives for us. I wasn't going to let their sacrifice be in vain. I was going to rebuild the school bigger and better. I was going to change as many lives as I could. I was going to show people outer beauty and help them reach inner beauty. I was going to show them how to find value within themselves.

I got up to leave, then Henry grabbed me by the arm and said,
"This meeting never happened. Our conversation is a secret that better be buried with you as you lay to rest. Trust no one, not even me."

His words were heavy and fell on me. They seeped into my soul. I pulled away and walked out the door.

Then I turned and said,
"I am keeping my promise."

Now that I was part of the *Partners,* I wanted to get on with my plans to open up the beauty school *Beautiful One.* This would be in remembrance of my Mr. Roberts and Mrs. Barbra.

Then my plans where heard about, and they were stopped in their tracks. I blamed Henry for that. I went to work in a beauty salon to make ends meet. I needed to take care of Angela.

Times were hard, but I did my best. I had the house, yet the up-keep of it was massive. I finally understood why Mr. Roberts never turned on the heat.

The house was mine, and there were still rooms in the house I never ventured into. When Mr. Roberts was living, I was forbidden to even ask about them. Now that he was gone, I wanted to go into them. I often felt like his presence was still in the house, and I wanted to respect his wishes.

However, one night while unable to sleep, my curiosity got the best of me! Every time I would even try to fall asleep, I would imagine what Mr. Robert could have possibly been hiding in there? I couldn't take it anymore. I went right to the door and turned the knob. To my surprise, it was unlocked! I walked inside to see the most elaborate micro clothing factory I had ever seen. There were drawings for fashions and some finished items. Now I understood what he was doing up there. He was making clothes. I looked around in amazement of his creativity, and his ability to re-create. As I was looking around in the corner, I noticed a safe. I walked over to it, turned the handle and it opened.

Inside were also stacks of money! On top of the money was an envelope. It was addressed to me.

I opened the envelope and pulled out the single sheet of paper that read,

"Mindy. If you are reading this, then I know you are no longer afraid. You are strong enough to handle whatever comes your way. This money, you see, is for you and Angela. But be careful not to bring attention to yourself as you spend it, because the secret of its existence comes with much danger and possibly death. Use it only as needed, and let it stay our little secret."

I fell to the floor turning the paper over and over. I wanted there to be more. I wanted him to say, "I love you" or "I had this planned all of the time". I wanted him to give me the plans for my next steps. Or more importantly, I wanted the secret of how to destroy the *Partners* and kill Big Mama. But there was nothing.

What else did I expect from Mr. Roberts? He was never a talker, but he was a provider. Even in his grave, he was thinking about Angela and me.

My husband was not perfect. I knew that. In reality, others may have even looked at him as evil. After all, he was my lover when I was only fifteen. But when I came of age and was old enough, he was also a good husband and father.

I still couldn't believe that it was my husband, who had created the famous plates! So many nights he must have stayed up chiseling the perfect replica of money. That was incredible. My man was incredible. And, I was not going to let his life be in vain! He was willing to go the extra mile to protect his family, and so was I.

I had money. My money troubles were over. I could now focus all my attention on my plans to resurrect the beauty school and nobody was going to stop me.

BEAUTY SECRET BLUES

Beautiful Eyes Behold

*Whoever said money can't buy you happiness was
drunk, jealous, crazy or just plain stupid!*

⌁Annie

~ For the first time in my life, I have more money than I could
ever spend. I sure am happy! ~

I remember growing up in that two block radius
neighborhood. I was never able to explore nothing
past the old laundry mat. I ate whatever Daddy
dropped off once a week. I played with the same kids. We
played them same old tired games day after day. I wanted
more, and I needed more. I knew I would figure out how to get
it! No matter how much it cost. I was determined to have
whatever I wanted.

Mamma wasn't the only one who could make money rain
from her ass. I was going to use my ass to rain hundreds.
Mamma was a hoe! She was a real street walk'n, pimp have'n
hoe. And her best friends, the Aunties, as she had us kids call
them, were hoes too.

Mamma, was called Sugar Cat by some of her men callers.
They said, "She was fine as wine and her body tasted like
honey." Mamma was beautiful! She was half-Puerto Rican
and half-Black. Her shape puts a coke bottle to shame! Her
skin was caramel, and she had the most beautiful freckles. She
had pretty green eyes that changed to hazel, when the sun hit
them just right! When she talked, the words were smooth and
flowing. To the unsuspected listener, she could talk you out of
your clothes. Mamma had that way about her. She had the
power to control men. Mamma was always named the #1 hoe.

Mamma kept it real! She said,
"Annie, this ain't the life for everyone. No one can choose
this for you. Whoring ain't pretty and it sure ain't cute.
The most beautiful thing your eyes will ever behold is
your money, 'cause that's the only prize! Once you have
money, no one cares about beauty, respect or love. They
just love the money! If you chose a life of hoeing, you
have to accept this life on your own terms. Remember, it's
a hustle! The beauty of this hustle is, if you hustle the
right one you never have to worry about money again.
Just make sure you're the hustler and never be the one
getting hustled. The hustler is the only one that gets to
keep the check."

I knew what she meant.

Mamma made her paper, but daddy was there once a
week to cash that check. What he left for us to live on was a
sharecroppers share. I loved my daddy don't get me wrong,
after all he was my daddy. But right is right, and my daddy
was pure down and dirty wrong. He was wrong right from the
start.
My daddy, Earl, and the other pimps ran all the houses.
They were all only out for themselves. There were four daddies
that controlled ten houses. Who really knew which daddy
fathered who? Each house had only one child, except Mamma
Jean. She was the only auntie who had two kids. The other
aunties started complaining about Mamma Jean having two
kids.

They said things like,
"Why is she so special? What she got we ain't got? Does
she think she's better than us?"

And before you knew it, she was back down to one child
just like everybody else. That day was a shame too, because Lil'
Syn was only about 4 to 5 or so! She was a happy child. She
was minding her own business that day, when out of nowhere
came a black car. It pulled up, put her in it, and as fast as it
came, it went away just as fast. She was never seen again.

From that day on, all the aunties got their stuff together. Whatever our daddies said, they did. Everybody was scared their child was going to be next. The sad part of Little Syn being taken away was watching Mamma Jean chase that car down the street. She knew she couldn't catch it, but I guess she didn't know what else to do. She ran until something happened with her leg, and she collapsed!

Not one of the aunties came to help her. She lay in that street, until nightfall. By the next morning she was gone. I waited a few days. I thought I would see her limping on her way to the street corner to make her money like everybody else. But, I never did.

You almost wanted to feel sorry for the Aunties. You could see it in their eyes. None of them wanted to be hoes, but somehow this was the hand they were dealt. In this game, there were no winners. The game ended when you did.

I was different! I wasn't going to wait for someone to get me out of this prison! I was going to make my own way out. All I needed was a plan, and then I could go and make my money. I told myself by the time I reach sixteen, I was going to be my own woman, making my own money, and doing things my own way! But for now I'll just sit back and wait out my sentence.

Out of the ten houses, there were six children. But after Lil' Syn was gone, there were five left. There were three girls and two boys. Henry was the oldest, me, Rodney, Joyce and Mindy. Lil' Syn was much younger than us.

The girls had it the hardest! We had no respect and were treated like mini-hoes. Henry's daddy was the worst! James was tall and lean, dark in color. He had the face that carried war wounds! He shaved his head bald and his eyebrows were thick like his facial hair. He wore a beard, mustache and chin-straps that he kept immaculate. He dressed in silk suits and polished shoes, and would slap a heifer for saying, "Hi," without permission.

James would tell Henry,
"A woman ain't worth a quarter, but her body is First National Bank! Make sure you get that account number and withdraw whatever is deposited."

James made Henry's life hell! Each day he would tell Henry how weak, he was.

"Why can't you be more like me?" He would say, while pointing at his chest.

He walked around like he was king of the mount. Henry didn't look like James. James was tall and lanky, while Henry had an athletic stalk build. James was dark, Henry was light. The more James wondered about it, the more he punished Henry for not being more like him, cruel and unfeeling.

Henry had a heart. You could tell that pimping and hustling wasn't in his character, so his daddy would call him a fag, a cock lover or a punk. He would punch Henry and slap him, to try and make him tough. James started prepping Henry, when he was very. I remember one day, Joyce, Henry and I were playing hopscotch on the sidewalk. When James came up behind Henry and went to town on him.
He beat that boy senseless for playing with us.

He told him,
"Don't you ever play with a woman. They ain't your friends. They's your money."

Henry just lay there whimpering, James stood over him in disgust. Henry's legacy was to take over this whole operation, since he was the oldest and all. But, the one who had the heart for this type of life was Rodney. Rodney's father was Steve. Steve was much like James. He was James' go to guy. He was the type who would shoot now, and ask questions later. When you looked at him, you saw a soulless human being, and Rodney was just like him.

Rodney had no morals, no values or a soul. He loved the pimpin' and hustling life from birth. The only problem with

him taking over was he was born after Henry. So the birthright belonged to Henry.

Rodney and Henry were forced to be best friends. They were all each other had. Yet, they were as different as day is to night. Henry represented the day and Rodney the night. Although they were very different, Henry loved him some Rodney. Rodney was like the little brother he never had. He protected him, coddled him and told him what to do. Since, Rodney didn't have the best sense of judgment.

Rodney on the other hand, hated Henry like a woman hates a snake. Henry was a thorn in Rodney's side. Rodney's every thought was how to pull it out.

They couldn't play with us. All their time was spent together, learning how to be pimps and the hustling game from their daddies. When Rodney wanted to mess around, I was his play hoe. I knew as soon as I was old enough, I would be his official one.

Henry on the other hand had his eyes on Joyce, but Joyce was so strange. She never really talked much. Around the age of ten or so, she stopped talking period. She hardly ever came out the house. She would just sit in her living room window watching the world go by. Joyce was strange, and I stayed as far away from that crazy hoe, as possible.

The boys did what they wanted to do. They were trained to walk in their father's footsteps. We were raised to 'walk on them streets' way behind them. They got all the nice clothes, ate like kings, and talked to their mammas like dogs.

It was a shame. How you could birth a child, then have your own child order you around. If their mamma's got out of hand, their daddy's would tell them to teach their mamma's a lesson. They would cuss them and even sometimes hit them, especially Rodney. It was a crying shame, but that's how the daddies did things.

They told them,
"Women ain't nothing, ain't ever going to be nothing. All they do is lie, cheat and steal, you can't trust them. All

they are good for is the bank roll that sits between them legs."

Although the boy's heard that crap all their life, they still saw their mother's struggles, and to us they were our brothers.

As Henry got older he learned how to put on a front for his father. Henry loved the Lord! One year when Henry was about twelve, a man with bibles came around. He talked to all of us about God, church and vacation bible school. When Henry heard the Word, the lessons from the church, he was changed and vowed to never be a heartless pimp. Joyce fell for Henry at that moment and he fell for her.

Rodney ran back and told James what Henry said. James was furious. He must have stopped the man from coming into *the hood*, because we never saw him again. The little Bibles were taken away, and he blamed Joyce for making Henry's heart weak.

One day a few years later, James and Steve went over to Mamma Jean's house. They beat both her and Joyce so bad, we didn't see them for a whole year! The next time I saw Mamma Jean, she was holding her a new baby. She had named her Lil' Syn.

When she appeared with that baby, the mess really hit the fan. All the Aunties were jealous! I don't know why? They couldn't feed the one child they had.

People are the same no matter if they are rich or poor. They always want what someone else got!

Never the less the question was asked,
"How was she rewarded with a baby after being punished?"

I think there was more to it, but perception is everything.

Rodney didn't have a problem with his lifestyle. He had no remorse for the pain he caused Mamma Jean and Joyce. He

liked life like it was. If he had to keep mess going to make sure
it stayed that way, he was down.

Rodney had big dreams of running this whole city, but
Rodney was dumb. He couldn't complete a sentence without
stuttering. His mind worked the same way. He couldn't keep
a thought for five minutes without losing track of it. The only
thought Rodney's mind could hold on to was Henry. He had a
hatred for Henry like Cain had for Abel, and this jealousy
consumed him. He wanted the birthright that was given to
Henry. He knew one day Henry would be the leader of
everything. He knew he would always be seen by Henry as the
weaker one. To be honest, Rodney deserved that birthright.
Rodney's heart was evil like the life we were born into.

Rodney tried every day to change Henry's heart, so one
day they could be partners. Henry would just shrug him off.
Rodney wanted Henry to be messy, lie and keep up commotion
just like him. Henry was fair and saw things differently. This
pissed Rodney off even more! You could tell Rodney wanted to
fight Henry. But Rodney was short and frail, if the wind blew
too hard, he would be blown right down the street! Let's just
say he was light in the ass.

He had a little boy's face. Not the type of face your mother
could love or anybody for that matter! I was the only one who
understood him and loved him. Henry on the other hand was
big and strong. His presence demanded attention. He was a
nice brown-colored. His lips were kissable, face loveable, and
he was smart as a whip. If you were held by Henry, you didn't
ever want to him to let you go. Every time Rodney suggested a
plan to get out, Henry would just shoot him down.

After a while, the pressure was too much for Rodney to
handle. He wanted out, because he was tired of having to take
orders from Henry. He couldn't go one more day living in
Henry's shadows. Rodney and I were on the same page.

I didn't mind hoe'n to get our release papers.

Rodney said,
"If we did ever take that step to be together, he would be a
better pimp to me than my daddy was to my mamma. He

wouldn't make me do no john I didn't want to. I could
keep some of my money and everything would be better."

I felt like that was a good partnership. After all, a girl
needs protection. At the end of a long work night laying with a
bunch of strangers, you still need someone real to hold on to. I
don't care what anybody says, a woman wants someone to call
her own, no matter how bad he may be.

Rodney and I never told no one our plans. We knew if it
got out, there would be someone out there waiting to destroy
our dreams. I wanted out of this place so bad, I was willing to
sacrifice my life for it.

"Sugar Cat, Oooh..... Babe I like the way you handle that!
Yea mamma deeper, deeper, oh yea…. That's the way I
like it, right there keep it right there….."

I heard coming from the other room, through my half
asleep, half awaken state. I hate when mamma is still working.
It's mornin already! Give it a rest! He must be paying overtime,
cause it ain't like Mamma to be up this time of mornin with no
job.

I rolled over in my bed and looked outside to see Mindy
and Joyce sitting outside on the porch looking all innocent-like.

I told Henry and Rodney,
"Wait till they realize they ain't going to be noth'n , but
old hoes just like they mammas. I heard Mindy's daddy is
already teaching her how to handle a private in her
mouth, and she can suck it like a trooper already."

We all laughed, but it was a shame how Mindy's daddy
took her innocence so early.

I wonder what those hood-rats are talking about.
Probably something dumb like the silly games we play on the
sidewalk. Sometime I wish, I was close to someone and had a
best girlfriend.

116

But Mamma always says,
"Put a woman too close, next thing you know, they are
more you than you are yourself. They will steal all you
got, and you be left with noth'n. But if you keep your
man close, he can't take nothing from you that you don't
let him have. You got the power, you in control."

I know Mamma's right, but having someone to play dress
up with or tell your most private secrets to sure would be nice,
every once in a while.

I pulled the curtains back down and rolled over hoping to
go back to sleep, so I wouldn't have to listen to what was going
on in mamma's room. Just as I was drifting into a sleep state, I
heard a knock at the door. I wondered who it could be? This
wasn't Daddy's day to come by. I stayed in my room. Mamma
didn't allow me out of my room, while she was working.

She says,
"Not all men are in the right frame of mind, and all
women body starts looking the same to them even if it's
aged or not."

I got out the bed and pushed my head to the door to see
what I could hear. I heard mamma's footsteps in the front room
to answer the door.

"Why the hell are ya'll here. What have I done?" Mamma
said in a loud sarcastic way.

I waited to hear a response, so I could hear a voice to see if
I could tell who it was. All of a sudden, I heard loud blows like
fists to a face. But who was the punching bag?

I thought.
"Lord no. Please, not my mamma!"

I could hear her body being thrown around, breaking up
our furniture. I knew that my mamma was in big trouble and

there was nothing, no one that could help her now. I ran and hid under my bed.

I started asking myself,

"What Mamma did? Was this a setup? Did she short Daddy on some money?"

My mind was racing trying to figure out,

"Why she was being beaten like this? Could this be a setup? Is she being robbed?"

I wanted to call my Daddy because I knew he would at least want to protect his investment, but the phone was in the front room. If I made any noise they would know I was here.

"What about Mamma?" I thought.

I could hear her begging for them to stop.

I pressed my ear to the floor,
"Please, please just tell me what I did wrong. Let me make it right. Whatever I've done, I'm sorry. I'll do anything just stop. Please stop."

Her voice was trembling. I never heard fear come out of my mamma's mouth. Then I heard a crash, and mamma's body hit the floor. I heard them drag her to her room. I couldn't tell how many exactly, but I was sure it was more than three.

I thought to myself.
"This was a setup. I knew it was strange for a job to still be here in the morning. He didn't want to pay Mamma her money. Now he is going to let his partners get in on the action for free,"

Men ain't nothing just like Mamma said. I could hear loud talking coming from mamma's room. She was screaming in pain. They must have been running a train on her.

I heard one say,
"My turn get out the way. This will teach this heifer for taking what's not hers. Move on out of the way, so I can put my pole in that."

"Just put yours in her mouth till I'm finished." I heard another one say. "That will shut this heifer up."

Then I heard another say,
"Move over so I can get that ass."

I knew if I could hear all of this noise, someone else had to hear something too! Where were my Aunties? Why ain't they over here helping my mamma?

Then I remembered how they did Mamma Jean, they didn't help her either. I was paralyzed with my ear stuck to the floor. I no longer heard Mamma screaming.

I thought.
"Maybe they were finished. Maybe they felt she had enough, and this whole nightmare was over."

There was silence for while I didn't hear anything. Then, I heard footsteps coming towards my room.
My heart dropped.

"Why were they coming to my room? Had Mamma dimmed me out to save her neck? Was her body worn out, so they were coming to use up mine?" I thought.

I took a deep breath and told myself,
"Annie you said you ain't no child no more. Now stand up and be a woman."

If I knew if I wanted the privileges of grown folks, I was going to have to do grown folk things.

I wiped my eyes. Yelling, I told myself,
"Stop crying like a spoiled heifer! You going to be a baby or take it like a women."

I was fifteen and someone needed to relieve my mamma. I crawled from under my bed and stood up. The door opened and my heart dropped. There stood my daddy, Earl. I was devastated!!

He was the one I was going to call for help. As I stood there, I knew I stood there alone. In that moment, I knew I had nobody. I never was one to cry, but being betrayed by your own father just does something to you.

"Daddy?" I whispered because I couldn't make a sound.

As I looked into his face, his eyes were cold. He stood in front of me like the pimp. He was not my daddy.

"Shut up! Take that gown off." He yelled. "It's time for you to pay for your dumbass mamma's mistakes! Next time, she will think before she disobeys me."

He snatched my arm, so hard I thought it was going to come out the socket. He took me into Mamma's room. It smelled like old ass sweat and blood.

I saw Mamma laid out, naked and bloody. It seemed like the blood was oozing from every hole in her body. Mamma didn't look like Sugar Cat anymore. She just looked like a worn out hoe.

When I entered the room, Mamma never moved. She just laid there motionless.

"Mamma!" I cried out, but she didn't respond.

I looked around the room. There were four men, including my daddy. They looked at me like I was their next victim.

They were half dressed in their t-shirts and boxers. Their privates hung out of the slit in the boxers, still wet from being inside my Mamma. They had blood on their hands. They stood there like apes ready to devour their next victim. Sweat ran from their foreheads. They were still high from the rush of the previously won battle. From the looks of their clean shaves and lined haircuts, I could tell that these men had money. They didn't need to take body for free. I knew they were here to prove a point.

I raised my gown over my head and stood there.

"Where have you been hiding little girl, you have a big debt to pay. I hope you have more strength than your mamma did." One said.

Then he pushed Mamma on the floor, ripped off the dirty sheets from the bed and laid them over her, like she was a dead dog.

I looked him in the eyes, because I never wanted to forget his face. I felt like the last slice of cake at the party and everyone was willing to fight over it to get a bit.

Before I knew it, one came up behind me and slammed me on the bed. I could feel his knee in my back, while the other man pulled my legs opened, and forced his hand in my inside, as if to shape it to the size of his pole. They poked and rubbed and spit at it me.

One yelled at the other, as he prepped me before the invasion,

"Make sure her tail is good and wet, I want to enjoy this."

Then one after another, after another, they all took turns, including my daddy! They forced their poles in me, ramming as hard as they could. I was ripped wide-open.

I closed my eyes and cried silently. In my mind, I thought of Mamma. All I saw was sadness in her face. Mamma talked so tough and put on such a front, about how good her life was.

But the truth was, Mamma lived a life of regret and forced bondage. When she spoke of how weak women were, how they couldn't handle this life. She was talking about herself.

Mamma wasn't bragging to me about her past, she was warning me of my future. Mamma never chose to be a hoe. Her life was full of fear and suffering. She was a slave to this life. She lived and died a slave. She had a life of pain and misery, and no one was even here to morn for her--but me. I was the very product of her unrewarded life.

My Mamma was dead, but her death taught me more than words. It taught me change. I blocked out the men's cheering and coaching each other on. I blocked out the punching and slapping. I blocked out all the degrading names I was being called. I just concentrated on my mamma.

By the time they were finished, it was almost night, and my nightmare ended. They left. I laid there. I was in so much pain. I reached down to feel my sore body and ass. I looked at my hand and saw all the blood.

I felt and it looked like I was stabbed. My body was swollen and I hurt all over. My thighs and butt were bruised from the weight of their bodies and from each thrust that entered me. My back felt bent, and I never was able to stand up straight again.

I rolled over, got on the floor next to mamma and put my ear to her chest. I needed to hear her heart beat just one more time. There was nothing. I closed her eyes and kissed her on her lips.

I whispered to her,
"I love you Mamma. Your dreams of a better life are with me. Thank you for the sacrifice. It will be worth it."

I lay next to mamma and pulled the sheet around us both to keep us warm, and went to sleep.

I heard a loud knocking coming from the front room. I was afraid to answer it.

"Who could be at the door?" I thought.
"Was it more men to pick up where they left off? Did they come back to finish me off so they would have no witnesses? Was it daddy coming back to say I'm sorry?"

I put my ear to the floor.
I heard a woman's voice,
"Come answer this door gal."

I got up, went to opened the door, and there stood Mindy's mamma.
"What did she want?" I thought. "Out of all of the Aunties she was the meanest. Why did they send her? I needed some compassionate words right now."

All she had to offer was some,
"Shut the Hell up witch."

Right now that wasn't enough. Right now all I wanted was a hug from someone who loved me. I wanted to hear someone say,
"It's going to be okay".

I opened the door for her. She stood there looking at me in disgust, as if I asked for it. I stared into her face, hoping for a glimmer of condolence. But like always it was hard and unfeeling.

"Girl, get something and cover yourself up," she snapped.
"Grab your things and come on. Hurry up! I ain't got all day to fool with this foolishness!"

I paused for a moment. I wanted to tell her about my Mamma. I wanted to tell her what they did. Instead, I walked slowly into my room and put on some clothes. I went back into momma's room and ripped off a piece of the bloody sheet that lay over my mamma. I folded it, in remembrance of her. I threw some items in a bag, and left with Mindy's mamma.

We were going to her house.

> As we walked, she scuffed,
> "What's done is done, ain't no need to discuss this no
> more, you hear me?"

I didn't say anything.

> She stopped and looked at me with them monster eyes.
> "Yes Auntie," I answered with a trembling voice, and we
> went to her house.

> "Girls, get your lazy asses up! This ain't no hotel, and you
> witches ain't just goin to lie up all day."

Her yelling was the first thing I heard, the next morning.

I hated living here! Mindy's mamma was insane. She
hollered about everything, and every word out of her mouth is
a cuss word. She wakes up in a bad mood every day and goes
to sleep the same way. I don't know how Mindy does it! A dog
would be treated better and live better too.

The house was filthy and smelled like piss mixed with ass,
then top that with peanut butter and tuna. Old food was
molded on the dishes and on the counters. The floors looked
like the catch all for all that didn't fit on the counters. The
furniture was sticky from sweat and cum. The house was dark
because of all the mold growing on all the walls.

The bathroom smelled so bad, you would rather hold it, or
do your business outside. The brown slime all around and in
the toilet made you think twice before sitting on it. You
couldn't take a bath in the tub or wash your hands in the sink.
They both held nasty clothes soaking in gray murky water.

When I tell you the house was gross? I mean gross. At
night I felt the bed bugs biting and the roaches crawling. I also
heard the rats in the kitchen for a midnight snack. The house

needed to be condemned. No one should be forced to live like this, especially a child.

Mindy's mamma wasn't any better. She was a cold alcoholic. If she had any money, it went on booze and cigarettes. She kept a drink in her hand, and a cigarette dangling from her mouth from dusk til' dawn.

Now I see why Mindy doesn't say much. She's always ready to fight, because she had no one to love her. In her room, there was only a bed, and a few clothes in a small pile on the floor. Those clothes were so nasty they needed to go straight to the trash. All the bad talking I did about Mindy made me feel bad. I felt sorry for her. My momma, Sugar Cat might not have been the ideal parent, but she did love me and she told me often. She kept a clean house and something to eat for dinner.

She said,
"You better love yourself Annie, because life doesn't give a damn."

I really miss my Mamma. I can't stay here. If I do, I will go insane too! There was no way I was going to stay here! My new plan was to leave this house as soon as possible, but before I leave I wanted to help Mindy. Seeing how she had to live, and the pain she must feel every day. I understand her so much better.

One night while we were sleeping, I felt Mindy moving around in the bed. I opened my eyes and was startled to see Mindy's father Rubert standing over her. His silhouette was massive. It blocked the moonlight coming through the window and the bedroom became pitch black.

His deep voice rumbled as he spoke,

"Get up girl and clean off this pole. Your mouth is the cleanest thing in this nasty place!"

Mindy got up and did what she was told.

When he was finished, he said,
"You better swallow it all witch." Mindy never responded.

After he left, she just lay down in the bed and went back to sleep, like it was the norm. I rolled over and cried for her. I was never the praying type, not even when them men were doing the unthinkable to Momma and me. Today, I said a prayer for Mindy, because although what happened to me was bad, it only lasted a day. But, this has been happening to Mindy her whole life. I needed an escape. I vowed a vow that one day I would make it right for Mindy. I was going to love her, because no one else did.

The next morning we woke up early, before her mamma started her raving, mad round of cuss words and insults. I knew Mindy was awake because of her breathing. It was heavy and labored.
I knew she was ashamed of what I witnessed the night before, so I whispered.

"Mindy. You woke?" But she was silent.
I continued. "I'm sorry, if no one ever tells you, I will... I'm sorry."

I heard a faint sigh leave her body. It sounded like she had been waiting all her life to release. She turned over, and we faced each other. Our eyes were locked. It felt like we could read each ones sorrows and pain.

"We are going to leave this place!" I said with conviction.
"We have to keep it a secret. No matter what, we will love each other. We're all we got." Mindy nodded in agreement.

We both laid there in silence, until our silence was invaded by Mindy's Mamma's regiment. Here we go. Another day, but now we had a plan. Soon, it was going to be another way, instead of just another day.

The days turned into weeks. The weeks drifted into months. My life at Mindy's was hell on earth. The verbal abuse was so constant and landed hard. Each word hit you like a baseball being hit with a bat, and they always scored a home run. The words shot out of Mindy's mom's mouth, so fast they broke your spirit and crushed your soul. After a while, the words began to soak in. Your body felt weak and heavy. It was like you were carrying all the bad in the world on your shoulders. The only strength I could draw was from my dreams to leave this god forsaken place.

I kept telling myself,
"I love you Annie," and before I went to sleep at night. I told Mindy that I loved her too.

I taught Mindy how to clean the house. I told her how important she was. I told her that she was a young lady, and young ladies needed to look pretty and smell pretty. I showed her how to keep her private clean. She started to take baths every day. She washed her panties out in the sink at night, before she went to bed, so she would feel and smell fresh in the morning. I gave her some of my clothes to wear. I took some of her old things and pieced them together to sew new ones. I did her hair and nails, before long her whole outlook on life changed.

I began to see hope in her eyes. I told her just because life dealt us this shitty-hand didn't mean we had to take mess. We could play the game by our own rules, and we could win.

Mindy was spending so much time with me that Joyce stopped coming around. Mindy and I became best friends. Mindy's mamma never changed, and Rubert still made her suck his private. The house was now clean, so he could no longer

use dirt as an excuse. But we didn't care, we had each other. And for the first time here, we both felt love.

We started playing dress up. We pretended and acted like we were rich and famous. We worked on our vocabulary and manners. We walked with books on our heads to improve our posture. We had a beauty regiment every day and practiced walking up and down the sidewalk like runway models. We would critique each other on how we looked. Mindy was tall and thin with petite features, pretty black hair and camel brown skin. She had just enough ass and tits to balance it all out. Her curves were small but sexy.

I told her,
"Stand up straight, show pride when you walk. Walk as if you are gliding on a cloud and someone was pulling you up by a string attached to the top of your head."

She practiced and practiced until she had perfected her walk, which was more like a glamour glide. Mindy looked stunning and elegant when she walked. She had a class of confidence about herself, even though we had nothing. I watched in amazement, as she grew up!

Who knew giving her just a little hope would change her whole life? Mindy strutted back and forth looking for my approval, and then she stopped to strike a pose. I could tell she was in deep thought, so was I. Mindy looked up to me! One reason was because I was the oldest, and I had the attitude that life had no power over me. The world was mine. But as I got older, I could feel the pressures of my life, and my perception of hope fading fast.

I once saw myself as the beauty queen of the block. I was a short little pistol full of fire and life. Now, I look in the mirror, and all I see is a short, insecure girl with fallen big tits, no ass and a fat-round face full of large freckles. I hated it all. The night of the rape left my back twisted, so I walked slightly bent over.

In one day everything changed for me. On that horrible day, I was left motherless and had more physical and emotional

scars than I could deal with. I had a constant reminder of that night. I held it close inside of me for nine months. Then one day, I let it go.

I wished the secret would just go away and never return.

> *Yet, just as the world goes around in circles, so do our deepest secrets. No matter how hard you try to conceal them, they grow out of control and there is nothing you can do about it, but wish you were never given the secret in the first place.*

I gave my secret away. A baby boy named Eric. He took with him the best part of me, a piece of my heart.

I woke up to a tapping on the window I got up and peeped out from the torn curtain. It was Rodney. I opened the window to see his tiny frame covered with dirt.

"What the hell do you want Rodney it's four o'clock in the morning?" I asked.

He looked at me in desperation.

"Come on, let's go. I got to get out of here, before I kill somebody or somebody kills me!" He pleaded intensely. Rodney's voice was pleading in panic.

"What's wrong, Rodney?" I asked.

I needed to know what I was committing myself to. I knew in my best judgment, not to leave. But, I had nothing to lose, and this might be my only chance to escape this hell. So, I took the chance.

Still pleading he replied,

"Everything, let's just go Annie! Please, let's just go right now."

I turned around there stood Mindy. My heart dropped. I couldn't leave her here, but how could I take her with me? Mindy was just a child. The life that awaited me was for grown folks. I had promised we would stay together forever. But for her, here was better than where I was going. Mindy had a chance to be someone and change her circumstances. She could be somebody great. Where I was going was a dead end road of despair.

In her mind, out that window was hope for better tomorrows. That was true, just not with me and Rodney. I knew Rodney's plans and hope was not in them for me or him.

I knew when I climbed out of that window, our relationship would change forever. Our bond would be broken beyond repair. The look of betrayal on Mindy's face was haunting. It left an engraved picture in my mind. I couldn't look at her.

I turned my back to her and said,
    "What I look like dragging a baby around?"

As the words shot out of my mouth, the tone was the tone, like her momma calls us. It was just as unfeeling as if her momma herself had said it.

I tried to hide my face from her, but out of the corner of my eye I caught a glimpse of Mindy's eyes filled with water. I knew with the next blink, tears were going to roll down her thin brown cheeks. I saw her heart drop. How could I be so mean? I love her and she loves me, and I was breaking our promise.

As my feet hit the ground, I felt her thin little fingers grabbing for my hand. When she touched me, my heart skipped a beat. I had the strangest feeling like I was leaving my blood-kin--- my little sister? I looked deep into her water-filled eyes. And, in them…. I saw mine.

Mindy was more than just a girl I once knew and grew to love, she was the only family I had, and I was going to protect what was mine. I could no longer keep up the charade. The

thought of us being apart touched my spirit, and full emotions came over me. I wanted to be strong for her. I wanted to be the big sister, she could be proud of and maybe one day look up too. I wanted so much, but my time was up! I had to go!

My voice quivered as I tried to fight back the tears and say,
"Mindy, I got to go, but I promise I will come back for you. I promise I will be looking for you, and when you need me the most, I will be there."

I quickly turned around. I could no longer look her in the face. My heart was breaking with each passing second. I quickly ran through the yard and got in the car with Rodney, refusing to look back. I had a knot in my throat. My gut told me not to go. I ignored them both, and I never returned to live in that neighborhood again.

I knew Mindy would never forgive me, but I had my one chance for escape and I took it. I knew my freedom would cost me a great price, yet I never thought it would cost me my best friend, my sister. The one person I knew for sure loved me.

I wish I could say life with Rodney was all peaches and cream. All I did was trade a nightmare for a horror story.

Rodney was all about making bank! The only problem was my body was the bank. Each day men made their deposits. Rodney was there making all the withdrawals, I never saw a dime. He made the deals, named the price, and collected all the money. He took plenty of lessons from his father, Steve, and turned out to be a real-life pimp. He was like no other, cold-hearted and mean-spirited. He didn't give a flying flip about me. All he cared about was me making that money.

Years went by, I watched Rodney get more hoes, buy nicer cars, and move in a nice home with his new younger and prettier heifers, while I lived in a weekly. He would pay for my weekly when he wanted to pay. If not, I had to walk up and down the street all night looking for the next john. I tried to sneak in a nap, while he was hitting it from the back.

Rodney ate like a king, steaks and lobster. I ate his leftovers he got from a restaurant. It was rarely a piece of steak.

The only reason I could tell he had a steak was the steak sauce left on the half-eaten baked potato. I hated Rodney just as much as I hated the men that killed my mamma. I swore that one day I would make them all pay for what they did to us.

Well, one day came sooner than I thought and my life changed forever. My eyes were fixed on a dried cum stain on a low budget motel bedspread. I was on all fours taking it doggie-style waiting for a job to finish screwinging me. He was pale, fat and sweating like he was really doing something. I could see why he had to pay for tail. He was ugly and had no skills. He was banging me like a jackrabbit on the run trying to find a hole. His fat stomach slammed against my ass as he tried to go deep with his two inch small private.

Somewhere between the dirty talks of, "ooh baby, baby," and "Keep it right here," and, "Oooh…. You're so big daddy,"

I looked on the floor and saw an old newspaper. Right on the front page in front of my eyes the headline read, *"Winner Paul Marshall for Mayor."*

The name didn't mean a thing to me, but the men in the picture were worth millions. Paul was standing in front of a podium with his hands waving in the victory sign high above his head. From left to right were two men on one side and two on the other. Their faces were engraved in my mind like a notary seal. They took everything from me, and here they are as bold as everything, looking like some innocent priest. I knew the men who came by that day were important by the silk boxers and expensive cologne, but the Mayor! These so called leaders were the ones who raped me and killed my Mamma! They were the ones that came in our house that day and destroyed my whole world. Then they just walked away satisfied like they finished a meal at an expensive restaurant.

Paul's face stood out the most. He was the one who pushed my mamma's motionless body to the floor. He was also the first to force his sorry private in me.

The heartless bastard was standing there with a smile on his face, with no cares in the world. But, I was about to drop a

doomsday bomb on them all, the size of Texas. When I am done with them, I plan on collecting for all the pain, for all the hurt, for the rape, for the abuse, for the death of my Mamma and the fathering of my son.

The last man standing to the right of Paul, I knew too well. He was Steve, Rodney's father. He was smiling and celebrating with them. Steve wasn't there that night, but he was going to be the doorway to get my vengeance from them.

The wheels of my mind began to turn. They hadn't done that in a long time. I had stopped thinking, and I had stopped caring. I was a bad-ass witch once upon a time! I was once a girl who people thought twice about, before they approached. I was the one with balls.

Then it hit me like a ton of bricks. What the hell was I doing? Here I was hunched over like a dog accepting whatever from this fat slob that I'll never see a dime from. Nor am I even getting any satisfaction from it. This wasn't the life I had planned for myself. I was told I would be a hoe just like my mamma, when I was small, and here I am. At least mamma had a home, I don't even have that.

I rolled my flat ass over and I got up, leaving the little limp private wet and hanging. He went from pale white to fire engine red in five point two seconds. He started screaming and yelling to the top of his lungs. It sounded like I had taken a bone from a pit bull.

"Heifer, where the fuc' ya, thank ya goin'? Get yo ass back here and 'sume the position." He yelled, pointing his finger to the spot where I was hunched over in just seconds earlier.

I looked over at the red countrified cowboy, unmoved by his rage. My eyes were locked on him like a shotgun ready to fire. I reached over and wiped my wet tail with the end of the bedspread, pulled down my dress, grabbed the newspaper and walked out, slamming the door behind me.

I could still hear him screaming with that western accent, as I walked to the street corner to call Rodney on the pay phone.

I reached in my bra to get some change. My hands shook with anger.

After a few rings, he picked up the phone.
     I didn't wait for a response.
     "Rodney," I yelled. "I'm ready. Come get me."

He hung up the phone like he always did, like I was some kind of inconvenience. I waited for about an hour until he pulled up. Rodney rolled the window down and to his surprise I got in.

     "What the Hell! Heifer you crazy? Who do you think you are getting in my car?" He screamed in my face.

I turned and looked at him with so much anger and fire in my eyes. It caught his attention. He knew the old Annie was back. It was the old Annie, who didn't take no mess.

My lips were pressed, my fists were balled, my tone was sharp and deliberate.

     "You shut the Hell up! You are going to listen to me, and you had better listen to me good." I scream in his face. My tone was steady and course.

Shocked by my aggression, Rodney waited for my next word, unsure of what I might do.

     "My Mamma's dead because of these heartless assesers and I want my part!" I yelled.

I held the newspaper tight in my fist and waved it in his face. I looked him square in his eyes, then yelled,
     "You let your daddy know that I'm coming for his friends for what they did to me. They better get me my money too, because I'm not no free tail. Neither was my mamma. If they don't, their whole lifestyle will be over! The next time they think about screwinging over some heifers I want they asses to think twice. All secrets surface sooner

134

or later. If they want this secret to stay hidden, they better contact me, or else the next screw they receive will be in the pen. It will be them getting screweded in the ass. Their party is over! You tell them my message. If something happens to me all of their secrets will be on the front page of tomorrow newspapers! You know where to find me."

I threw the newspaper when I got out of the car. He grabbed it in midair, anxious to see what had stirred up all my emotions. As he looked at it to see what I saw, his eyes lit up in shock like a little kid on Christmas day. He saw one of the men in the picture was his daddy!

After Rubert was killed, our daddies disappeared, including his daddy. I think it bothered Rodney the most. He wanted so much to be just like him. His daddy just walked out on him. When Rubert was killed, everyone knew it was a paid hit. None of them wanted what happed to Rubert to be their fate.

I was happy our daddies left. They only saw us girls as future hoes with a tail that could one day make them money. When Rodney's daddy left, he realized his father left him like he was an old hoe too. This killed some of his spirit as a man.

When I got out the car, I lifted my head for the first time in years. I walked down the street with new confidence and pride, because for the first time in my life I was in control and no one could stop me.

Whoever said money can't buy you happiness was drunk, jealous, crazy or just plain stupid. For the first time in my life, I have money and I sure am happy!

Rodney gave them my messages. The price to keep my secret was 2.5 million. One thing I know is, if you rub shoulders with the right people you will find out that everyone has secrets

and depending on how bad they are, sometimes they are worth their weight in gold. It's funny how life changes you in one moment, whether good or bad.

While you're going through your situation you don't even realize you're changing with it. One day you are discarded like a piece of trash. The next moment you're sitting on top of the world. I once walked these streets. Now I own lots of them.

I took some money and got myself some things. The first thing I bought was the non-profit organization called *Loving Holms,* the two blocks of houses called *the hood* that made our lives hell. The *Loving Holms* were meant to help prostitutes get off the streets. This time it did exactly what it was designed to do. It didn't just help prostitutes. It helped anybody who needed a second chance in life.

I became business associates with the Mayor and the men in the photo. They all had success through the government or the community. They had no problem donating and funding any of my ventures. They knew as long as the money came in to me, their secrets were safe with me. They were all positive leaders now, including my daddy who it turns out wasn't my daddy at all. That didn't change what they did. But at least they would pay for all the wrong they did.

Like mamma used to say,
"Keep your friends close, but keep your enemies closer."

We formed an alliance and called ourselves the *Associates.* Together we opened old and new businesses, including the corner store and the old dry cleaners to help empower the old neighborhood. I cleaned up the two blocks of houses that once imprisoned us. I made them a safe haven for women with children. I rebuilt the houses and made a real community. My life was beginning to be more like a storybook fairytale, instead of dreams of horror. It seemed like when things are going good someone always had to come and mess it up. My mess up was Rodney.

He was like a booger on your finger that you just can't flick off. He saw my new found fame and titles of prestige in the city, and he wanted his piece. I felt like I did owe him

something, after all he did blackmail his father into getting his friends to form the *Associates* with me.

When he realized the pimping and hoeing game was pennies on the dollar compared to the money coming from the organization daily, he begged me to let him join the *Associates*. So I gave him the same proposition, I gave to all of the members of the *Associates*. I told him I had to be the keeper of one of his deepest secrets. So if he ever thinks about getting out or dimming the rest of us out. The secret will be the ball and chain that hangs around his neck like a noose. With one screw up, I would tighten it around their throat and hang them with it.

Rodney agreed to my terms. But when he told me his secret, it was one so big that if I let the other *Associates* or the *Partners* in on it, Rodney's life would be over.

The day Rodney spilled the beans and lifted the weight of his secret off of his shoulders changed our lives forever. We sat facing each other as equals. Before, I was his worthless hoe, and he was a greedy pimp that treated me badly. This was a grown and mature conversation, which demanded his full attention and for him to give me respect.

Rodney began with a story much like the one I knew to be my own, with a twist. He began and I became engulfed in the story like an unreliable fable.

"Annie what I am about to tell you might out-weigh any pain that you have ever felt. I don't want to be judged by what I am about to tell you." He said, looking me eye to eye.

I shook my head in agreement.

He began his story saying,

"When I was around fourteen or so, the pressure of life was so unbearable that it interrupted my thoughts and controlled my mind. I felt like I was going insane sometimes the pressure was so intense I just wanted my

life to end. I had nobody. I was taught that women were nothing but property with no heart and no soul. Their only value was to be used to make money. I saw the struggles of you, Mindy and Joyce. I saw you all as my sisters that I could not protect. Then there was Henry. I was beaten everyday for not being big, strong and smart like him."

"My life at home was hell with my mamma. No one knew what was going on behind those closed doors... They never knew how many times Rubert would stop by and..."

Rodney hung his head down.

I looked at him and saw tears as they fell from his face to the floor. I knew then that his secret was great. I could never understand what the hell happened to him back then that caused him to be so heartless and cruel?

I could feel his pain and suffering. His emotions overwhelmed him. I felt sympathy for Rodney, a feeling I had never felt for him before. His body shook as he tried to contain himself. I felt pity. I came closer to him, and put my arms around him and held him giving him the love I had been holding back all of my life.

"It's okay, you can tell me." I said, "I promise your secrets will never escape past these walls." I told him with a soft voice that was full of compassion, a trait I never possessed before.

Rodney looked up at me and I could see his soul for the first time. He wiped his face and gained his composure.

Then he continued.
"Rubert was an evil man who never wanted nothing good for us. That's why my heart rejoiced when I saw him get killed. No one saw me, but I was there."

My heart dropped as he talked about Rubert's killer, but I managed to keep a composed face.

Rodney kept talking.

"Rubert was a drunk and a heroin addict. When he was on that high, he would have nightmares of the spirits and demons that haunted him. He would scream out 'leave me alone, it wasn't me.' He was like a madman. They would possess him and hurt him. While in this state he would relive the days of how men used to rape him with everything imaginable and beat him when he was growing up. His life was hell, and it made his mind sick with perversions. Rubert raped me over and over."

"Then, my so called mamma made me do to her what her johns wouldn't do. She made me give her pleasure. She would force my head down on her. I had to suck and lick on her, until she would scream with pleasure. It was only then that she would let my head go." He cried.

"Rubert was there because he liked to watch, and thought it was funny. I hated her and I hated Rubert."

"I swore one day I'd get revenge. Then that one day came. I was in my hiding place under the house, I heard Rubert, James, Earl and Steve talking. At first I didn't understand what they were saying. Then I heard Rubert say."

"Once we get them, we can get out of this pimping game and burn this whole hell down. With the flames will burn our secrets of these hoes and their bastard children?"

I knew he was talking about us.

"Rubert went on to say, one of my business associates said he had a tip on how to get our hands on some moneymaking plates. He says he knows a man down in Mexico who can duplicate anything he sets his mind to.

The money he produces looks and smells just like the real thing. We got to get our hands on them plates. Then I want him dead."

Then James said,
"Why can't we just cut a deal with the Mexican and have him make us some money?"

Then I heard Rubert say,
"You should be the first one to know, motherbastarder. I don't make no deals. I am the deal breaker. I want those plates! I want to be the only one who has them. I want those plates, and I want that Mexican dead! Do you all understand me?"

They all said in unison,
"Yes Rubert." Like soldiers receiving a command.

I sat there wondering to myself, am I that worthless? Are all of us are nothing but hoes and bastards to him?

"A few months went by. Again, I heard them having another meeting. This time Rubert had your mother Sugar Cat in the room. He told her there was something he needed her to do. He told her that some of his business partners would be coming by to pay her a visit and to do what she does best make sure they are happy. She agreed."

A few days later Rubert and the daddies were talking again.

Rubert said,
"The word is out on the streets about the plates. Everybody is trying to get their hands on them, but I stole them and I have the plates hidden. If anybody finds out I have them, I will be dead. So I told them that one of my old hoes had them, and I had to go get them from her."

"I followed Rubert everywhere, until I found out where the real hiding place was. He began to carry a silver steel briefcase. I knew the plates were inside. He stashed them in Mamma Jean's house under her bed. Mamma Jean never liked me, and she was always at home. I didn't know how to get into the house to get them. So I told James and Earl that Mamma Jean was filling Henry's head with that Jesus stuff. I told them that he was going to run away with Joyce and leave the pimping game. And, they were going to tell all the secrets of *the Partners*. They were furious and went over there. They beat Mamma Jean, then they did the same to Joyce. After that what they did to Henry, I would of never expected. They went and got Henry and brought him around to the back of the house. Joyce's bloody naked body lay in the dirt, they made Henry rape Joyce. Joyce belted out a scream so loud that it pierced your eardrums and touched your soul. She never spoke again. Henry jumped up and ran down the street. The daddies laughed at them and left."

"I went into the house and saw Mamma Jean lying unconscious on the floor. I reached under her bed, found the briefcase and ran. I waited until it was good and dark and no one was around. I dug up my mamma's flower bed and buried the briefcase deep into the ground."

"When Rubert heard what happened at Mamma Jean's house, his hiding place, he was mad as hell. He went over there to retrieve the briefcase, but it was gone. He accused James, Earl and Steve of stealing the plates."

"They all ran scared, because he said, 'they would all die by his hands.' Everybody went into hiding, especially Rubert. Years went by, everyone was still searching for the missing plates."

"The day the men came by your house and killed Sugar Cat, I was hiding behind one of the cars. When they came out I told them that Rubert had the plates and that Sugar Cat was just the scapegoat, but it was too late. When

141

Rubert heard about Sugar Cat, he got really scared. He didn't know who was after him. It could have been the business men, the Mexicans, who he stole the plates from, or the daddies whom he had threatened to kill."

"And after years of hiding, Rubert reappeared and went over to Mindy's house. He stayed there a while. When he came out, a short, fat man was waiting on him. He escorted him behind Sugar Cat's house. He told Rubert to get on his knees."

Rubert begged for his life. He told him, he didn't have them.

"He screamed. We're family. You have to believe me. Our plans never changed."

"The man didn't let Rubert finish his sentence. He raised his hand. His fist was tightly wrapped around a knife. He planted it in the center of Rubert's chest. That was Rubert's final day. The man left. Later I found out the man was Mr. Roberts, the owner of the *Beautiful One Salon.*"

Rodney continued his story.

"I knew what I did was wrong. Rubert is dead because of me. He had a debt to pay for all of the wrong he did to me, to us, and to our community. If he hadn't gotten killed, he was going to kill all of us and burn everything. There would have been nothing left but ashes. Had I done nothing Rubert would have carried out his plans to burn us and our neighborhood of hell."

"I had to leave that night when the plates never resurfaced, everybody was looking at me. All the lies were coming back to haunt me. The night we left, I had the plates in the trunk of the car. I kept that old car for a reason. I had the trunk sealed shut so my secret would be safe there."

"The *Associates* are made up of killers with the Mayor, Police Chief, business owners and more. They are no better than me! The only difference is I don't have a title to hide behind. The *Associates* killed Sugar Cat for nothing. The word on the streets is that I have the plates. I need you Annie, you are my only protection."

Finally, I truly understood Rodney and I saw him in a whole new light. I didn't know how to make him an *Associate* without the others knowing his secrets. I needed to ensure his protection from the *Associates* and the *Partners.* One of his secrets was too personal and the other would have him killed, so we got married and formed our own alliance---- the keepers of each other.

I never broke my promise to Mindy. I would watch her from afar. The day she left, I followed her around all day. I watched as she looked in all of the windows of the downtown stores too afraid to enter. She walked around until night fell. I was afraid for her. I didn't want no one to hurt her, so I drove up behind her. I was putting the car in park, when all of a sudden she ran into the *Beautiful One Salon and Beauty School* owned my Mr. Roberts. He took her in. I set up a private meeting with him to ensure her safety. I tried to give Mr. Roberts money for Mindy so when she turned eighteen she could have her own money. However, Mr. Roberts wouldn't accept my money and told me Mindy found her own way.

To my surprise, she did. She became business partners with the school and the salon. She didn't need me or the money. She was stronger than I thought.

After Mr. Roberts was killed I wanted so much to comfort her, but his death was a paid hit by the *Partners.* I wanted no parts in that. I didn't want her to think I had anything to do with it, although I heard Rodney was the one who set the bomb that killed him.

I made sure the money was left in a safe place for her and Angela. I never let her see me, but I had kept a close eye on her.

She opened up a small hair salon called *The Beautiful One.* The word around town was that she wanted to open up a beauty school and help girls who had no hope for a future.

Then suddenly it changed. I had heard she was trying to get *the Partners* to help her, but that organization was weak with Henry over it. They didn't have the money or the power that they once had. Henry was a minister. He was so busy trying to win souls for Christ that he didn't make sure that the streets were being run right.

The Partners were comprised of our daddies: Earl, James, Steve and Charles, when Rubert was killed. Henry became the leader of it all. As the leader of *the Partners,* it was now his job to make sure the hoes got their fair share and the pimps didn't kill them. He also gave the say on who won the elections and what businesses would succeed or fail. Henry was the Godfather of the city. With that title came all kinds of the respect. Henry never wanted the life or the respect. He was quite content to pray to God and lead his church, so he left a lot of street business unfinished. I was going to finish it.

I set up a meeting to let Henry know what I wanted to do. I wanted to be more of an overseer of the city. During the meeting, Henry reared up at me and said the birthright belongs to him, and he wasn't going to let some old hoe call the shots. I told him the *Partners* had grown weak, and the *Associates* had some good ideas on how to make things better. He accused me of threatening him. He said my *Associates* were nothing but killers and thieves. In some ways he was right, but I had something to keep them in line, their secrets, which Henry knew nothing about. Let's just say the meeting didn't go well.

I never professed to be a Saint, plus money is money. It all spends the same. The secrets kept by the chair members bound us together. If one secret got out, we all went down the same. The funding was sometimes gained illegally, but in all fairness, so was the funding for the *Partners.*

> *I hate it when someone wants to see the twig in your eye, when they have a whole branch hanging out of their own eye.*

Henry was always so judgmental. He didn't realize the power I now possessed. I needed to do something to bring him down a notch or two. I wanted control of the city, and if I had to strong hold Henry to get it, I was up for the fight. I loved Henry, don't get me wrong. After all, we grew up in the same hell hole. That bonded us together. But his reign was over, and I needed him to step down peacefully and let me take over. It was time for me to do right by the city. He was concerned about the *Associates* and their past history, but I had it all under control. He just needed to swallow his pride and accept the fact that he was no longer in charge.

I told Rodney of Henry's unwillingness to hand over the control of the city to me. My evil-hearted husband did what he did best. He planted seeds of lies and deceit on Henry, like he did in the day of Rubert, but worst! It was hard to tell the truth from the lies, even for me. He took the heat off himself and accused Henry of having the moneymaking plates. Before long, a paid hit was sent out for Henry's life. Then one was put out on my life! Everyone was putting hits on everyone's life. No one trusted anyone. With each new waking day, you didn't know if it was goin' to be your last! Everything was whirling out of control with no end in sight. It's funny once shit hits the fan there is no way to see where the mess is going to land. In all our cases, this held true.

When the shit hit the fan for Henry, his whole church went on a save Reverend Henry campaign. The town was at war between the good and the evil, or should I say between the *Partners* and the *Associates*. The only problem with that was, some of the *Associates* belonged to the *Partners*, and some of the *Partners* belonged to the *Associates*. No one trusted no one. Life was havoc! I never wanted all of this! All I wanted was control so I could change the city for the better and make things right.

One day while sitting in my office, Charles and Earl walked right in unannounced and told me, I was being summoned by Big Mama. In all of my days I never heard of a Big Mama? I knew of Mammy and from what I understood,

she was killed in the explosion with Mr. Roberts. But this Big Mama person was a new player in the game. If she had the power to make Charles and Earl walk up on me, knowing the power that I possessed. Then yes, I needed to meet her.

They escorted me to a black car similar to the one I saw so many years before. It was one like the one that took little Syn away. I sat in the back seat and the windows were pitch black. It seemed as though we were driving for an eternity. Charles and Earl never said a word. They were focused and eerie like we were on our way to see the Queen of Hell herself. I could hear the sound of gravel as the tires rolled to a slow stop. Earl got out and opened my back door.

I was blinded by the light, because I had sat in darkness for so long. We walked up a long entry way with heavy foliage growing around it, which kept the walkway shadowed. We entered through a massive copper door and stood in a cold, empty foyer. I stood there looking around trying to see more of the house, but the lighting was so dim, it was concealed. Earl walked away. Charles and I stood there in silence. The house had a strange feeling and was silently haunting. Soon Earl came back. We followed him up a winding flight of stairs to an upstairs bedroom.

Inside sitting in a chair was an old woman. She had a strangeness to her face that was hard to describe. The best description would be like the devil himself with all of his evilness. She had a scarf on her head and big-rimmed sunglasses, even though the room was almost dark. I sat in a chair arm's length from her. I waited patiently for her to speak.

After a few minutes of silence, she spoke and her voice pieced me with fear. She talked slow and each word was cold.

"My name is Mabel Holms known to you as Big Mama. I am the grandmother of Rubert and the creator of the *Partners*. I have sacrificed my soul and cursed my future generations to have the power to control this city. Now I sit here and watch you grow into someone much like me. I know you've had a hard life, yet you have managed to

survive and become head of the *Associates*. With this you
feel that you have enough power to challenge me?! I will
tell you now that you will never be powerful enough to
challenge me!"

"I have called you here today, because I feel you are strong
enough and wise enough to understand what I am about
to tell you. The death of your mother was unfortunate.
Her death was a loss to me also, after all she was one of
my best moneymaking hoes. The death of my grandson
Rubert changed me and now I no longer know who I can
trust. I am old and with the death of Samuel and Barbra I
know my days are numbered."

"I have to make peace with God and this world before I
move on. I have caused more pain and suffering to more
people than I can number. There is no way I can change or
fix my wrongs. Now all I can do is try to right my wrongs
and end the curse of my bloodline."

"I killed a powerful Voodoo priestess when I was young.
She was the mother of Samuel and Barbra you know her
as Mammy. Together we were the original *Partners*.
Power consumed me and was the only future I could see,
but what I didn't realize is, there is more to life than power
and money. Having it all is good. But once you have it
all, you are left alone with no one there to share it with.
I'm old and alone my heart is cold. I can no longer feel or
love. Now I know the most important thing in life is the
love of family and I have cursed mine, because I never
knew their value."

"I never thought I would need help from anybody, but I
need your help now. I have the power to smash you like a
grape, and you would never even be missed, but I'm not
going to threaten you, but my request of you is required. I
have something that belongs to you, your son Eric. The
son you gave away years ago, I have kept him alive. I also
have something that will ensure my bloodline, Lil Syn, the
daughter of Joyce and Henry. She is in danger and needs

protection. I will not be around to do it. You will protect them both with your own life, if necessary."

"You will also end this war you and Rodney have started between the *Associates* and the *Partners*. Henry was given the birthright of the *Partners*, because his mother sacrificed her life for him and his heart is pure. I made a promise to her. He will keep it. My advice to you is to get out of this power business before it's too late. If you want to have power, you have to be willing to sacrifice something more than the secrets of others. If you want real power you have to sacrifice something more precious than gold, your soul. My question to you is, is your soul worth the sacrifice? Your answer is going to be written in eternity."

My heart struggled with each beat. My mind was on overload. This evil that hovered over our neighborhood was a relentless storm cloud. Yes, I wanted it all. But if this is what was at the end of my reign of power. If this is my future, then my answer is,
"No, I do not want to sacrifice my soul for power," I responded out loud.

Big Mama turned her head and responded,
"That's the right answer. I also have some advice for Rodney. He was hurt in the exchange. He has hurt many and caused a lot of pain. But you have the power to help him now. You can give him the love he never had, but always deserved. As for Eric he must never know you are his mother, Lil Syn must never know that you were sent by me to protect her. Do you understand?"

I looked over at her and shook my head,
"Yes."

Earl grabbed me by the arm, and they escorted me out of the house. I got back in the back seat and thought of all that was said, and all not said. I knew my reign was over, and I was at peace.

When I arrived back to my office, I packed up my personal belongings and locked the doors to the *Associates* for good. My future had been altered by one simple answer to the question. Was the price of my soul worth hell's eternity? Again, I have to say no.

I never told Rodney about the meeting I had with Big Mama, but I did let him know I was done being the baddest heifer in town. I came to realize, there is always going to be a heifer bigger and tougher than you. So I was content to be his wife, and he was happy with that.

I still was haunted by dreams about my childhood. I missed my mamma, and everything wasn't perfect. But now I had money and power, I could do some good. I couldn't help or change what happened to my mamma. However, I could help change the situations of others. My life now had new meaning. Instead of trying to take over the whole town, my only job now was to protect the lives and success of Eric and Lil Syn. Plus both Rodney and I needed to change our ways, or a hit would be put out on our lives.

I now had a bigger responsibility. I decided that I would find Syn and bring her to her mother. I would right a wrong that was created long ago. I would give back what had been taken away so many years before, Lil Syn. She needed to know she was a part of something great. She needed to know she wasn't alone. She needed to know she was always loved and her family was waiting for her to come home.

SYLVIA HARDIE

Beauty School Blues

*"Today is your first step in a new direction, a
direction that is going to change your whole life.
No more will you stand on the sidelines and watch
your life play out in front of you. You are the main
player. No more will you listen to other people make
important decisions for your life, while you sit
quietly and say nothing. No more accepting the
ordinary for your extraordinary life. No more!!!!"*

ᴧSyn

I rritated, I slammed my hand down onto the buttons of
an old school cassette tape player on my boom box.
My fingers tingled from the force of my hand
slamming across the keys. My boom box was my only
companion as it rode shotgun on the passenger's side of my
seventies Buick. Our Buick and the boom box were both
eyesores, but they are the two most expensive possessions we
owned. Although, the paint on the car was cracked, it was a
protection for us and our babies. The foam cushion looked old,
dry and split. I wedged the 50lb boom box in the foam to
anchor it from the twists and turns as I raced to my destination.

Eric my man said,
"One day, we would have all the money we needed."

He said,
"He could feel a change in the air and our days of having
nothing were soon over."

151

I believed Eric, because he was all I had.

"I wonder," I said to myself, "am I making the right choice? Is this time the right time for me? How is beauty school any different than high school? I couldn't even finish that? After, all I've been through, I hope this is not going to be a whole year of beauty school blues."

I shook my head as if to shake the doubts that were swarming around in my mind.

"Syn. Stop talking to yourself! You know this is the right choice for us and we don't need a dumbass motivational tape to say what we already know. What a bunch of crap!"

The tape and the boom box were Big Mama's, my owner. Her evil words destroyed my spirit like a wrecking ball colliding into an old abandon unwanted building. When my will to live was at an all-time low, I would listen to a motivational tape to lift myself back up. I was sold when I was small to Big Mama. When she died, I was lost with no direction or clear future. I had grown accustomed to someone ordering my every step and determining my every move. Now that she was gone, my head was filled with so many questions and no real answers.

Big Mama was a true business woman. I was her slave. She reminded me every day that I wasn't worth the price she paid. I had to work until the debt was paid in full. Whatever demeaning job she could think of, I did. Men would come by wanting disgusting things from me. She would let them do it to me, for a price of course. She owned total rights to me. She had total control over my life, over my thoughts and it seemed like over my soul. My thoughts were her thoughts, my actions were at her command, and I did as I was told.

Now that she was gone, I don't know what to think, how to feel or what to do. I feel like a puppy with no master, no home and no direction. I am just lost in a world of confusion and doubts.

Knowing I'm on my own, caused my nerves to get the best of me. I have so many doubts, no real focus, no real answers and crazy undirected thoughts. I can remember when I was growing up, the men would cause me such pain. I would let my mind wander in dreams. The one I loved the most was of me playing in a yard. There wasn't much grass, but the feeling of the sun on my face and watching the breeze blowing the flowers across the street filled me with joy. A beautiful woman with a smile would pick me up and hold me. She would rock me in her arms humming the sweetest melodies. In her warm and gentle touch, I knew love. The dreams would always end looking at the cold face of Big Mama.

The reality of my life would erase the warm sun and gentle touch of the dreams. I wanted so much to trade my dreams for my reality. I wondered how much it would cost to be loved. For, I would surely pay that price. I would think what if my dreams are my reality and this is just a dream? My mind would go back and forth sending me into thoughts of confusion. My only sanity came from the hope that I belonged to someone out there, and they loved me.

The day Big Mama died, my days of being her slave were over. The cloud of oppression was lifted. Now I wake up each day looking forward to a new life, a life of freedom. Today was my new start. I was on my way to *The Beautiful One Cosmetology Institute.* For the first time in my life, I felt free to be who I wanted to be. I would be a professional, a Cosmetologist.

"Syn." I said, screaming at myself with a stern voice, "See all this daydreaming, you passed up the entrance. Damn!" "Syn what the hell are you doing? Stay focused!" I continued quarreling with myself in a one-sided argument in my head.

Big Mama used to tell me all the time,

"Girl, pull your head out your ass and pay some damn attention to what the hell is in front of you, before I kick you from behind."

Her cold words echoed in my soul as I tried to regain my sanity and focus on my day. I was so deep in thought that I missed the turn into the entrance of my new school.

The street had one of those concrete dividers in the middle. I had to go all the way to the light, make the whole block and come all the way around again. That's how my whole life had been, never easy, always missing the right turns and full of obstacles. I sometimes wonder what the city planners were thinking. We need more open lanes instead of creating more obstacles. Frustrated, unfocused and confused, I came around to the entrance again and pull into the packed parking lot.

I notice the clock on the dash. It was eight after the hour. "Hell, I'm late!" I said.

I remembered from the long three hour orientation. One of the many, many rules was you had a seven minute grace. After that, you were late. I drove around, until I saw a compact space. I knew there was no way in hell I should be puttin' my big Buick body into this small ass space, but I was late. I was fat, also and too damn lazy to walk any further. Plus, I was in a hurry. I didn't have the time to drive around to find another spot, so for right now this space would have to do.

I eased the car into the space inching in ever so carefully, so not to hit the cars beside me. I threw the car in a hard park. My Buick jerked, shook and smoked, then cut off. I grabbed my purse, my paperwork and opened the car door. The space between me and the car parked beside me was closer than I thought. I figured I could maneuver it. I tried to blow all the air out of my oversized body, hoping to decrease the size of my wide ass. I slither one cheek out at a time, cleared my booty through the crack, and then pushed the door shut with my hip. I held my purse in one hand, paper work in the other and run for the door.

By the time I reached the entrance, I was breathless and even more late. I entered the most beautiful place I have ever seen. I looked around in amazement! I couldn't believe I was

really here! The receptionist sat so proper. Her hair was in a professional curled style. Her nails were well-kept and her makeup was flawless. Her lashes fanned me with each blink.

She had a pleasant face and smile.
"Can I help you?" She asked in the most personable manner.

"Yea, my name is Syn Jackson, and I am supposed to start school today?" I replied.
I could hear my unpolished voice and felt so out of place. She looked down at her list using her freshly, manicured finger to scan the sheet to find my name.

"Ahh... Here you are. Go down the hall to the second door. They are in the middle of orientation soooooo......." She had a look of uncertainty on her face.

I held my breath, hoping she wasn't going to say I can't stay, because I was so late. She didn't understand, today was a big day for me. I had tried so hard to get here.

Irritated, I answered, "So what?"

She could see my irritation and tried to explain.
"Well, Ms. Mindy doesn't fair well when students are late."

I could see she was just trying to warn me and meant no harm. I calmed my voice and softened my posture.

"Thanks for the warning." I replied, as I scurried down the hall.

She smiled back and said, "You're welcome, good luck!"

As I reached the second door, I took a deep breath and proceeded in. I was willing to take whatever my next step had to offer. I was late, but past this door held my future. As I walked in my eyes locked on a lady standing in front of the

class. My uninvited entrance stopped her lecture in the middle of her thought.

I assumed she was Ms. Mindy. Her sharp eyes cut through me like knives. In her presence you knew who was boss. My shoulders dropped and my knees got weak. My confidence left. I glanced away from her cold stare to gaze at the frightened students. They looked back at me with terror.

"What the hell did I just walk into? I'm only ten minutes late! These students look like they have been here for hours enduring inhumane abuse!" I thought.

Ms. Mindy walked over to me, looked me up and down like I was a stray dog or something.

"May I help you?" She asked in a very sharp tone.

I regained my composure and tried to reply with confidence.
"Yea, I'm Syn Jackson. I'm your new student."

My poor girl slang echoed through the room like a ghetto call.
She replied with a sarcastic smirk on her face.
"Yea? What kind of answer is that? Were you trying to say, Yes?"

Embarrassed she called me on my inappropriate grammar. My mind went into combat mode.

Before I knew it that old Big Mama tone came out of me.
"Yes maim, I am one of your new students."

I balled my fist up. My eyes locked on her, ready to strike. She could see my aggression by my warrior stance, and she withdrew her attack.

She calmly extended her hand.
"I would like to introduce myself. My name is Ms. Mindy. I am the owner and senior instructor of this school."

I looked down at her extended hand. We shook hands, as if we had entered into a secret treaty of peace.

She continued,
"I believe in order and discipline. If you look around you, you will notice all of you are new students. The difference is the other new students managed to make it here on time. What is your excuse? Is your next 2100 hours going to be full of excuses?"
Ms. Mindy's tone was soft but stern. Her words bordered the sarcastic line.

"No maim." I replied.
"No maim what?" She asked.
"No maim Ms. Mindy. I will not have another excuse for the next 2100 hours." I answered.

"Good." She replied. "Because if you were, you can leave right now. Let someone who is serious. Now take your seat." She continued.

Biting my lip to keep from cursing this old lady out, I take a seat right in the front. It was the only seat left available.

"Does she know who I am? I was raised by Big Mama! She taught me to cut a heifer now and ask questions later. She needed a good cutting, just for being rude. I have love for the elderly, but she is out of line. We could go toe-to-toe. I be puttin' a whoopin' on her and not even feel bad."

I thought to myself with my head down, shaking it from side to side. My body language captured Ms. Mindy attention. She put me on blast again.

"Syn. Can you please stand and tell us a little about yourself, since you seem to have more to say? Start first start with your name Syn? That is different! I only knew one other person with a name like that." She said with a look of wonder on her face.

I replied, "I don't know much about my name it was the name I was given. Big Mama, the woman who raised me, told me I was made from sin and pain. I was the result, Lil' Syn that came out of it."

Ms. Mindy's eyes locked at me in amazement. She looked like she had seen a ghost. Then a smile came over her face, like a lost treasure had just been found. As quickly as her smile came is as quick as it left.

"You must be one of those girls from the *hood*?" She asked.

Her question was said like she was fishing for something. Big Mama would threaten me with a place called the *Hood*, but I never knew where it was or if it was even real. She told me that once I was grown, I would live there. I would pay off the rest of my debt and men would rape me and beat me. She said I wouldn't have her protection like I did at home. She told me that's where all the old hoes like me lived, until they died. I knew if it was anything like the life I had already seen, it was a place of despair and death.

I escaped that fate, by the death of Big Mama. For Ms. Mindy to even mention it was an insult, a spit in the face. Her insult was like a match ignited the fire of anger that had been raging in me for all of those horrific years. I released the inferno on Ms. Mindy like she was the source of my pain.

"What?" Loud and aggressively, I responded. So she could understand the degree of insult, I felt. "I might not speak your proper English or wear your fancy clothes or even know where I'm from," I continued. "I may have been sold into slavery, when I was small, and don't know who my Mamma or Daddy were. But I sure as hell am glad, I escaped going to a place like the *Hood*. I would of sacrificed anything to keep from going there!"

"Look lady. I already know how to do hair. I just came to get these hours from y'all, so I can get my legals and make me some real money. Now there are two ways I can get it. I can get it in peace or at war. Either way I will be walking up out of this school with my papers. Y'all understand?"

My teeth were clenched together. I took a deep breath in hopes to keep my blood from boiling over across this whole room. Ooh.... I felt a release of hurt and pain. I had been holding all that in for so long. I cut my eyes and rolled my neck. Then I turned to look around the classroom to see if I had any more challengers. I popped out one hip, did a slow hip dip, and eased my big-ass in the small desk seat. The room was silent. You could hear a pin drop.

"Had I said something wrong? Man, why the hell did I wake up and rush to get here for? I could have stayed at home for all this drama." I thought.

She glanced back at me. She could tell that my patient was short. Her attitude let you know she's been through some things not all good. I wouldn't be surprised if she didn't keep a forty-five in her top desk drawer to back up all the mess she talks.

Before I realize it, I saw a lot of me in this stranger. It was much more than that I could imagine.

Mrs. Mindy walked up to me humbled and apologetic,

"I am so sorry I wasn't trying to offend you. Being from a place does not define who you are or who you will be. Everyone has the power to change their circumstances. Everyone should have an opportunity to dream for something better and have it. That place called the *Hood* is where I'm from. Yes, my mother was a hoe and my daddy was her pimp. I survived. Everything you see here is because I had a dream. I didn't let my past interfere with my future. I wanted something better for myself, so I changed my circumstances. My sacrifice is the reason everyone here has that same opportunity to be better, if they work hard and show up every day."

"I promise each and every one of you will have a chance to change. I hope that change will start today."

I looked at her kind spirit. I felt like a total ass. I always thought my life was abnormal. Now I see I was a lot like so many others, unloved and unwanted. Ms. Mindy rambled on

for what seemed like forever. I saw her years of wisdom and experience. She walked with her head raised high. She was engulfed with confidence. Her words entranced me. I was under her spell. I was willing to do anything she said. I wanted so much to be like her.

Ms. Mindy was tall and slender with a model-type body. Her brown-skin flowed like creamy whipped chocolate, carefully glazed over her flawless stature. She seemed to glide with elegance and grace, when walked around the room. My eyes were fashioned on her every move. I was intrigued by her perfect grammar and refined demeanor. Her hair was long with natural curls. It was graced by a small patch of gray, more like white, in the front. She had that type of pretty gray every old person wished they had, but didn't, so they dyed it black to cover it up. I was ashamed for staring at her. I led my attention to the other ladies, who seemed to share the same dreams as me.

I looked around the room to see all types of ladies. There were fat, skinny, pretty and ugly ones, all as eager, as I was, for the opportunity to change for something better. I bet they were all undercover kitchen beauticians just like me, with kids and a sorry ass baby daddy, just like me. It's funny how you always believe you are the only one dreaming a dream or going through something that seems impossible. Then you open your eyes and look around, you realize you are a part of a whole society of people who are dreaming and thinking. They all are going through the same life as you. I knew I found my niche. Somehow just sitting here, I knew I was where I belonged.

Cosmetology was not just a profession, it was a way of life. At *Beautiful One Cosmetology Institute* they mastered the process and success was the only outcome. I may not have agreed with Ms. Mindy's tactics, but I was willing to do and go through whatever it took to become a professional cosmetologist. As we exited out of the classroom we got a tour of the school and my heart dropped. The school was beautiful with soothing, warm, inviting colors like the ones you find in a high society salon you could never afford to go in. I saw the clinic floor. It

was run like a well-oiled machine. The seniors were dressed in all-white uniforms pressed to perfection. They shared the same confidence as Ms. Mindy. Each student was well-skilled and beautiful. Now I understood the name, they were the "Beautiful Ones."

Like they say, "a diamond only becomes a diamond under immense pressure."

Ms. Mindy's personality was enough pressure to change anybody. I was up for the challenge.

I killed Lil' Syn that day. I allowed the *Beautiful One* in me to emerge. I didn't want to be known as the sins of others. I changed my name to Synthia, a name to be proud of. Lil' Syn had always been the victim. Synthia was victorious! And, I wanted more!

I don't know much of my childhood. I remember the first time I met Big Mama. I guess I was about five or six. She was a thin, lanky woman who kept plenty of snuff in her jaw. If black spit wasn't shooting out of her mouth, bad words were.

Big Mama cursed about everything good or bad, and at everybody. Her bad attitude was the school I took my lessons from. I used it as my shield of protection from the world. Big Mama never had a bit of trouble from me. I was just too scared of what she might do.

The first day I met her. She looked me up and down and said,

"Okay little heifer. There ain't going to be no trouble, is there?" She stared at me with one eye and never blinked the other.

I stood there in terror.

So, she said,

"Sit that ass down before I slap your ass-crack to your forehead."

I did just that! Wherever I was, I sat too scared to move.

Then she said,

"Heifer. Move your lazy-ass!"

I did.

Big Mama didn't believe in repeating herself. Her words were never threats. They were promises. So, if she said she could slap my ass-crack to my forehead? Well, you better believe she could. I sure did.

Big Mama ran an illegal gambling hall in the basement of our house. It was big and mansion-like. She was treated like royalty. She was the leader of some underworld society called the *Partners*. With one word Big Mama could end your career or end your life. She held all power and no one, I mean no one crossed Big Mama.

It was my job to mind my own business. I made sure everyone had a fresh drink in their hand. By the time I was ten, I could mix any drink just by name. Big Mama was the dealer, the pit boss and the security. In her establishment, her word was law. When the men had a problem, didn't want to make good on their bets or showed signs of resistance about paying their debt, Big Mama's temper would flare up in a rage. Her voice would raise, and before long they knew there was going to be trouble. Everyone ran. It was a fight for the closest door to escape before Big Mama got to you first. I would crouch down real slow and ease my way out the door. I didn't want to be the victim of a stray bullet. I'd peep around the corner to see who would hit the floor first.

One time, Big Mama jumped on three men at one time! She kicked one in the knee, sending him to the floor. She pimped slapped the other so quickly, the man just sat there in a daze wondering, "What happened?" Then, she swung around and punched the one standing, so hard that spit and a tooth shot out his mouth. The three men were so embarrassed by the whole ordeal. They were too ashamed to return.

Big Mama was always the last one standing! She was the devil in person, a cold blooded, ass-whoopin' machine. Nobody, I mean nobody, messed with Big Mama. If there was a fight, she thought she couldn't win, she would shoot first and

then ask questions later. I believed everyone was scared she'd cast a spell on them.

Big Mama ruled. She was her own god on this earth. As the years went by, she seemed to get more evil with each new day.

One day, Big Mama didn't wake up.
Some said, "It was foul play."
Others said, "She was too old, too mean, and death did all of us a favor."
Big Mama never had a friend and folks had become so corrupt you really couldn't tell what was what, or who was who. I just know I was lost on that day.

I never knew anything about myself like, who was my mamma and daddy? Did I have any siblings? I remembered having one friend growing up, Eric. I would see Eric from time to time with one of Big Mama's grandsons. Sometimes he was with Earl or Steve. He was like the little boy nobody wanted, but needed to be raised. Eric was a few years younger than me. At first I saw him as a baby, as he got older, we became allies. The difference between him and me was I was a bought slave with value. He was discarded by his own mamma and daddy, when he was first born. He was treated more like a stray-mutt. I felt sorry for him.

When he came by we would play in the back room, while Big Mama and her boys had their little meetings. Over time, me and Eric formed a bond of friendship. We both saw life just as it was. There was no glitz, no glam or the fairy tales of Santa Claus or the tooth-fairy. Both of our lives were hard. It was full of horrors and disappointments. I knew his pain. He was aware of mine. Then suddenly, I didn't see Eric anymore and I was totally alone.

Eric re-entered my life when I needed him the most, the day Big Mama died. The day of the funeral, I saw people I had never seen before. Eric appeared out of nowhere. He sat right next to me. I looked at his now grown sculpted body and my heart raced with attraction.

He leaned over and said,

> "Are you going to be okay? I'm here for you. You are going to be with me."

I didn't question him. I had no one else and no place to go.

That evening Eric took me back to Big Mama's to get my things. As I was searching for my few possessions, I felt Eric's body close to mine. Before I knew it, Eric had bent me over the dining room table. In one quick motion, Eric had my dress hoisted over my hips ripping my panties off. I could feel his fingers. He checked me to see, if I was wet and if there was room enough for his thick private. Then, without hesitation he plunged his private so deep and hard into my body. The force was so strong it took my breath. Back and forth, in and out each of his movements were more intense than the last. He grabbed the back of my hair, holding it like the reins of a horse. I could hear the slapping sound of our bare flesh. Our bodies collided, as his groins bounced off my fat-ass. He took his open hand and slapped my ass, so hard it jiggled like a bowl of jelly. I could feel the sting of his hand as he repeatedly slapped it over and over. It burned like fire.

Eric was on a mission! His force was so strong and deliberate. He was establishing his power to gain control over me. I had just been released from Big Mama's strong hold. I was not ready for a new master. I held my breath as I tried to wiggle out of his controlled position. I moved. He countered my every move, preventing my escape. Once I understood I was caught, I ended my resistance.

He leaned over holding my face with his hand and coldly whispered in my ear,

> "Heifer, you aren't going anywhere! You belong to me now. I'm your daddy and you're my woman. You do what I say do, you understand?"

I was defeated, plus I had nowhere else to go, so I replied,

> "Yes, I understand. "

Unhappy with my response, he plunged his private even deeper into me until I yelled out,
"Yes, I'll do what daddy says do. Yes, I'm your woman."

Satisfied, he made his final plunge and came, while yelling,
"Oh shoot!"

His body grew limp and our roles were established. He was my new king, and I was his submissive servant. I'm sure that was the night I got pregnant. Eric said we were all we had and nobody's bond was stronger than ours.

Once I realized Eric was right, and we had no one but each other. I realized no one cared? No one else mattered to me, but Eric. He was my love and my life.

Eric and I just coast on through life. We had money to get what we needed. I never questioned where it came from. I just trusted my man. He always made sure I was okay.

One thing I could say, Eric was making some attempts to pay bills. He was at least trying to hustle a little.
When he was coming up, he said,
"If I ever had a place of my own, I would take care of it and never took it for granted."

We both did our part so I guess we made a good team.

I remember Big Mama telling me,
"a lazy-ass is a broke-ass, so keep that ass in motion."

She instilled in me to be a go-getter, so I got getting, doing what I did best.

I found a job cleaning up hair in beauty shops. I worked my way up to the shampoo girl, then I built a clientele. I went to their home to keep from having to pay booth rent. When Eric was in the streets, he told folks that I could do any style you asked for. I did my best, but I never had proper training. But, I did the best I could. If I messed up someone's hair, Eric would

tear my ass up, and I'd figured out how to do it better the next time.

He said,
"His reputation was on the line and he didn't need me screwinging it up!"

I wish sometimes I could tell him what I really wanted to say, but like Big Mama would say,
"A closed mouth keeps teeth,"
And I need all of mine.
Eric had that way about him. There were no real emotions or tender loving moments like you see in the movies. I knew that deep, deep down inside, Eric had a good heart. But his pride got in the way. He never revealed it to anyone, not even to me. I know his type, attitude larger than life. That's how Big Mama was. One day, late at night, I heard Big Mama crying, and I knew then even the devil has a heart when alone in the dark.

When you saw Eric you knew not to mess with him. His expression was solid and unforgiving. It worked for him. He was 6'0", size 12 shoe and 225 lbs., before breakfast. He was built like a perfectly-crafted masterpiece of machinery!

My man woahhhh..........
He's fine!

He had carmel flawless skin that is only complemented by his green and hazel mixed eyes. He has black curly hair tapered around the sides with pretty curls on top. His hands were so soft to the touch. They could rub your body into a perfect fantasy world. When he got dressed, his clothes lay across his tall, tight body like a freshly made hotel bed. Perfect in every way when you saw it, all you want to do is pull back the crisp sheets, climb inside and stretch out across him. Eric's smile showed off the whitest teeth. He had the prettiest lips that drowned you into submission.

All Eric had to do is look at me. There wasn't anything that I wouldn't do for my man. I loved him, and sometimes I

believe he loves me too. Somehow we got along and life made sense.

Soon after we got together, I was pregnant with Ledell, then Louise, and then Lee. We had three children in four years. I can't remember what was worse, watching my body go through hell from being stretched out in mass proportions, or having a three, two and one year old. Everything changed. Life took a toll on us both. When it was just Eric and I, we could sit up all night in a 24-hour diner or hustle enough money to get a room for the night.

When you got babies, your whole game has to change. You need diapers, formula, clothes and a permanent place to stay, and Eric wasn't the stay in one place type of guy. If Eric had to choose between buying things for the children like food and clothes or taking a chance on a sidewalk craps game. Well, let's just say we rarely won. A hustle always came first.

Life came at us so fast we didn't have time to recoup. It was harder and harder for me to keep it together. I couldn't stand to see our babies hungry and without. I wanted to go and get us some welfare. When I asked Eric if I could go, he got all pissed off and said,

"Why you want them motherbastarders in our business? You are just a dumbass heifer,"

His words were so cold and heartless. I knew he didn't mean anything by what he said. He just didn't want someone asking me questions about what he did. I was raised by Big Mama. She taught me to keep my big mouth shut. So I did. Big Mama always had enough for me to eat and a place to sleep. I wanted the same for my babies.

I can say this. Eric's fine-ass did make me some pretty babies. Even though, he wouldn't get a father of the year award for his parenting skills, our babies looked like angels. I never knew how to love or take care of a baby. But the first time the doctor placed Ledell in my arms, I knew I would lay down my life for him. Sometimes I would have to choose the babies over Eric to get us a night in a shelter and a hot meal. The babies and

167

I could stay, but not Eric because they had strict rules, no men allowed. I love my man, don't get me wrong. When he found out that I went to a shelter, I knew an ass-whoopin' was sure to follow. I loved my babies more, and they were worth it.

Trouble always found Eric. He was a thief and a born hustler. He could steal the white off rice before it even realized it was brown. He was just that good of a thief. When Eric was growing up, he never had his essential needs met. For that matter, he never had enough of anything, like food, clothes, a role model, love or a hug. Big Mamas grandsons felt he didn't need anything extra.

Big Mama's grandsons were pimps. In the pimping game, there is no time to be sitting around babysitting a bastard child nobody wants. They say his mamma was a hoe and gave him away, because she didn't know who his daddy was. Eric basically just raised himself. As the men drove around town taking care of their business, he was often in the back seat. Or, he sat in the back room of the houses with the men, waiting for their hoes to finish a job. So they could collect their money.

Eric said,
> "He learned how to steal by watching the hoes seduce their johns."

He said,
> "While the men got all entranced from the hoes rubbing their nut sac, she would grind on them, talk sexual smack in their ear, and would be robbing them blind."

Eric learned from the best. He could look you right in the eye, while stealing the clothes off your back. You'd be so busy listening to his fine ass. You wouldn't even notice, you were standing there butt-ass naked. Eric always wanted to be seen. So while Eric was in the street hustling, I worked really hard to make a life for us. And, although I tried hard, my efforts seemed minimal. For every dollar I made, Eric needed to pay off some bad dealings or to invest in some ghetto-get- rich quick scheme.

When I could no longer pay his way out of the trouble, we had to move into our car.

Eric said,
"He had met some girl that could set us up for life, if he played his cards right."

I knew he was up to another hustle. I wasn't too keen on the entire idea. I was the jealous type. I didn't want no heifer too close to my man. That's why I was so glad, when we met Mrs. Annie. I felt better depending on her than some girl Eric had met in the streets.

Mrs. Annie just showed up one day. She found us living in our car. She had that hustle mentality that Eric could understand, so he allowed us to receive her help. I was glad Eric lowered his pride, for once.

I didn't know what to do. Mrs. Annie gave us the support we needed. She took us under her wings, and helped us get on our feet. Mrs. Annie had long money from some nonprofit organization she chaired. Plus, she had connections with the big dogs, like the Governor, Police Chief, Judges and the Mayor.

Mrs. Annie knew people. She never got into our personal business. Word on the street was she used to be some hoe that became a high roller. Then something went bad and she got out of the game to marry her childhood sweetheart. She doesn't talk much about that.

Mrs. Annie put us in her nonprofit program called *Loving Holms.* She introduced me to my new case worker Angela. Angela worked for the state. I told her I always wanted to be a hairdresser, so she suggested beauty school. She said I could gain a skill to take care of my family. She even got me a scholarship, where my tuition was paid as long as I did the right thing.

Ms. Angela was young with dark smooth skin and perfect bone structure. Her eyes were like big saucers. Her hair was silky with a slight wave. It ran down to her mid-back. If I had to say so myself, Angela was pretty. She knew it too. She

carried herself with class. You could tell she was raised with money. She worked because she wanted to, not because she had to. I envied her life. She had it all a nice car, no kids and she never knew struggle a day in her life. Angela took a special interest in my case. She gave me a lot of one on one attention. She said it was because she knew Mrs. Annie, but my womanly instincts smelled a hood-rat hiding in the shadows. I just couldn't put my finger on what it was.

Angela enrolled me in every program, *Loving Holms* and the State offered. They had everything from Parenting Classes to Cooking Classes. They cared about women like me. They held you responsible and ensured you reached your goals. I got enough food stamps. It was like food Christmas on the first of every month. I even got a check! It wasn't much, but it was better than nothing.

The *Loving Holms* program gave us a home in a small neighborhood. You could always tell when you were in our neighbor, because you entered in through a gateway and the whole neighborhood was surrounded by a tall brick fence. There was only one way in. All the houses looked the same. They were small little cottages that made you really feel at home.

One of my neighbors was Mrs. Joyce. She didn't talk. She just sat in her window every day, keeping an eye on everyone's comings and goings. Her careful watch over our neighborhood took the place of the police. We really never needed any police. There was such a peace here and every neighbor's life was like ours.

I was grateful to have Ms. Angela in my life. She seemed to care. Angela was cool. She also gave me extra money to do her hair at the house. Being so close to her, I never had to worry about my benefits getting cut, or my paperwork getting lost. All I had to do was keep her an open appointment every Friday.

I gave her the usual one of a kind hairstyle, which causes her to be the envy of the office. She's corny though. She told everyone she got her hair done at this expensive ass day spa across town. Her co-workers all dreamed of going, but could

never get an appointment. I was her little secret. For me, it was a fair exchange.

It helped to have a friend with lots of connections like Mrs. Annie. She knew everybody. When she wanted something, her request sprang back faster than a screen door. I don't know what we would of done, if we didn't know Mrs. Annie.

I never questioned her motives, but my Eric sure did. He would ask,
"Why is this old heifer always hanging around and being in all our business? What's in it for her?

Then he said,
"Don't say nothing when she asks for something in return and the cost is more than it's worth."

I would just listen to him talk. I just saw it as a good hustle. There was no way I could have fed my three babies, and take care of my baby daddy, Eric, without Mrs. Annie's help. Plus, I was tired of just surviving. I was ready to live. So to me, Mrs. Annie was our Savior.

After we moved into our new home, we took a family picture. It was a vision of perfection. Everything in the picture looked perfect. The children were smiling and looked so happy. Eric and I looked so in love, so I hung it over the couch. This way, when you walked in the house, it was the first thing you saw. That picture was the only solid and secure thing in my life. Every time I began to feel depressed, I gathered strength from that perfect picture. I guess I thought, if I worked hard enough, the fantasy perfect family portrayed in the picture would one day be my reality.

I was lying on my couch drained and reminiscing about my day, when a loud pounding came from the front door. I

knew it was my five o'clock weave, Mrs. Annie. But, today my nerves were already at their breaking point from Ms. Mindy's first day of Cosmo Boot Camp. Plus, I didn't' feel like trying to make Mrs. Annie's two inch hair into an ass length flawless Diana Ross sexy do. So, I lay there as quiet as possible, hoping she would just leave and come back another day.

I was almost in the clear, until my noisy son Ledell ran up to me screaming at the top of his little lungs,

"The door mamma! Somebody's at the door! Mamma get up! Get up!"

I tried to pretend like I was asleep. He began kissing me until I gave in. Ledell was so cute. He was a mirror image of his beautiful father. I kissed him back, until he begged me to stop.

"Mamma the door!" He said.

"I know, thanks baby! Go see how sissy and baby are doing?" I told him.

I gave him another kiss on his forehead. He disappeared into the back room. I gathered myself together, painted a smile on my face and answered the door.

"Hi Mrs. Annie, how are you today?"

She answered,

"I am fine girl. I thought you would never get the door. I've been out here at least ten minutes waiting for you."

Mrs. Annie looked over to the house next door. She acted like she was rushing in before my neighbor opened her door.

She ask,

"I see your crazy neighbor peepin' through her front window. Have y'all met yet?"

She stood there with sweat rolling off her forehead. In one hand she held her cane and the other hand held a tight grip on her eighteen-inch deep wave bag of the Indian silk weave. She entered the house, walking slow. She was bent over with a limp

and acted all old and tired. Mrs. Annie looked much younger than Ms. Mindy, but she moved like she was born right along with old man time. She was a heavy short lady, fair-complexion with large freckles that sprinkled her chunky cheeks. They looked like chocolate chips melting in the sun, warm plump and chewy ready for someone to take a bite. And when she smiled, deep dimples appeared out of nowhere. She had thick pink lips already in pucker mode. You could tell in her day she was a high- stepper. No one could tell her nothing because she was so fine.

Now when she walked, her steps weren't very high. She did more of a shuffle than a walk. Every step she took, looked like she was ready to fall over. The weight of her big breast came just short of her stomach. Her stomach shifted from side to side as she walked. I guess she needed the cane for balance. She always complained of her back pains. Maybe if she stood up straight and lost some weight, ninety percent of her problems would probably be solved. I waited patiently as she walked.

Mrs. Annie stopped and looked at me waiting on my response about the lady next door.

I said,

"Oh yea, I met her. One day when I was trying to get the kids in the house, Ledell fell. Before I knew it, she came running out, picked him up, dusted him off, then kissed him on the forehead. I thanked her. Then I realized she doesn't talk. She has a way about her. You can tell she has a good heart. She just sits in her window watching life go by. I don't have to worry about anyone breaking in here with her living next door. It's like having your own personal alarm system."

Mrs. Annie continued her slow walk again, still in thought.

Then stopped to turn and glance back at me.

"You are sure right about that. Joyce has always been strange like that."

Shocked by her response I asked,

"You know her?"

Mrs. Annie looked like she didn't know what to say,

"Yea, I know that no talking strange lady. We grew up together right here in the hood."

I could tell she needed to take a seat, so I said in an uninterested tone,

"Oh?" Like I didn't care to know more.

But the truth was, there was something about the lady that lived next door. I wanted to know about her, like why didn't she talk. Who is she looking for when she sits staring out of her window from sunrise to sunset. I knew there must be some juicy gossip lingering around that strange lady. I just needed to play it calm, until Mrs. Annie mouth got warmed up. Then, her mouth was going to run all night.

Mrs. Annie finally reached the dining room table. Before she sat, she turned around to look for the chair to place her wide-flat butt in. I secured the chair from behind, so it didn't move as she eased herself down to it real slow. I took a deep breath to prepare myself for the long night we both had ahead of us. I tried to make conversation before she started in on her gossip.

She said,

"Girl, what took you so long to get to the door? You and that nigga ain't trying to make no more of them babies are you?"

I looked down at her shining bald spot in the middle of her head. I could almost see the funky expression on my face.

I was thinking to myself,

"She better watch what she says about my man before I set it off in here."

I took a deep sigh and responded,

"No, I was coming. Just trying to get some shut eye from my long day."

She responded.

"That's right, you started beauty school today! That's right! Now that you're going to that fancy school your price might go up?" She said pausing to see, if I was going to respond.

I pretended like I didn't hear her.

"My prices are going up rather I finish beauty school or not." I thought to myself.

Mrs. Annie was that kind of client. She just cheap for no reason. I started doing her hair soon after I moved in. Mrs. Annie was nice. The only issue I had with her was, she was just so nosy. She had her ways of finding out everybody's secrets! Some she kept under lock and key, and others, she shouted them out like a police car siren.

She said,

"Tell me how your first day went? How's Mindy doing? Not waiting for a response, just planting seeds to grow into conversation, that old goat?"

Pretending to act surprised because she knew everyone.

I asked,

"You know Ms. Mindy?"

She replied,

"Yea, we grew up here together too. We all grew up together: Mindy, Joyce and I. Mindy and I lived across and down the street. Joyce grew up in the house, she is living in now. Oh... we had some memories here, not all good either. Yea... coming over here bring me back to those days. I sometimes wish I could forget. Henry lived right across the street. My husband Rodney lived next door to him."

"Joyce and Henry married." She continued. "I guess she was just too strange for him, because he left her. Then she moved right back to this place. She had her a mansion with maids and everything."

"That Joyce," She said, while shaking her head from side to side in disapproval. "She and I were never close. She was a dumb, simple girl, who was content to accept our horrible life. Mindy and I wanted more. I stayed as far away from her as possible. What made things worse, something really bad happened to her, when she was twelve or so. She never was the same again. When that happened, we all were changed."

She kept talking.

"Now Mindy and I that was a different story. We were just like sisters after my mamma died. I lived with Mindy and her evil mamma, until I was sixteen. We made a promise to one another and I broke it. I left the hood, and I left her behind. Mindy never forgave me for leaving her. We never spoke again."

She took a breath and continued.

"Mindy left shortly after I did. She got married to Mr. Roberts. He was her father's wife's only brother. Her father's wife's name was Mammy. She was the original founder of *Loving Holms*. Mr. Roberts was the original owner of *The Beautiful One School and Salon*. They were both killed by some crazy accident where the school and the salon burned down. It was a big deal, we all felt sorry for her. But she ain't that feel sorry for type. He had a big insurance policy. With that and some city grant money, she rebuilt the school. She used it all for *The Beautiful One Cosmetology Salon and School*. I have to give it to her. The school is beautiful like her. Mindy is a hard woman. She runs a tight ship. She is tough! Back in the day, she would beat a heifer down just for staring at her too long. We were raised in the *Hood* with pimps and hoes. You had to be tough if you wanted to survive. No one expected you to be nothing but a hoe, just like your mamma. Man we were treated like dogs. We all share secrets and understand each other's pain."

Mrs. Annie stopped talking, turned around and gave me one of those looks that meant, if I repeated it Mrs. Annie would deny it.

As she talked about Ms. Mindy, it reminded me of being raised by Big Mama in the speakeasy, as her child slave. I had no love and no friends. I wish I could recall memories of people I knew. I was told to mind my business, to keep my head down and keep everything to myself. I knew if I said anything about how I was raised, it would hit the floor running. Everybody would know my business by the end of the day. One time, Big Mama was the only family I had. Now my family is Eric and our kids, those are the only memories I hold dear.

Trying to take my mind off my past. I said,

"I had a run in with that Ms. Mindy today! What a trip? Yea, she's a trip alright!"

We talked more shop talk, which is a nice word for gossiping about everybody's business. Soon her head began to bob around. I knew she was asleep.

"Mrs. Annie?" I said with a loud voice pushing on her back to getting her attention, while handing her the mirror.

She always fell asleep when I did her hair. Her head bobbed and weaved so much, it was like trying to return a ball in a one-sided tennis match.

"Finished already? She asked. "Girl you know you are fast and good, and like always the right price."

She hands me a balled-up knot of cash. It looked like money she had probably stashed in a jar or something. I never count it, because it's always there.

"I guess I'll see you in a couple of weeks." I asked.

Trying to give her the hint that it was time for her to leave.

Pausing for a second, she turned to look at me.

> "I am going to give you some advice and it is free. You
> can take it or leave it! Everyone one has a past, whether
> good or bad. Life is strange that way. Everyone is
> somehow connected to one another. Some folk you're
> connected to are good folk and some folk are pure evil.
> Just watch your back and question everyone's intentions
> and I mean everyone."

She reached for the table to get support, gave a grunt, got out of
the chair and left.

     .

That night, I laid in my bed thinking about what Mrs.
Annie said. Ms. Mindy was right, I did live in the *Hood,* and so
did they. Big Mama said I was going to live here one day. I am
sure glad it's not the way she said it would be. I still questioned
what she meant when she said we are all connected. What does
that mean? Who am I connected to? Is this where I belong?
Did my family come from the *Hood*? Did Mrs. Annie knows
who my family was? I don't know anybody, so why did I need
to watch my back?

I lay there tired of all the questions running through my
mind and disgusted because my man wasn't home. My body
sure wished he was here to put me to bed properly. I put my
hands between my legs and stroked my toot, until I dozed off to
sleep.

> "Hey babe, hey where you at?" I could hear Eric
> screaming and the yelling from the kitchen.

> "Shoooooooosh! The kids are sleep! It's three in the
> morning," I yelled back from the bedroom.

> "Get up! I am so hungry! You knew I would be hungry,
> so where's the grub?" He asked.

I got up and headed for the kitchen where he was opening
up every cabinet and pulling out all kinds of crap.

I said,

"I had Mrs. Annie tonight. So I didn't have time to make you something. Sorry babe."

I pushed my ass up against him to shove him.

"Move Eric, you always coming home after the kids are sleep. Why can't you come home before they go to sleep, so our babies can see who gave me the sperm to get them here? " I said, talking with a smart mouth, full of attitude and pissed off, because I was still horny as hell.

He looked at me and said,

"Alright now, don't let your mouth write a check your ass don't want to cash tonight. Unless you want this ass-whoopin'?"

Quickly humbled, I ran to the stove and begin to cook not saying a word. I slammed the pots and the refrigerator door, letting him know that I was pissed. But I was not pissed enough to fight.

He got up from the kitchen table. I could feel him behind me. Before I could turn around, Eric pinned me up against the counter, kissing me, rubbing me where I needed it the most. I gave in and the love making began. He had his ways to get me where he wanted me. I was like a tamed puppy accepting abuse just as long as a pat on the head came along with it. After a quick nap to recoup from his long dong, I gathered myself together, got off the kitchen floor and prepared a feast fit for my king. I love taking care of my man, especially when he knows how to take care of me.

All of the homes in the two block radius were built the same. When you walked in the front doors, you could see out the back. The house was separated by one long hallway and all the bedrooms were on one side of the house. The living room, kitchen and front room were on the other. The small kitchen fit a table and four chairs. Across from the kitchen was the two bedrooms, both about the same size, except in the master bedroom was an extra closet. In our room was a queen sized bed and a small table on one side of the bed The other side of the bed was pushed up against the wall. Of course, that was my

side of the bed. The mattress frame was on wheels. Between Eric's big-ass turning and me trying to stay out of his way, the bed would have moved during the night. I woke up every morning wedged between the wall and the bed.

The children's room had one single bed that Ledell and Louise shared. Baby Lee still slept in a crib. We all shared one small bathroom. It was just big enough to do your bare necessities with no extras. The one thing I can say is the folks here had money. You could tell because of the things they gave away. The thrift stores were like a fancy department store. They had everything you needed to fix up a house. I put the house together the best I could. It was simple, but cozy. I tried to decorate, but decorating was never my thing. I hung pictures wherever there was space on the wall. I put a chair where I thought you might want to sit. The house had no rhythm, reason or rhyme. It was just fit for our needs.

Raising the kids was my job, along with the cooking, cleaning, and going to school. Eric believed the woman did all the house things. His job was taking out the trash, doing small house repairs and pumping the gas. He kept the kids when it was convenient for him. Sometimes I would get Ms. Joyce next door to watch them. She didn't seem to mind. I think the kids were her company, since no one ever came over to visit her. The more life I made for myself, the less I saw Eric. I never questioned him, I just focused on what was important. That was getting done with beauty school.

Life in school wasn't what I thought. If someone had told me, you had to read a book in order to do some hair, I would have been the first to call them a liar. I didn't finish high school lessons. Now I'm expected to learn chemistry, electricity, anatomy, business, diseases and disorders of the hair, skin and nails, infection control facials, manicuring and the list goes on and on.

Cosmetologists even have their own vocabulary,

"We wash clothes, we shampoo tresses;" "We fry chicken in grease, but on tresses we use pomades;" "We scale a

fish on tresses; we do a systematic brushing to remove excess scales on the scalp."

"Who the hell comes up with this stuff?! All this was just part of the introduction."

Beautiful One Cosmetology Institute also had other programs. While becoming a Cosmetologist, you could also get your GED and get a degree in Salon Business. Theory was grueling. Once a week, we sat in a classroom for hours listening to lectures and learning procedures after procedure. There is a procedure for everything from draping a client to a simple haircut. At *Beautiful One Cosmetology Institute* they believed everything should be done in proper order with professionalism and grace. Ms. Mindy made sure you were able to recite the three B's of Beauty;

Be Professional, Be Beautiful and **Be on time.**

Every morning before we started, Ms. Mindy would have us stand up and check out the person standing next to you. We critiqued each other on our appearance.

Then she would say,

"Look at your partner! What do you see? Do you see a future beauty professional or a kitchen beautician?"

She wanted our hair to be combed, our clothes to be clean and ironed, our make-up to be on and a smile on our face.

She said things like,

"If you pulled up to a burger joint and they were out of burgers you would be upset because that's what they do. They make and sell burgers. Well the same goes for us, we sell and make beauty, If someone walks up to you, and they don't know what you're selling then there is a problem. That problem begins with you! They should at least know that you are in the beauty industry, right?"

Everyone would answer,

"Yes maim, Ms. Mindy."

As each word flowed from Ms. Mindy's lips, they rung in my ears like the sweetest song I had ever heard. I knew for the first time in my life someone cared. My world was all of a sudden larger than life! I found somewhere to belong. Who knew I would have a new found respect for Cosmetologist and for myself. I even begin to look down on my fellow kitchen beauticians who believed as I used to. One of the rules you dare not break was doing hair at home.

Ms. Mindy says,

> "Here at *Beautiful One Cosmetology Institute* what you did in the past is in the past, but once you become part of our
>
> family you will see yourself as a Professional. If I find out you are still practicing your kitchen beautician habits at home, you will be sent home and your funding will end. You have two choices: change and be better, or just stay the same."

I believed in her words and ended my home business. With each new day, I could see myself changing and growing. Before I didn't care what words came out of my mouth, I'd just say whatever popped into my head. Now I choose each word, thinking first before I speak. Ms. Mindy ran a tight ship, she and her staff were in total sync. They had one mind set and one goal. That goal was to change all of her students from the ordinary to the extraordinary, and half-stepping was not an option.

Mrs. Sarah was our freshman instructor. She was an older real strict woman. She never smiled and her voice was real raspy and thick. When she talked, it was like someone's nails going down a chalkboard. When she gave you an instruction, you did it immediately because you didn't want her to have to repeat it. Plus, she had one of those old people smells that got right underneath your nostrils and stayed there. So, you made sure you did each procedure right that way she wouldn't have to come to your station and show you again.

In my freshman class, there were twenty students. We were housed in a separate area from the rest of the school. The only time we saw the seniors was during our breaks and lunch. After you finished your ten weeks in the freshman class, you graduated to the clinic floor as a senior and you worked with clients. When you saw a Senior, you felt envy in your soul. They had a certain air about them and were disciplined in the craft. Their demeanor was refined and beautiful. When the seniors walked passed, you gave them respect. They demanded it. I knew they had been trained by the best, Ms. Mindy. The girls in my class were nice, but they lacked what the seniors had. I didn't want to socialize with them. I felt that I was so much more advanced and mature than them, because of my experience with working in a salon and doing clients at their homes. I had way more talent and expertise. I was old school in this hair game.

I kept to myself in my own little corner and dared any of them to even speak to me. All I wanted was to finish these ten weeks, so I could get to the clinic and really show off my talent. Ms. Mindy let us know that not all of us are going to make it to the clinic floor if she didn't see quality in your work, if you didn't give her 100% or if you fell behind in homework or the theory exams. You would repeat the ten weeks again. If after you repeated the ten-week freshman training, and you still couldn't master the concepts, then this is not the profession for you. Attendance was mandatory. If something kept you coming every day for the ten weeks and you miss more than three days, you will be dropped. You would have to wait for another enrollment period and start again. I vowed a vow that I would not miss one day. I wanted to finish school and really make some money for me and my babies.

The school was great, but Mrs. Sarah treated me like I was everybody else. The first couple of weeks I didn't mind. I was getting into the swing of things. By the second month, I was expecting her to see how good I was and give me a waiver. That way I didn't have to finish the whole ten weeks of training.

They would just put me with the seniors. Plus, between her voice and that smell I was going insane.

One day while doing a perm rod set, Mrs. Sahara came over to me, picked up my mannequin, looked at it with her nose turned up and gave me a list of all the things wrong with it.

She started with that annoying voice,

"First off the parts are not straight. Second, you did not put equal tension on each rod. Third, your rod sections are inconsistence."

Before she could get to number four out of her wrinkled lips, I grabbed my mannequin out of her hand with pissed written all over my face.

I yelled,

"Heifer move!"

I felt the spirit of Big Mama coming over me and I was going to give this hoe the ass-whoopin' of her life. She stared back at me, neither one of us willing to back down. It was a standoff and I had nothing but time.

Before long I could feel the presence of Ms. Mindy as she approached us. The air changed and I knew this was a fight, I had no chance of winning.

"What seems to be the problem?" She asked in a calm disregarded tone.

In one instant I was eye to eye with Ms. Mindy. My head and shoulders dropped simultaneously. I felt weak like a child that is about to be scolded. I changed my tone and attitude.

"Ms. Mindy, I have had enough of this lady picking on me. She was just looking for something. I could tell she never liked me from the first time she saw me. I'm doing the best I can and all she does is find the wrong in everything I do."

Ms. Mindy's face was like a book with an empty page. I couldn't read her. I didn't know what angle to use on her.

She replied,

"What has happened to make you feel this way?" In a compassionate voice.

I let my guard down and words raced out of my mouth like a runaway train.

"Well, for starters, I have worked very hard here at *Beautiful One.* I stay to myself, I have been ethical, professional and respectful. I stay out of trouble and follow her directions. I am a good student, I just don't think that my talent has been recognized or appreciated. I was working on my perm rod set and Mrs. Sarah comes over and criticizes it before I could even finish."

Ms. Mindy walked over to my station and picked up the same mannequin. She held it in one hand and began to twirl the head around. Then she started where Mrs. Sarah left off.

"I can see for starters, your parts are not straight. This is important in order to have even sections. Your tension is not consistent, this is important for proper perm solution absorption."

She kept going on and on. The more she talked, the more defeated I felt.

"I am so sorry to disturb you Ms. Mindy, it won't happen again." I said.

She looked at me, waiting and tapping her foot on the floor.

"Don't you have something else to say?" She asked.

I wanted to keep how I was truly feeling to myself, but I blurted it out without recourse.

"All I'm asking for is one chance to show off my one of a kind masterpieces. I have many clients and they all rave about my greatness. I mean if you only knew who I was, you wouldn't treat me like the others. I have ten years of doing great things. I could probably teach you a thing or two. Don't you know that I'm doing you a favor because I chose this school? I am Syn the extraordinary never to be confused with the ordinary."

Ms. Mindy just looked at me act a total fool. When I was finished with my self-confidence speech, she responded.

"You will have your chance to shine in the hairdo completion that will tell us all that we need to know."

With that, she walked out of the room and we resumed the day as if nothing ever happened.

Every freshman from the first week looked forward to the up-do competition. It was the finale of the ten weeks, and it concluded your freshman training. It was your chance to show off what you had learned. You were no longer limited to assignments or styles critiqued by Mrs. Sarah. Nor did you have to do boring procedures over and over, day after day. For a freshman, this was as good as it gets. This competition was going to be my day of truth. They say every dog has their day. Well, today is going to this woman's holiday.

I put all I could into the hairstyle. I got real creative and sampled a little from every style, I had ever done. I wish I could have brought my own props or had live models. However, I was going to make the best of the mannequin head I was given.

I stood back and looked at the style which I had created. In my mind, I was going for the Statute of Liberty with Shirley Temple curls spiraling from her torch. I used green and gold spray paint to give her the color, so she would look lifelike!

It was true the design in my head fell a little short from my creation. I figured talented stylist like myself, would be able to understand my concepts. I was pleased, though it was a little busy. If you had an open-mind and a real flare for style, you would see its greatness. I glanced at my competition and to my surprise some of them were good, really good. A glimmer of doubt entered my mind for the slightest second, but I held my head up. I knew mine would still outshine them all. I was on pins and needles, when it was time for the competition. Each mannequin head was numbered, so no one would know which mannequin belonged to whom. I looked at mine. It was lucky number seven. I was glad I had that number.

The judges included a few of the seniors and four of the instructors, and of course Mrs. Sarah. I stood back to see everyone's expression as they passed by my creation. My hair style was the largest one there. I was going for volume. As the judges passed by, I could hear snickering and finger-pointing.

I wanted to yell out,

"What are you laughing at number seven is mine."

Did they think I was a joke? My temper went from zero to five-hundred in one-point-two seconds, and was getting hotter and hotter. It was like steam in one of those old school pressure-cookers ready to blow. I did all I could just to keep my composure, until the results came in. I didn't even place.

The platform I once placed myself on was crumbled underneath my feet. How could they not see my greatness? Had I put myself into an unrealistic place of existence? I was devastated! I felt like I was the last to know there was no Santa Claus. How could I have been so stupid! I listened to Angela and her friend rave about my work. Was it all a lie? Was I the butt of the joke? I wanted so much to be special. It turns out. I am just like everyone else. Even worst, I am lower than them. I didn't even place.

I hate this place. They fill your head with false hopes and dreams. At the end of the day you're still a nobody. They made

me out to be a joke. I was a laughing stock. I felt embarrassed and hurt all at the same time. I forgot everything Ms. Mindy had taught me about the three B's. My hurt turned into anger!

"Laugh at me, I could give a rat's ass about them or this school." I thought.

The anger consumed me. I was no longer myself. I could feel the tears falling down my face, when I began to shout uncontrollably,

"What the f***! Are you kidding me? Y'all chose this s*** over mine! Are y'all all blind!"

Before long, I lost all control and begin throwing mannequin heads left and right, students and instructors alike starting running for cover. I was so out of control and full of so much anger, I didn't want to stop. I wanted to hurt someone. The mannequins happen to be the unsuspecting victims in this case. All of a sudden, I heard a voice and it shook my soul so deep it rocked me back into reality.

"They might do this crap in the country, but in my school! You will have some sense and control! And, I mean have some sense, right damn now!"

I looked up from the floor, peering into a set of bold bloodshot eyes. Gasping for air I felt her hands around my throat. I could feel the rest of her weight on my chest. Ms. Mindy traded in her proper clothes for a cowboy outfit, and she had just wrangled, pinned and tied her first heifer. Her grip around my neck was strong and unforgiving. I thought I was going pass out.

Squeezing with all her might, she looked at me and said, "Do you hear me girl?"

Searching for air I tried to respond. I tried to move her off my rib cage, so I could gather just enough air to whisper,

"Yea." Her Kung Fu grip around my neck got even stronger.

"Yea?" She answered, still gripping with even more persistence.

"I mean, yes maim Ms. Mindy" I replied.

"Don't you have something else to say?" She answered.

My brain was fried because of the lack of air. I was willing to do or say anything to end this fiasco a humble,

"Sorry?" eased out.

"Sorry, what?" She asked, still unsatisfied.

I realized this was more than just two battles of pride. This was her platform of total respect. She wasn't just going to accept any imitation. She wanted it from the heart, so we never had to venture down this road again. I showed myself the white flag of surrender. I let go of my pride, my attitude, my anger and conformed to her plan of excellence.

"I am so sorry, Ms. Mindy. I promise it will never happen again." I conceded.

With that, she effortlessly got up, dusted herself off, and continued her day as if nothing had ever happened. From that day on, me and Ms. Mindy had an unspoken understanding. I had a new found respect for Ms. Mindy.

Home life was better. Eric saw all the attention I began giving myself, and he began to pay attention to me too. I guess it is true what they say,

"people are going to treat you as well as you treat yourself."

If you look like you don't give a damn they will treat you like you're not worth a damn. I began to see me too. I am pretty. I never thought I was before. My hair was long. I started to flat-iron it, instead of pulling it back into my normal pony tail. My face cleared up from years of acne. My clothes matched with purpose. They were not just something I picked up and threw on, because it smelled clean. The house was clean and organized. The kids now went to daycare, instead of destroying the house all day.

I had a routine for each day and it worked! I started using my slow-cooker so every night we could have dinner, and we sat down together as a family. The kids loved having their daddy around. I could see a change in their behavior. I began acting like a lady and he began to treat me like I was his queen. Eric even began to hint around 'bout us getting married.

One day in the middle of dinner there was a knock at the door. I got up to answer it. It was my case worker, Angela. She peered in the door to see a clean house, and our perfect little family sitting together having dinner.

"Hey girl did we have an appointment?" I asked.

"No, you were due for an inspection" she replied cold and distant.

"Well, we are right in the middle of dinner right now. Could we schedule it for another time?" I asked.

"No!" She responded even colder, she pushed the door open and walked right in.

Without even acknowledging my family, she went right to the back of the house into our bedrooms. She began opening up closets and drawers. She went into our most personal areas. I felt violated, even my children were not spared. Angela's vengeance went into their toy box, like she was looking for something. She continued in the kitchen, opening up my

cabinet, looking in my pantry. She even went through our refrigerator. I finally reached my boiling point, when she pulled out a pen and pad and started jotting things down when she left each room.

She continued into the bathroom and opened up my medicine cabinet.

She said.
"I see you are out of birth control pills. Do you have any intentions of filling the prescription?"

I replied.
"No, I have more. I just keep the extra under the sink."

"Well, I need to see them. We can't have you people lying around having all these babies and expect the state to take care of them, when they have a perfectly healthy father in the home." She sneered.

"Sure." I answered with no reaction.

I reached under the sink and grab a bag filled with birth control pills. Angela snatched the bag from my hand, trying to get a response from me. I refused to give her that satisfaction. Plus, Eric was a damn fool. I didn't want it to escalate into an event, where he got involved and our perfect family would be pulled apart by him ending up in jail.

There were two things Eric hated. One was people in our business. The other was his family being disrespected. Today, Angela had done both. I knew I had to keep my cool or else all hell's fire was going to be let loose.

I smiled back at Angela and asked,

"Can I help you with anything else?"

"Nope, you've done enough!" She said.

With that, she walked out the door. I didn't want to look at Eric. I knew everything he wanted to say to her, I was going to get it. I sat back down like nothing had happened.

As she went out the door, Eric turned, just stared at me then said,

"What, you are going to just sit there and not look at me? What the Hell Syn? What, this woman thinks she can just come into our home, like we just some worthless trash? She thinks she can just come in here and disrespect our kids like they ain't nothing? I mean, come on, what is going on? I thought y'all were friends? I thought she liked the way you did her hair? Now she gone come up in here like you're a stranger?" He yelled.

I looked up at him, fighting back the tears, with all I had. He was right. I was so caught up in my happy new family that I stopped taking care of business. I didn't want to get put out of school, so I stopped doing clients at home like Ms. Mindy said. But Ms. Mindy didn't have babies to feed and a home to run. Now I have put us in jeopardy.

I thought,
"I should of kept doing Angela's hair, if no one else."

But it is hard to feel good about yourself, when you have to give a service to someone who makes you feel like trash. Plus, I sometimes wonder if she liked me, because I did her hair, or was it so she could see my man. I notice'd how she would try to come up with conversation with him to get his attention.

I'm not stupid. I'm not the old Syn and I liked the new me. I liked doing better and feeling better. In one day, I let her take all my hard work from me.

Eric could see my crushed spirit as I tried to explain,
"Babe, I am so sorry I didn't know what to do."

I tried to explain and stay calm, but the tears were flowing down my face. Eric walked over to me and held me close. I don't ever think we had been on the same accord before. I felt at one with him, and he felt at one with me, for the first time.

"You did everything right love. I should have stepped up a long time ago and a lot of this wouldn't have happened." He said. "I'm sorry."

I looked at him so deep! In all our years together, I never remembered Eric showing me compassion. For once, Eric was taking the blame for our situation and apologizing for his shortcomings.

I thought back to what Mrs. Annie said to me, "People are going to pull against you. It's your job to make sure their pulling doesn't pull apart all you have worked so hard to hold together."

I knew that I couldn't repair the relationship between me and Angela, so I just braced myself for the worst.

I stopped doing clients at home cold-turkey, especially since that incident with Angela. I didn't want it to get back to Ms. Mindy that I was still doing clients. Plus, after my hair competition fiasco, my confidence wasn't what it had been.

Some of them were pissed, but understood what I was trying to do. With more time on my hands, we did more family outings. I could truly say for the first time in my life I felt like we were a real family going in the right direction, but Angela made my life hell. I started getting all kinds of letters in the mail from the welfare office that I hadn't gotten before. I never read all of them. Most of them said how my benefits were being reduced. I knew she was tripping'. I thought she would get over it. After all, it was her idea that I went to school in the first place.

Then she started leaving phone messages saying that I needed to come into the office, because I was under investigation for fraud. I knew doing hair under the table was

wrong, but now I can see it becoming personal between me and Angela. After a long day at school, I didn't have the patience to listen to any drama. I thought if I ignored her, she would find another beautician and get off my back. I knew it had to be more than just me doing her hair.

Angela was beautiful. She had it all. She had the nicest house, a fancy car and more money than she could ever spend. The only thing I had that she could possibly want was Eric. I began putting two and two together. Who was Angela? Why was she so eager to get me into beauty school? Was it to get me out of the house?

I began to remember how Eric and Angela would look at each other, when they thought that I wasn't paying attention? Then it hit me like a woman's intuition does. That woman is sleeping with my man. That explains why she came to our house that day. It was to check up on Eric. I knew something was up, because Eric had been coming home, giving me sexual attention every night.

I was furious. Not at Eric, I knew he was a dog way before Angela. I was furious at her, because she came into my home posing as my friend. Angela's anger was just basically jealousy. I had the man she wanted.

As the months went by, my money was funny and my change was strange. What little welfare money I got once a month barely paid the rent, and my food stamps got cut in half. I knew it was because of Angela. I just had to budget the little I had.

One morning I dreaded getting up, I knew my babies wanted their oatmeal and milk. I knew that there was nothing in there to eat. I laid there and laid there, with all types of thoughts running through my mind. The first thing that popped in my mind was,

"Where the hell is Eric?"

I've been so caught up in school, kids, and the Angela's drama. I haven't been able to keep an eye on what he's been up to. Now that I need him the most, he is nowhere to be found.

How could I be so dumb! For once I wanted to believe Eric was going to be a real man and take care of home. I thought he'd be here, not prowling the neighborhood like a dog sniffin' the ass of the first woman he saw. I guess I am supposed to put on my super woman cape. Then figure out a way to make meals with no food and drive the car with no gas. Oh yea, I forgot I'm super, so I don't need gas. I will just fly to the store that's miles away. The last thing I need is to have some of my classmates drive by me, while I walk down the street with three children behind me, looking all tired and frustrated.

I glanced at the door to see three little people looking back at me. Before I knew it, they were all in the bed jumping up and down,

"We're hungry, we're hungry mommy."

Their little voices gave me the strength to put on my cape to make something happen. I rolled out of bed and opened the refrigerator door and to my surprise there were milk, eggs, bacon and bread. A smile came across my face, then a tear.

I was feeling alone, angry and hurt. My partner had left me all alone. Why do I always think the worst? Before the guilt set in, a flashback ran through my mind of how much of a dog he still is, but that was the past and this is now.

I made breakfast and sat in the living room. Then noticed fifty dollars on the coffee table with a note,

"Babe get some groceries. I know it's not much, but you have the skills.

Eric."

With new found energy, I quickly got the babies ready. I always liked to dress them in their Sunday best, especially if I was paying with food stamps. I never wanted to look like one

of those welfare moms with bad-ass acting, dirty kids with raggedy clothes.

I did my final inspection of all us and left for the grocery store. Even with a super cape on, trying to keep up with three kids while looking for the cheapest deals was overwhelming, frustrating and working on my last nerve.

In the front of the cart was baby Lee, whose little feet kicked me repeatedly. Louise was sitting in the cart with the food. Every time she tried to stand up, she smashed the bread, caved in all cereal boxes and the fresh vegetables looked pureed. My big boy Ledell was under the cart, propped on top of the bottled water. As I went down each isle, his little hand jutted out and pulled down items from the neatly arranged shelves. On every isle, we left had a trail of items on the floor.

I'm in beauty school learning how to be beautiful and glamorous. This reality went against all Ms. Mindy had drilled in my head from day one until today.

I saw my reflection in the frozen food glass door. If I had to say so myself, I still looked fly! I tossed my head back like I was in a photo shoot striking poses. I placed my hands on my hips and shook them from side to side, changing my expressions from smiles to serious to ooh... I'm so hot!

I could feel the people in the aisle looking at me. So after I had my moment, I continued on like I was a superstar's wife. I ran into Mrs. Annie in her power chair. I felt sorry for every innocent bystanders that happen to cross her path. I think they should make old people get a permit before they set them free to drive those motored carts. I guess they will do something, when someone gets hurt.

I said,
"Hi Mrs. Annie, long time no see. How you been?"

I was happy to see her looking good, although her weave had been replaced with a cheap wig.

She replied,
"I've been just fine. I guess I can't say the same for your situation!"

I was thinking to myself,

> "What scoop does she have on me? How many shops had my name and knew my situation?

> "My situation, what's up?" I asked with irritation in my voice.

She began to say,

> "Well, you know the girls at the welfare office done told me how that Angela is trying to put you in jail for welfare fraud. They say, she done called up to your school trying to get your funding revoked. She says your precious Eric has been hustling them streets selling or making... Oh, I can't remember which one."

I couldn't believe all that she knew!
"I mean lady get a life and give me a break."

I can see some things never change. Like Big Mama use to say, a dog that will bring a bone will sure carry one back. I looked down on her while she sat in her chair.

I must have looked like I wanted to stomp a hole in her forehead. Because she looked at me and said,

> "Girl don't get mad at me. Your business came knocking at my door. All I did was answer it. Angela got a hold of your old clients' numbers. She called them up to let them know that she was recording the whole conversation. She told them they would do time for not cooperating in her investigation. They say she got enough on you to put you under the jail!"

She paused, shaking her head.

Then she said,

> "One thing I can say is that the only reason you're not in the slammer right now is because of Mindy. She stopped

that Angela right in her hateful tracks. When she called up to that school, Mindy let that hussy know that she was messing with one of her girls. She say what was done before you entered her school was done before. That was no concern of hers. You belong to her now.

Then she said,

"if I am not mistaken, wasn't Syn the one that does your hair also?"

She laughed and said,

"Yeah. Mindy read her rights like a true mamma can. Boy you could of bought Angela for a quarter then."

I was shocked I couldn't believe Ms. Mindy had done all that for me and never said a word.

"You supposed to be my friend, what part of my back did you cover?" I asked.

"Syn you must know I had your back or else I wouldn't be in this supermarket with this cheap-ass wig plopped on my bald head. You might not know this, but don't anybody do anything in this town without my permission. Angela works for me, I have the power to make or break anybody I please. I just stay on the down, until a thing gets out of hand, because when I step in, all hell will break loose." She said.

She sighed,

"I approve the budget for some of the programs in her office. Let's just say I put a major bug in her ear." She said winking and continued saying, "Angela got the message, I told her to cool it. I'm not saying that your ass is out of the frying pan, but at least the fire is turned down. Welfare fraud is federal. If she takes it there, there's little any of us can do. Just know this, we are pulling for you."

I wanted to give her a hug. This was the first time I felt like I had some family in this place even closer to me than the family God gave me.

Then she said,
"My suggestion to you is, you need to watch Eric. I think he's got his head some place it doesn't need to be."

With that, she turned around and went to the next isle.

I thought,

"What the hell is she talking about? Does she know about him and Angela too?"

Now my mind was really racing. I finished my shopping and went to the checkout line. With every beep the machine made to add up my purchases, my eyes were on the balance. Forty nine fifty. Wheeww... I thought I was going to have to put something back.

I handed the clerk that brand new crisp fifty dollar bill Eric had left for me. The clerk looked at the fifty, then at me strange.

I looked back at him strange, then I smarted off,

"Is there a problem? What? You don't think I can have any money? All food ain't bought with food stamps you know?"

The clerk began to turn red from embarrassment so I lowered my voice a little. The manager looked at the clerk, and he quickly gave me my change. I snatched the receipt from his hand, grabbed my groceries, and headed for the car.

On the way home, I began thinking to myself,

"What a strange day? First, I didn't know how I was going to feed my babies. Then, I run into Mrs. Annie. Then this stupid clerk, with his racist ass, was acting like my money wasn't good enough. Plus, still don't know where the hell Eric is?"

I finally made it! Ten long weeks of this mannequin looking at me, and ten long weeks of being pissed off for having to work on her every day. This has been the longest ten weeks ever! I had named her Sandy. Today I gave her hair one last glance. I had dyed, highlighted, burnt, cut the top and shaved one side and permed the other side of this hair. Many a day I had gotten so frustrated and wanted to quit, but today it had all paid off. Today was my crossover day.

We had a little ceremony. Ms. Mindy gave us a speech on how proud she was of us. She said don't make her regret this opportunity to be something great. Then she personally gave us our white smocks. I was sooo…. emotional. As I looked into her eyes, I could see the reflection of myself in them. All I could feel was her pulling for me. I knew I was not going to let her down.

When, I walked onto the senior floor and I knew I was somebody. So many times I saw the seniors in the lunchroom discussing the many tips they made that day, or how many clients requested them. How I wished I could have that same chance to show off too.

Ms. Mindy stood in the middle of the clinic with all of us. She gave a speech on how we were going to conduct ourselves in her clinic. She reminded us of the three B's. We all looked at her in total agreement.

She began saying,
"If I see once, and that's all it takes once, where you are not conducting yourself in a professional manner, you will be removed from the clinic floor immediately and placed back into the freshmen room. You will stay in the freshman class for an additional ten weeks. If you still are unable to present yourself in a professional manner, then you will deal with me."

I looked around to see the terror in each student's eyes. I felt the same fear deep in my soul. Ms. Mindy was a fair woman. She had that grandma insight, like she knew the future before it happened.

She continued,
"I have placed you in the sections that will be the most
beneficial for you. It is none of your business why I
choose your placement or how long you will be placed
here. Do not come to me later and ask if you may be
moved. If you do have any objections to where you have
been placed that is fine with me, just keep it to yourself.
Neither I, nor your fellow students, nor your instructors
need to hear it." Does anyone have any objection? "

An even more distinctive hush filled the room. Ms. Mindy
slowly surveyed the room, making eye contact with every one
of her students to see if there were any objections.

Then she continued,

"As I was saying," looking down at a thick packet of
papers in her hand. "I am holding the clinic floor rules. I
will go over a few of them and in your spare time, you
may read the rest. **Rule Number One**. There is no
chewing gum in my school or on my clinic. You may eat
only in the student lunch room. **Rule Number Two**. No
one will touch, move, borrow accidentally, take home or
disturb your fellow student's supplies, tools, implements
or anything else that does not belong to you. **Rule
Number Three**. You will not refuse any client that is
assigned to you. You will have five minutes to set up after
your name has been called. Each client that you receive
will be done in a timely fashion. If you are unable to do
your clients in a timely fashion, you will be removed from
the clinic floor and placed back into the freshman
classroom for more practice. **Rule Number Four**. You
will greet each client with a smile and treat each one of the
clients with respect and courtesy. Each client is to be
pampered and will enjoy their experience here at *Beautiful
One*. If you find yourself with an attitude when you wake
up in the morning, that's fine, just remember to leave it at
the door, because attitudes are not welcomed here at
Beautiful One, nor will they be tolerated. You will be sent
home immediately. **Rule Number Five**. You will be in a

201

uniform that is inspection ready at all times, which means uniforms are to be clean without stains, pressed and creased. Your shoes will be clean and you will wear white socks. Your hair will be done and face pleasantly made. Your hygiene will be at its highest standard at all times, which includes fresh breath. **Rule Number Six.** You will not ask clients for a tip. If your services are appreciated, the client will tip. If not, that's fine. If they request you again, it is the biggest tip you can receive. These are my most important clinic floor rules, but there are many more. My goal is not to weigh you down with rules. But there are rules in life, just as there are here. If you cannot learn to follow the rules here, you cannot succeed in life. Greatness began with rules. Success is how well you are able to follow them."

Ms. Mindy took one last final look at each one of us and went into her office.

The clinic was divided into three sections. Each section had twenty stations with chairs numbered one through 20. There were 60 stations in all. Each section had an instructor assigned to it. Mrs. Ruby had Row one. She was a light-skinned lady, who reminded you of a gypsy. Although she looked flighty, you could tell she didn't play. She wore her hair in a free-flowing natural style with long earrings. She had at least eight beaded necklaces around her neck and twenty or so bangles on her wrist. You could hear her coming a mile away. Row two was Mrs. Mercedes. She was a tall, slim, model-looking type. She walked, talked and acted stuck-up. She wore high-fashion all name brand clothes. She owned a salon. Only the elite students were invited to work for her after graduation. Even then, you still had to start as a shampoo girl, until she felt you were worthy to rent a chair from her. Row three was Mr. Cummings. He was a short, Hispanic man, who had an artistic flare, but not the kind that is feminine or nothing. He could just whip the hell out of some hair. All kinds of hair, it didn't matter he could do it. Although he wasn't exactly the

handsome, he had that "I am the shit" swag about him. And he smelled like a man god every time he walked by.

I patiently waited to hear my name called,
Synthia Jackson, row three, seat number ten."

I gathered up my supplies and went to my station. I was right in the middle of a long row of twenty stations. I felt lost and unimportant. If I was good, how could Ms. Mindy put me in the back in the middle of nowhere? I knew when I came here I had a lot of work to do. But I had put in the work and improved my skills, plus I had mad talent. Thinking to myself as I was getting my supplies out of my bag, I looked up to see Mr. Cummings looking at me.

"Synthia is it?" He asked.

A smile came over my face because he called me by my new name.

"Yes, " I replied, "although some people call me Syn for short."

"Are you okay?" He asked.

"Yea, I'm fine, just trying to get use to my new station." I replied with memories of my last thoughts.

Then he said,

"I'll let you in on a little secret. Back here is the best place to be, because when you shine from back here no one will ever wonder who you are, it will be brighter than anyone."

He gave me the biggest smile, a wink, and a warm feeling came over me. I felt honored that I was in his row. He understood me without me saying a word. Once a month, there was a clinic competition. Each row competed against the other. Whoever won in our row was head chair and moved to the first seat of that row. I could just imagine myself in first chair for the duration of my hours.

The school was set up more like an upscale salon than a school. It was packed with clients from the time the doors opened, until we took our last appointment. In the mornings the clients would be standing outside. They signed their names on a list to hold their spot, until the receptionist could collect the money and write up their ticket. One of the school rules were no students were allowed to walk up to the receptionist desk to hustle clients.

When your name was called the client was escorted back to you. I could see out the gate that if you were a kiss ass to the receptionist, she would make sure she gave you a high- tippin' client. If you were a nobody, she would give you one of those screaming kids. If you got on her bad side, she would give you one of our haircut specials that cost four dollars and you know they ain't tippin'.

I looked around to check out my competition and see what I was up against. I mean these ladies were bad! Their hair was always fashion show ready and their nails should be in a magazine. We had to wear all white smocks with white shoes and pants. They better be starched not a stain on your clothes and not a scuff on your flat rubber sole shoes.

At the end of each day, there was a station inspection. Over the loud speaker you hear, "Station inspection," and everyone stopped what they were doing and scrabbled like a military drill cleaning and scrubbing each station. The clinic had to be cleaned and sanitized like it was new, each mirror was streak-free, and all station drawers didn't have even the smallest hair-clipping in it. The base of each chair sparkled like a brand new nickel. The floor around your station needed to be hair and product free.

Mr. Cummings inspected our row at the end of each day. We all lined up like soldiers behind our chairs, and if your station didn't pass inspection Ms. Mindy was there waiting for you in the clinic floor. At the end of everyday Ms. Mindy stood there alone, because who wanted to be the one that was pointed

out as nasty and too lazy to clean up behind their selves? No one at *Beautiful One,* that's for sure.

My first client was hell! That stupid receptionist must have given me the nappiest, thickest hair I have ever seen. It didn't help that the little girl was tender headed. I tried everything to make the hair soft enough to comb, but it was no help. She squirmed, cried, and screamed. She flipped and flopped out of her shampoo cape and everything. I looked down my row to see Mr. Cummings peering at me. I knew I had to get the client done in a timely fashion, and keep in mind the three B's (professional, beautiful and on time). The last thing I wanted was to be sent back into the freshman room for another ten weeks. I spun my chair around and was eye to eye with this little Tasmanian devil.

"What is your name, sweetie?" I asked in the kindest and gentlest voice I could muster up.

Wiping her eyes, she replied,
"Myanna."

My heart was soften by her soft, innocent voice, she reminded me of my little princess Louise at home. I took a deep breath and began treating her like the princess she was. I made small talk and before long she felt comfortable with me. A smile came across her face. When I finished and walked her to the front to meet her mother, I could see the shock on her face. Her mother immediately began questioning little Myanna to see what type of spell was cast on her demon seed. I just stood there with a smile plastered on my face.

She asked,
"Baby, are you ok?"

Little Myanna looked back at her giggly and said,

"Yes mommy, I want some ice cream."

Amazed, the mother looked at me and said,

"I don't know what magic wand you have, but we are requesting you for next week and every week after. Her hair is so soft and straight. I can't do anything with it at home. She looks great and she's happy! Usually by the time she leaves here all of our nerves are shot. She always gives all the other students so much trouble kicking and screaming, we are here all day."

She grabbed my hand and put a balled-up ten dollar bill in it. I was ecstatic!

She said,
"Thank you and I will see next week."

I gave a little wave to Myanna, and she gave me a hug. As she ran back to her mother, she yelled back,

"Bye Ms. Syn."

I could see the other clients looking at me.

Then one said,

"So your name is Syn?"

"Yes maim" I replied.

"Well is it ok if I request you too?" She asked.

"No problem, I would be honored." I replied.

I hurried up and left from the front desk, because that was one of the rules and returned to my seat to prepare my station for the next client. Before I could get there, I heard my name being called to set up for my next appointment. I could feel all eyes on me. I knew then that I didn't have anything to prove I was shining. The rest of the day flew by. All I wanted to do was go home and tell my family my good news.

On my way home, I had the most satisfying feeling inside of me. I knew everything I had worked so hard for was coming together. As I came up my street, I could see police cars all over the place. What on earth is going on?

I said to myself,

"Folks always letting these ghetto bunnies with that baby-daddy drama move-in and bring down every property value. Why can't we as a people just get along?"

Before I could finish my thoughts, I saw my man, my beautiful, precious Eric, on the ground in handcuffs. My three babies were sitting on the curb beside a female police officer, with Ms. Joyce standing close by. The lady in me left. I could give a damn about some property value. This was my family that they were messinging with!

Leaving the car running in the middle of the street, I jumped out and I ran to my babies. In one scoop, I grabbed all three still in motion.

Then, I ran to the officer that had his knee in my man's back. Me and all three babies transcended on the officers back like a pack of wolves defending the Alpha.

Their little feet were kicking as I was screaming.

"Get off of him, he ain't no dog, get off of him!"

The kids could feel my pain. Then they started screaming and hollering. Four officers came out of nowhere running to the other officer's rescue. Each one tried to pull my babies from my arms, but I had that mamma grip that was not letting go. My little ones were not going to let anyone rip them from their mothers' arms. My babies held on to me just as tight as I was holding on to them. I felt like I was being tag teamed in a WWW fight, and I was the underdog everyone was cheering for.

Then I heard a calm voice from an older officer,

"Miss, Miss, calm down. This ain't about you or your babies. Just calm down, this ain't even your fight! Just calm down, please. "

I stopped fighting and the officers backed away. Still holding my children, I looked up to see this monstrous statue of a man looking down at me. He could crush me with one blow. He ordered the officer off of Eric and ushered me to the porch. I sat down to catch my wind.

Fighting back the tears I replied,
"What is going on, what happened?"

"Well maim, it seems that gentleman over there has got himself into a little trouble." He replied.

"What kind of trouble?" I asked.

"The kind of trouble, he's going to have to go downtown and explain to the prison guard in the jail house kind of trouble." He answered.

I could see that he was trying to say as little as possible because the kids were like little sponges hanging on his every word.

"Why don't you see if you can get someone to watch the little ones for a little while so we can talk?" He asked.

I could tell he wanted to help. I looked up to see Ms. Joyce with her arms opened to receive the children. Although Ms. Joyce didn't talk, I felt her heart and it spoke to me,

"Is everything alright?" Her gentle spirit calmed me into a perfect peace.

My heart was full of emotions, and it replied

"No, everything ain't alright!"

Our eyes locked, I knew she felt the pain I was feeling.

My whole perfect life was crumbling before my eyes!

I turned away,

> "Hell no, everything ain't alright," I mumbled to myself as I walked back to the scene.

They put Eric in one car and me in another. I knew I was safe, because I didn't know what the hell Eric has been up to and for once I was glad. When we arrived at the police station, they escorted me into one of those little interrogation rooms like in the movies with the two way mirror and all. The room had an uneven table with one nasty hard little chair. I sat down. They left me in there about two hours. Finally an older black lady came into the room extending her hand to me.

She introduced herself.

> "Hi, my name is Mrs. Potts. You were brought down here today to answer some questions."

I have seen enough court shows to know not to say a word, so I asked,

> "Am I under arrest?"

In shock that I asked her questions before she had a chance to ask me, she said,

> "Well, no! You're not! But we do have the right to detain you until we get more information on this case. You are under investigation."

> "Well then, I need to speak to a lawyer." I replied.

She got up and exited the door. I knew what she was trying to do. She was trying to get me to tell her some negative things about my Eric. That was not going to happen. He was not perfect by no means, but he is one of the main ingredients that makes my world complete. So, she was not going to disturb my recipe for my future life of happiness. Oh no, not today. More hours went by, and then they came in, handcuffed,

fingerprinted me and put me in a holding cell. I sat down content, because whatever trouble Eric was in, I wasn't going to give them any rope to hang him with. I sat back and waited to meet with my attorney.

Thoughts of my babies overwhelmed me. Who's going to take care of my children, while I'm here? I only expected to be gone a few hours. This could easily turn into twenty-four hours, especially if they are able to tie me to Eric's crap. What about school? I just got on the floor and got my respect. Now with just one drive home, all that has been taken away. I sometimes wish that I didn't love that man so much.

Over a loud speaker I heard my name being called,

"Synthia Jackson."

I stood up to see the guard at the door,

"Your attorney will see you now." I was escorted into another small room with a table.

My attorney was a Public Defender. I knew he had no intention of representing me or Eric. He was not looking out for our best interest. He just needed to close a case as soon as possible, so the state could impress some more folks. I mean another black couple behind bars just helps the statistics.

I came out with it bold and direct.

"So what the hell am I under investigation for?"

I looked at this twenty or so thin, fragile little man as he peered at me through his bifocals.

"Well Ms. Jackson, my name is Mr. Thomas. I will be representing you in this case." He said avoiding eye contact and looking through my file.

"My question to you again Mr. Thomas is, what am I under investigation for?" I repeated.

He replied.
"Um... From what I can tell it is counterfeiting in increments of twenties, fifties and hundreds."

"Counterfeiting? Counterfeiting what? I don't have a clue what you are talking about?" I exclaimed.

He removed his glasses and placed them carefully on the table. He folded his hands together and looked at me face to face, then spoke in a calm voice.

"Money."

I jumped out of my seat outraged!

He reared back in his chair, as I went through my enraged fits, yelling in anger.

"I haven't ever even touched no fake-ass money. If I had some money you think I would be sitting up in here talking to you, what the hell?"

Then, my good sense kicked in, that damn Eric ain't got the sense God gave a duck. I sat back down to get my thoughts together.

Eric is always out there trying to find the easy way out of everything. While I am working my ass off trying to get through school, take care of the house and kids. Here he is coasting through life like it is going to be handed to him on a silver platter.

I gained my composure and resumed my conversation.

"So what are they offering him, and what does this have to do with me?"

"Well, Eric and you have been under investigation for about eight weeks now. The only tie you have to this operation is the money you spent at the Ready Market." Pausing as he thumbed through more papers. Then he continued, "From what I can tell, you made a purchase

and paid with a counterfeit fifty dollar bill. They were also able to trace that your utilities were paid with counterfeit monies as well."

I looked at this stranger as he told me about the events in my life. I felt so dumb that he knew more about my world than me. I couldn't blame anyone but myself. I never even asked Eric where the money came from. I was just happy that for once he was taking care of us. I was happy that we were a family that he stood up as a man and took on the responsibilities for his family.

Now what am I supposed to do? I have too much at stake to take the rap for this. Plus, I don't know where it is manufactured or who his contact person is? But I can't let my babies down, we are a team. I stood up to walk around to clear my head, thinking to myself, "what to do? What to do? Think Syn, what is your next step?"

"So how much time is he looking at," I asked, looking at my occupied attorney?

"Well, for now, it looks like Eric is taking full responsibility for the whole incident. He wrote a statement that clears you of all knowledge of his actions, so from what I can see, you are free to go Ms. Jackson."

Then he said,

"I will have them start on your paperwork and you should be out of here in a couple of hours or so."

They took me back to the holding cell. While waiting for my release, I began thinking about how my Eric was not coming home. How was I supposed to make it without him? Even though he was doing everything the wrong way, his intentions were good. What am I going to tell the children? My life had reached a breaking point and the rope that tied me to my fantasies broke. The clouds lifted and I began to see things clear.

I looked around to see where Eric's bullcrap had landed me. I stepped over the nasty ass crack hoe lying on the cell floor in vomit. Her body was so thin. She looked like she hadn't eaten in years. Her weave was like a mop full of a milky-colored vomit. The toilet was connected to the cement wall in the middle of a thirty by thirty cell. Loud grouts come from the fat woman sitting on the toilet trying to take a dump. They could have at least hung a curtain to give some privacy to her keep from exposing her big, fat, yellow pimpled-filled ass. Or they could have some funky-booty spray for all the body fluid smells.

The harsh reality of it all came to a head. Eric has never really been there. It has always been me all the time, so why am I giving him so much credit? Am I just that dumb or desperate for a man? I wanted to tear the bars off this joint, find him and beat his ass for once. I knew it wouldn't be long before I got out of here, so I crossed my arms, sat on the steel bench and waited to hear my name called for my release.

On my bus ride home, I plotted out my next move. First, I'm going to have to drop out of school and resume doing clients at home to pay the rent and feed us. Next, I'm going to that welfare office and beg Angela to start my benefits back. I'll give her free services for the rest of her life. My life was great until Angela put that dumb idea in my head to go to school and change my life.

Now look what has happened, my whole life has been turned upside down. I walked the four long blocks home from the bus stop. I knocked on Ms. Joyce's door waiting for her to answer. I sat on her stairs. She opened the door, came out and sat down beside me. Then she put her arms around me, held me and didn't let go. I felt her heart, her soul and I felt one with her.

I broke down and I could feel the tears saturating my face.

"I am so tired, tired of trying to do well in school, tired of living, tired of that man. I'm so tired of trying to be a good mother. I'm just tired of everything."

She held me, rocked me and her heart spoke,

> "It's okay to be tired. When you feel tired it just means
> you need to take a short rest, and that's okay. But you just
> can't stop! Cry for now. When you're finish crying, it's
> finished. Dust yourself off and keep fighting, because
> your blessing is waiting for you just around the bend."

> "The devil knows you are so close. Why do you think
> your world is falling apart now? When you were doing
> wrong, everything seemed great. The second you change
> for the better, he starts working on you overtime. The
> devil don't want you to change. He don't want you to do
> well. He just keeps you looking through smoke-filled
> goggles and you never see the true light. For all you knew
> life was great, but in reality your life was hard. "

> "You never took care of yourself. You always put Eric,
> before yourself and those babies. But the second you
> changed your life, the devil knew he didn't have a chance.
> So he put obstacles in your way to get you so tired, you'd
> give up. That is his plan, to make you give up right before
> the race is over. If you give up, then you will never get
> your prize and God will never get the glory."

I slowly began to stand up feeling better behind her
comforting words. She stood up also. She held my hands,
raised my head up and looked into my eyes. Her eyes were
filled with tears, then the tears began pouring down her cheeks.
I dropped my head again, feeling bad for making her cry.

Then her heart spoke to me again, it said,

> "But God will have the glory. You were stolen from me,
> when you were little. Now God has given you back to me.
> You were gone. Now you are here. Once you were lost
> but now you're found."

As those words went flying out her mouth and into the air, my whole world shook. My mind went blank and I could no longer think.

There was a silence so thick I could hear nothing for about one whole minute or more. It was like life was placed on pause. Everything went dark and silent.

Then suddenly her distorted words came flying back and smacked me in the face, mind and body. I jerked hands away, looked at her and my quivering lips said,

"WWWait! WWWhat! WWWhat the.."

My eyes locked on Ms. Joyce, and I stared at her like she was crazy. She was one of those old church going praying women. Every Sunday you see the church bus pick her up early in the morning, the bus didn't drop her off till late that night.

I asked myself,

"What was she talking about? I was lost but now I'm found? Has she lost her mind?"

Then her words hit me again.

"You were stolen."

Her eyes locked with mine and she managed a slight smile. I paused. I knew her smile. It was the smile from my dreams. And.. And.. Those eyes… My heart began to beat so fast, and I could hardly breathe. Fear, excitement, sadness, joy, anger, hate and love all hit me at once.

I was shaking all over. I closed my eyes. I was trying to get my exploding thoughts together.

My mind said,

"Ms. Joyce is… She is…" My mind could not wrap around the thought of her being my, my…

"Could she be?" I asked myself between the bouts of insanity now racing around in my mind.

"No! No! No! God No!" I heard myself scream as the thoughts of Big Mama and all the Hell I received from her everyday evil intentions now joined in the race for my mind.

Tears fell from my closed eyes like buckets of water being poured down my face. My lips trembled uncontrollably. I couldn't look at her.

"I won't look at her!" I told myself. "I'm mad! No, I'm sad. Hell, I don't know what I feel." I cried more as the thoughts now ran in my overcrowded mind.

Then suddenly my heart cried out, saying,

"How many nights did I cry wanting my mamma and hating her at the same time for selling me to that evil Big Mama. How many nights did I fall asleep looking at the stars wishing, hoping and praying that my mamma would be there to take me away the next day. Only to awake to those evil eyes of Big Mama's staring a hole through me."

Back then I told myself,

"My mamma was a crazy. A wicked woman who sold children and had no soul. I hated her, and I learned to live by never caring and never thinking about her."

"Now I find out, I was stolen? That my mamma wanted me! God help me. Please God Please! I can't breathe! I can't breathe!" I screamed inside as my thoughts again managed to piece themselves together for a moment.

I gasped for air amongst the crying and tears, but couldn't find any. I could get my words together. My only sound was,

"Ahhh...ahhhh... ahhhh... ahhhhhhhhh..."

"Ahhh...ahhhh... ahhhh... ahhhhhhhhh..." I cried and cried and cried.

Through all of the crying and crying and crying, silent screaming and tears, I finally opened my eyes to find that I was no longer standing. My legs had given out long ago. My legs and my body had completely surrendered. My entire body, except my head, now lay stretched out on the porch.

"Ahhh...ahhhhhhh..." I cried again.

Finally, as I came more and more back to myself, I was now able to swallow and tried to calm down a little. Still sniffing and crying, I managed to get out a muffled,

"Mamma," realizing the woman rubbing and holding my head was my mother and I was home.

Synthia you have a client!

"Girl, get your head out of the clouds. That is the third time they called your name. Are you okay?"

I looked at the station next to me it was Pee Wee. Well, that's what we called her, but her real name was Priwillim. It was one of the ugliest names you could put on a girl, so we all just called her Pee Wee. Her parents were creative and made up the name like so many of us do. You could probably guess her mamma's name was Pricilla and her father's name was name was William. She was no bigger than a pea. She stood about four foot ten with her shoes, and weighed no more than one hundred pounds. We started off together in the freshman class.

She was a loner like me, but we did manage to exchange a word or two. I guess you could say we were friends, because she never did anything to piss me off.

"That is the third time they have called your name you better snap out of the world you're in and get back to reality before Ms. Mindy snaps you. You know she will come over here and all of us will get in trouble."

I knew she was right. So many things were going on in my head. Life seemed more like a dream than a reality.

I was just going through the motions moving just enough to tread water, but not get anywhere. I got up quickly and began to sanitize my station. When out the corner of my eye, I saw Ms. Mindy. I pretended I didn't see her coming, until she was right up beside me.

"Is there a problem Syn?" She asked.

I acted startled, and then nervous. Turning over everything on my station, I acted like I was looking for something I had lost.

"No maim. I was just getting my station set up. I just need one more thing. Oh, here it is!"

I immediately picked up a comb that had been sitting there all along and raised it up to her like I had found a lost treasure.

She looked back at me unamused and unbelieving.

"I can see what you are trying to do. My question to you is, why wasn't it set up five minutes ago when they called your name the first time?"

Searching for a good excuse I replied,

"Sorry Ms. Mindy, I guess I was so busy looking for my comb I didn't hear my name being called. It will never happen again."

I looked down at the floor to avoid any eye contact. I was hoping she would just let it go this time. But like any other day there are just some things you cannot get past Ms. Mindy.

"Syn," she started. "I have been getting only good reports about you, since you got on the senior floor. It would be a shame if you were taken off the clinic floor and placed back with the freshman. I'm sure they wouldn't mind seeing you act a fool again because your mannequin didn't win."

I knew what she was trying to do, piss me off. But I refused to give her that satisfaction. My fuse was already lit. I didn't need her hot air blowing on it or it might cause an explosion. I swallowed a big piece of humble pie and didn't say a word. She stood there a few minutes more to see if she could get a response out of me. I just stood there like a soldier at attention. She gave me one more hard glare, then continued down the aisle checking every student as she walked by.

I ran to the front to greet my client. It was an older lady with the kind of posture which carried authority. You could tell she had a certain kind of air to her. You could tell she ran stuff, and no one ran her. I extended my hand to greet her. She looked at me like I hadn't washed my ass in months.

"Oh, she must be one of those stuck-up heifers who feel like they are superior to everyone," I thought to myself.

I retracted my hand and placed both of them behind my back, pinching the inside of each palm to keep from telling this woman what was really on my mind. I took a deep breath and I let the air softly leave my lips.

It was followed with a pleasing smile.

"Hi, my name is Syn. I will be doing your service today. Would you care to follow me?"

I grabbed her ticket sitting on the counter and glanced at it. I could see the words "THE WORKS." She was getting the

works! That meant I was going to have this hateful cuss all day. What did I do to deserve this? Then I noticed she was a request. I kept a constant smile on my face, hoping to melt her cold demeanor. She just stood there as if I was invisible.

I waited for some type of response. After receiving none, I said.

"Follow me please."

I proceeded to my station looking back periodically to see if she was close behind. I sat her at my station. I spun her around, so her back was away from the mirror. I placed her drape for the service. I looked at Pee Wee. She shook her head. That was our signal to each other that it was going to be one of those challenging clients. Those were the ones requiring a piece of magic to change their attitude. I showed Pee Wee the ticket. She gasped, then continued setting up for her client. I looked at her hair and did my own quick analysis of her tresses. Her style was a mess. She had a round fat face and all these curls plastered around her full face. It reminded me of the hair the evil witch had in the Wiz.

Her length consisted of about fifteen strands of the hair that rested on her shoulders, because she had no neck. The hair was dry. It was in desperate need of a deep conditioner and a trendy cut. For her to be so high saditty, her hair was a hot mess.

I led her to the shampoo bowl. I leaned her back into the bowl, so that her head was suspended in a restful position. Then I began with the most magical shampoo, I could give. I knew I was going to have to win her over early or else this was going to be a very long day. I stroked, rubbed and massaged her scalp until I saw her eyes roll to the back of her head. I knew I had her, when she let out an unexpected orgasmic groan. I breathed real softly, so not to disturb her. She drifted into a total restful peace. By the time I applied her conditioner, she was my new BFF (best friends forever).

As we made it back to my station, she was Chatty Cathy.

"That was the best shampoo I have ever had. Angela said that your hands were magical."

"Angela?" I thought to myself. "Now, how does this lady know Angela, and furthermore, what kind of conversation were they having that involved me?"

"Angela you say?" I asked.

"Yes, we work together in the same office." She replied.

I didn't know how to respond. Did this lady also know that Angela had me under investigation? I didn't want to say anything that might incriminate me.

I quickly changed the subject,

"So, how would you like your hair today?

Surprised, I didn't join in her conversation. She changed her train of thought and focused on her hair.

"Well, I normally wear a lot of curls in the front and straight in the back. I like to see the length of my hair and the curls on top give me a little height." She said.

"May I suggest a couple of options for you?" I asked, keeping it professional.

"Sure!" She answered in agreement with respect to my craft.

I ran my fingers through her still wet hair.

"For starters, we need to give you a trendy haircut to get rid of some of this weight on top. Next, we are going to spit your bangs and bring them over to the side. Then, we are going to add some movement by cutting in some layers." I told her.

Looking at her in the mirror, I could see her nod her head pleased with my suggestions. I started with the cut then I flat-ironed it. By the time I was finished, her whole style popped!

She shook her head from side to side. She ran her fingers through it.

"Oh.... My hair has never looked like this." She said, "and it feels amazing!"

I felt so proud! I gathered up her things and took her to the manicuring area for a full set of acrylic nails. The finishing touches were when I put on her artificial lashes and did her make-up. She began to bat her eyes, while staring at herself in the mirror. By the end of the day, she looked like a brand new person. Her stuck up persona now fit her well.

"I can't believe this is me! I haven't looked this good in twenty years. Syn you have done a miracle on me. I am so glad I had the opportunity to meet you, before I made my final decision. So what I need you to do is, tomorrow call me. Here is my card, so I can get a written statement from you. We already have a statement from Angela, but I know that there are two sides to every story. Now that I have met you, I can see what type of person you are and what you are trying to do. There is no way all that Angela said about you could be true. We also need to talk about the new programs that are available to you, while you are in school. It gives you extra money for home expenses and child care. Your benefits will be reinstated and I personally will make sure your name is the first one on my list. I can see you have a passion for what you do. So many times young ladies get discouraged, because there are too many obstacles in their way. So I am going to help you with a few of them. I am willing to go the extra mile for you, but you have to promise me one thing". She said.

I didn't know what to say, so I just nodded my head in agreement.

"You don't stop what you're doing no matter what is going on in your life. Just don't stop until you finish school, okay?"

"Okay," I answered. My voice was soft and full of emotion.

She walked out the door with a brand new pep in her step, and I just stood there like someone who had been handed a mega-million dollar check.

Too shocked to move, I just whispered to myself, "Thank you God."

I looked at the card she had handed me the day before, as I sat in the welfare office waiting for my appointment. Mrs. Rosemary was her name. When she was at the school, I never did get her name. Mrs. Rosemary... her name was like music every time I said it. Mrs. Rosemary, oh..... Mrs. Rosemary. She has completely changed my life. What a blessing, she has been to me and my kids! I grabbed my purse to find a piece of paper to jot down my little song, when my name was called. I went up to the side door and was escorted back to her office. I followed the receptionist as we weaved our way through countless cubicles. I felt like we were rats going through a maze. In the far back corner of the office was the only door, on it was her name. That sweet name Mrs. Rosemary.

The receptionist knocked. Then, we proceeded to enter. When Mrs. Rosemary saw me, she got up with the biggest smile on her face.

"Hey Syn, have a seat." She said.

She looked at the astonished receptionist. I guess she was also surprised by the greeting she gave me.

"That will be all and please hold all my calls." She told the receptionist.

"Yes, Mrs. Rosemary." She replied and closed the door behind her.

"You would not believe the greeting I got when I came home. My husband, the Mayor, was staring and smiling. He has not been able to keep his eyes off me. Thank you, in case I never did thank you before." She said with much appreciation. "Have a seat."

I sat in the most comfortable chair.

"Would you like anything?" She asked, looking behind her in a little refrigerator that sat behind her desk. "Let's see I have coffee, iced tea, soda or water?" Turning back around to me in an eager to please tone, or are you hungry? "I can have one of the girls go out and get us something if you like?"

I didn't know how to act. No one ever asked me for anything before. I thought if I say yes, I'll look greedy and hungry, which I am. I held my hand over my stomach, so she wouldn't hear it growl and responded,

"No, I'm' fine, but thank you."

I looked around her office it was like nothing I had ever seen. You would have thought you were at Queen Elizabeth's office the way she had it laid out. When they decorated it you could tell they held back no expense. She wasn't Angela's supervisor. She was the supervisors, supervisor. She was the HNIC [Head Nigga in Charge] for real.

I came to the welfare office many times and sat in the waiting area next to hollering babies and single mothers with their bad-ass kids playing musical chairs. Just so I didn't have to sit next to the smelly, homeless people begging for money and things. They all waited right along with you. I've sat in one of those cubicles and told them my whole life story, so that I could get crumbs. The workers have a way of taking every ounce of dignity from you just because you need a little

assistance right now. They act like they are giving you their money. But today, was a new day! I am in the head office being treated like a queen.

"Syn, you have given me a new perspective on life! I have so many responsibilities most of the time I don't have any time to spend on me. Now I see what a difference a little time makes. I will be seeing you once a week! I have

already set up a standing appointment with you every Tuesday at ten, if that's okay with you?" She said.

"Sure, I would love to be your stylist," I said, answering like I was an aristocrat of something.

She sat down looking at her notepad and continued speaking.

"Like I was telling you at the school, I had your funding restarted. Since it was a misunderstanding as to why it was stopped in the first place, I am having them prorate it from the time it ended. I already took the liberty to have a statement written up explaining the whole situation. All I need you to do is read over it and sign the bottom and date it. I have placed you in the *Women's First Program, which* converts your food stamp money to cash and you get an extra two-hundred dollars to help with school supplies and other expenses. They also pick up the tab for your daycare expenses. Do you have any questions at this time? I know it is a lot of information."

In my mind all I could say was,

"Thank you Lord… over and over." I tried to talk over the lump in my throat.

"No, I don't have any questions. You just don't know what this means to me," I finally got out.

I could feel my voice getting shaky.

"You have been such a blessing to me and my children's lives. Yesterday I didn't even know where our next meal was coming from and the lights are scheduled to be cut off. Thank you so much I am forever thankful."

I could see her eye's watering too.

"Girl I know how hard life can be. Don't look at this office and think my life was always peaches and cream. We all need a little help sometimes. We all got a story. I'm just glad I could help you, while you are on your life's journey."

She gave me the warmest reassuring smile. I knew things were going to get better.

Mrs. Rosemary called her secretary to come and show me my way out. I stood up and extended my hand. She came around the desk and gave me the biggest hug ever. A warm feeling came over me. I knew she did the things she had done from her heart. When the secretary arrived, I said my goodbyes and left.

"See you on Tuesday Syn." I could hear her yelling out before the door shut behind me."

The secretary led me to the front office and gave me the check. When I left there, I went to the bank to cash my check. While standing in line, I recapped on the events in disbelief. This must be what people call blessings, and God had just saturated me with them. I was never ever going to doubt there was a God above and he didn't care about me. I couldn't wait to get home and tell Ms. Joyce about my good day. As I came up to her door, the excitement ran through me and the anticipation was overwhelming.

"Ms. Joyce are you in there?" I said, knocking and yelling at the same time.

Before I didn't understand what all the hype was about. Having a mamma now, I knew she was someone who you can't wait to talk to, because she only wanted the best for you. I wasn't a big believer in God before, but I saw his love through Ms. Joyce. She was truly God sent. She had watched the kids for me and never asked me for a dime. She even fed us when

we were hungry. Too many days I'd wake up and open the door to look outside to see a bag of groceries. She didn't think I knew it was her, but I knew. So today I was going to share my blessings with her.

As she came to the door our hearts spoke in their own language without our mouths saying a word. It felt so good having a mamma and our bond was strong. I reached in my purse and handed her five hundred dollars. She looked at the money without even counting it and handed it back to me.

Tears filled my eyes, because I was raised by an evil woman who would say,

"Everything has a price, ain't nothing in this world for free."

And before I realized it, I said.

"Mamma you have been such a blessing in my life, I just wanted to give you something to show my appreciation."

She wrapped her arms around me. I could feel the warmth of her body and the scent of her skin. I had never been this close to a woman before and it felt like paradise. I loved her as much as I hated Big Mama for taking me from her. I was not alone. I had a mamma.

Our bodies were as one and our thoughts were one.

Her heart said,

"You don't know how many years I have waited for you to come back to me, and to hear you call me Mamma you have fixed my heart that has been broken for so many years. I want you to know that I love you. You are not a sin. You are life that has been breathed back into me."

Her unspoken words were a comfort to my lonely heart. Never again did I have to wonder if someone loved me. No matter what happed in my life from this day on, I knew real love. This was something Eric was never able to give.

School was great! Bills were paid, and my children had a grandmother! Mamma and I were so close. It was truly a joy to have her in my life. I should have known life was going too well. If the devil sees you enjoying life, he gets jealous. Then he comes knocking at your door to pull you from your joyous high.

One day while lying on the couch in the spirit, I heard a knock on the door. I went to the door thinking who could be at the door, while looking out the peep hole.

Unable to make out my visitor through my distorted view I yelled,

"Who is it?"

To my surprise the voice from hell itself answered,

"It's me, baby-daddy's home."

Things had been going so well. I hadn't even thought of Eric ever coming back.

Praying it wasn't him I yelled back,

"Who?"

I could hear the sound of desperation in his voice.

"Baby it's me, Quit playing, let me in."

Still hesitant, I opened the door. There stood my Eric in the flesh. He looked like a puppy left on the side of the freeway. He grabbed me smiling and full of the joy that was just stolen from me. The only thing missing was the wagging of his tail. He grabbed me and held me so tight.

I didn't know what to feel anymore. I finally realized that life was better without him and now he's here. Was I supposed to forget all the lonely nights without him or how he had my ass in jail? Am I supposed to forget how he never stepped up to the plate when it came to our family? How he left us over some

dumb butt? I mean, who counterfeits money anyway? What, he didn't think that the federal government would catch on or the local grocery store? They know we ain't got any money in the middle of the month, and here I come with a brand new fifty dollar bill? Didn't he think the store was going to be a little suspicious?

So many questions ran through my head, I tried to ignore his full of bull conversation.

"I missed you so much love, you and my babies. I was worried sick. All I was thinking about is how are they going to eat? How is she going to pay the rent, electric or put gas in the car? Is the car still running? I have never felt so helpless and alone without you by my side. I love you Syn and I want you to be my wife. Will you marry me Syn? Will you give me the chance to be to you, all you've been to me?"

I looked at him and with everything in me, I wanted to believe he had changed and everything was going to be okay. But after all I had been through, I knew he could never love me, take care of me or treat me like my God. God had become my new man. God had held me when I was reaching for the empty spirit of Eric. How could I take him back and betray the one I knew loved me? How could I love him when our love could never have the bond my God and I had? I felt torn, I knew Eric needed me and my heart wouldn't allow me to turn my back on him. So I looked in his eyes and told the biggest lie of my life.

I said,

"Yes. I love you Eric and I would love to be your wife."

The words flew off my tongue like the slick words he had said to me so many times before. I saw a sigh of relief all over his face.

He held me, and he broke down and cried. For a brief moment, I believed he had a heart. But my past retraced my memories soon reminded me, and I knew it was a facade. I held back, knowing my feelings for him were full of betrayal.

That night when we made love I knew I was cheating on my real love.

As the days went by our lives went right back to the empty existence I had ignored before. Now the distance between us was greater than perfect strangers. We both had other lovers. His was the empty life of hustling, lying and cheating. My life was full with school, family and God. I also kept the biggest secret from Eric---- Mamma, who lived next door. He still believed she was just our nosey neighbor not, Mamma. I felt it would be better that way. I made a promise to God, if Eric ever led me back into his world, then I was going to have to make a choice and Eric would be on the losing side.

The next morning the children were so excited to see their daddy. Even though the feelings soon faded, it made my heart feel good that we were a family again. Ms. Joyce still kept the kids every day as I went to school and my schedule stayed the same. As the weeks went by, I wondered if Eric was going to bring up the proposal again or was it what he thought he needed to say to get in the door to come back home.

One Saturday morning Eric was up early, made breakfast, and we all sat together at the breakfast table. I sat across from Eric. He had an odd look and demeanor about him. He stood up to make an announcement.

As he began to speak his tone seemed sincere.

"Ledell, Louise and Lee and my baby Syn, daddy is so sorry for not being here. I am sorry for putting you all in this bad situation. I just want you all to know that I'm going to make it up to you, we all going to be a real family soon."

The children were lost in the speech. I knew it wouldn't be long before the relentless questions would come spewing out of their little mouths.

"What's a real family mean daddy?" asked Ledell.

Eric stands there unaware of the bombshell of questions that were about to attack him.

Eric answered,

"We are all going to be in a wedding."

The children didn't have a clue what a wedding or marriage meant to be honest neither did Eric nor I. Of course we've heard of them, but never went to one.

"What's a wedding," asked Louise?

I could see that a grown conversation with a four, three and two year old wasn't going to get far, so I interrupted.

"What Daddy means is he's never going to be gone again."

He looked at me with doubt. I knew we had a lot to talk about, but right now I didn't want to deal with confused kids and bad news. That night when the children were in bed, Eric and I sat on the couch and talked, we really talked all night. I felt like I was talking to a stranger at first, but by the end of the night I think we became friends. That was something that our relationship was missing.

As it turns out Eric really wasn't that tough dude at all. He had the size so people treated him like he was a tough guy. He had acted the part every since he was a child. I believed that's what protected him all those years in the streets. It was hard to see Eric as a regular man for so many years. I had put him on such a high pedestal that I couldn't reach it myself. Now to see him as an average man was kind of disappointing. Even looking at him face to face, seeing him without my fantasy goggles on, I realized he wasn't even that handsome. His eyes were pretty, but all those years of drugs and alcohol had taken a toll on his body. His eyes were bloodshot and his weight was out of control. His once pretty teeth were stained from the cigarettes and coffee. How could I be so blind? And please, don't blame it on love.

If I was going to make the commitment to be with this man for the rest of my life, it couldn't be based on love, because

I didn't love Eric all the time. It couldn't be for looks because over time all looks fade. It couldn't be for friendship, because I have a many of friends that I can't stand. So I decided I would only marry him in the presence of God and to him I will make the promise to stay till death does us part.

My wedding day was nothing like I had imagined, Ms. Joyce set it all up. I didn't get the privilege of walking down the aisle with some Luther Vandross playing in the background. Nor did I have a long floor length gown full of lace and pearls with the matching veil. I didn't have a beautiful bouquet of fresh flowers. No maids or groomsmen all matched up in coordinating colors.

We met at the biggest church in town early Sunday morning before the members were there. Ms. Joyce introduced us to Pastor Henry Jackson. He was a medium height stocky built man and his face was pleasant to the eye. Something about him reminded me of someone, but I couldn't put my finger on it. As we were introduced, he extended his hand to me. When I reached to shake his hand, he held my hand so tight, it was almost a fight to get him to release his grip. It was like he wanted to hold on to me forever.

I thought to myself,

> "What kind of Pastor is this? Is he trying to make a pass at a woman on her wedding day?" I looked over at Eric to see if his jealousy detectors had noticed the advance, but Eric was so intrigued by the church that he hadn't taken notice.

The church was an awesome sight. I don't think I had seen a more beautiful place! The size of the sanctuary alone was breathtaking. From where we stood, behind us was the altar surrounded by flowers that smelt like pure summer. The ceiling had a glass dome that allowed the rays from the sun to warm your skin. I had to say I could feel God's presence here. Although I didn't have the wedding of my dreams, I knew God was there. My guest list consists of the Pastor, my children, Ms. Joyce and, of course Eric.

Pastor Jackson stood there in a robe made for a king. It was the deepest purple you could get before black. There was gold embroidery across the front with gold ropes that hung to the floor. Just to be this close to him, you had a feeling of homage to him. We felt so out of place standing there in our everyday clothes. I looked over to see my pretty babies sitting on the pew, with Ms. Joyce. My heart was at rest, because I knew our family was about to bound together by God.

Pastor Jackson ran so fast through the vows, and we gave an even faster response. You could tell he had said these vows a million times before. Less than five minutes later, he said to Eric, "you may now kiss the bride." We kissed and for some reason, I thought now that we were married, things would be different or at least feel different. But it was the same emptiness that our relationship had always had. We walked over to the piano, used it as a table, to sign the license. Then just like that we were married.

I couldn't believe it. I had dreamed of being married, and this was it. A sudden feeling of depression came over me. I thought,

> "What the hell was I thinking? I should have held out for something bigger and someone better. The whole ceremony was just like me and Eric's whole relationship, pointless. Now I was bound to this fool for the rest of my life. "

I knew Eric could feel my frustration. I didn't even give him eye contact. I just turned around thanked Pastor Jackson, got the kids and sat in the car.

On the way home, Eric began yelling, pissed off!

> "What's with this attitude? I thought you wanted to be married and be a family? Well, now you got what you wanted. I suggest that before we reach this house you get a major attitude adjustment and a smile on your face. Or

you are going to have a very hard and long ass-whoopin' tonight.

I looked at him with as much anger as I could muster. Eric saw the nonverbal threat as I looked at him like he was small.

"You look at me like you want to fight Syn?" He shouted. "I can't grant you that wish now, but just wait until we get home. I'll make sure those dreams come true."

I was so mad I was shaking and crying.

"How could I be such a sellout? My life was going great without you, and I was happy for once." I thought.

I was having a private conversation with myself. Then I felt an unexpected slap across my face. My head ricocheted off the window from the force of his massive hand slamming me upside my head. It almost knocked me unconscious.

As my head hit the glass, it split wide-open. I could feel the blood running in my eye. Peering over at Eric with the good eye, I saw his lips moving. I could barely hear what Eric was yelling past the ring in my ears.

"So you were happy when I was gone, huh? You're a sell-out for marrying me, huh?"

I was finally able to make out what he was saying. I couldn't believe he knew my thoughts, until it dawned on me, I had vocalized all of them.

"Now y'all know you got these babies in the car." Ms. Joyce?

I had forgotten Ms. Joyce was in the car too. I felt so embarrassed. I couldn't look Ms. Joyce in the face. I knew I had sold my soul to the devil. I closed my eyes and held my head down. I held the end of my dress over my bleeding wound in silence for the rest of the trip home.

I felt the car stop and heard a car door slam. I looked up to see Ms. Joyce walking away from the car heading home. I helped the kids out and took them into the house, not acknowledging Eric at all. Little Ledell held my hand. I knew

he wanted more for his Mamma but was too small to kick his Daddy's ass.

His little voice was pure as he said,

"Mamma do you want me to make us some breakfast?"

We had left so early we didn't have breakfast. I looked down at all three of them, and gave them a reassuring smile.

"No Mamma's got it."

I gave them a bowl of cereal. Eric came in the house a few minutes later and walked right passed us not saying a word, and went into the bedroom. After the children ate, I put them down for a nap. Then I went into the bathroom to survey the damage from the incident. It wasn't as bad as I thought, so I cleaned it up and put a bandage on it. Before I could finish I could hear Eric calling me from the room.

"Syn you have some business to take care of so hurry up." He yelled.

I dreaded going in there, I had a headache. I was still pissed from the car incident. I took my sweet time. I removed the breakfast dishes, then proceeded to clean the kitchen. I turned around and there was Eric. He was in a kill-a-heifer mood.

"So you just not going to come when I call you? What type of wife you going to be? A good one or one that I'm going to have to beat that ass?"

I took a deep breath and let out a sigh as if I had any other choices. I could choose not to be his wife at all and take this ass-whoopin', but right now, it wasn't even worth it.

So I answered,

"A good wife."

"Good answer." He said, "Now come on and stop playing. Come give your new husband some loving."

We went into the bedroom and had sex without love. That's all it could be.

"Is that it?" Eric asked, "You gave me better loving, when we were just shacking up. What is wrong with you? The other night I thought we were buddies, and today we are strangers."

I didn't know what to say, my heart was split in two parts. Part of me wanted a family, but the other part of me wanted a family without Eric in it.

"Nothing Eric. I guess it all happened so fast. Two weeks ago you came home. This week we are married." I said, looking at him.

Then I began to ask questions.

"Why the rush? You never even told me what happened with your case. Is it over? Do you still have to go to court? Is there jail time involved? It seems like we talk about everything, but we say nothing. Before you left, where were you all those nights when you were not in the bed with me? Were you in the bed with Angela?"

A stunned look came across his face, by the mention of her name.

I continued,

"See Eric, you just go through life like everything is smooth and it ain't."

I sat on the bed waiting for a response. He looked at me, got dressed and left. I didn't see Eric for months.

Life at school was great! I made first chair, and I was the envy of all. I got special privileges, because I had so many requests when I got to school. I didn't have to do the classwork part. I could come right in and start on my clients, so sometimes I had the whole clinic to myself. I felt special! Mrs. Rosemary kept her appointment. She spread the word and more of her friends started coming. I was making *Beautiful One* a lot of money, and my tips that I took home weren't bad either. I made a few more friends. We would sit back, dream about our salons and how fabulous they would be. We all knew they

were only dreams, because none of us would ever have the money to open a grand salon like Mrs. Mercedes. It was still a lot of fun just to dream with friends who shared the same dreams as you.

One day Ms. Mindy called me into her office. I didn't know what to expect. I conformed to the rules at *Beautiful One*. I was so close to graduation. I didn't want to mess up. I came in and sat down in a somewhat comfortable chair. It was the kind that didn't hurt your butt, but wasn't comfortable enough to encourage you to stay too long.

She sat at her big desk looking at me with her reading glasses resting on the tip of her nose.

Then she said,

"Synthia, I want to be the first to congratulate you on your success here at *Beautiful One*. It is not often that a student turns around as quickly as you have. The passion that you put in your work shows every day. I called you in here to let you know that next month, at your graduation, you will be graduating with honors. With that comes a five hundred dollar voucher to buy new supplies and to help with the cost of licensing."

I wanted to reach over the desk and give her a hug, but Ms. Mindy wasn't the hugging type. So, I just thanked her respectively.

"Thank you so much for giving me the opportunity to be a student here. I have learned so much. Not just how to do hair, but how to live life. I learned no matter how hard life gets, I can't let it affect my performance. I just want to thank you for all the things I learned that wasn't in the curriculum. Thank you Ms. Mindy! I will never forget you."

She sat there like she was bored with my speech.

"I know you will never forget me. Because wherever you go, I will be there to check on you. I have a personal investment, you are one of my girls and you will always be a part of the *Beautiful One* family. Mrs. Mercedes has

also given you an invitation to work in her salon after graduation."

She stood up and extended her hand. I extended my hand, and she held it for a long time like she could feel her life inside me. At that moment, we shared a bond that would never be broken.

Mamma never changed. She treated me like nothing happened and didn't intervene into Eric and my problems. She kept the kids for me every day. I would go over to her house after school to pick up the kids. I would just talk about my day. Mamma would just sit back and listen. You could tell by her attentiveness that she had good intentions for me and my babies.

One day Mamma's mood was strange. I could feel it in the way her heart spoke. Our love was so strong we communicated without saying a word.

My heart asked.

"What's wrong? Is everything okay?"

A distressing look came over her face. The look a woman has when they are missing their man. I knew that look. I used to have that look all of the time. Maybe after all of these years of living in this house all alone, she just needed the touch of a man. I never saw anybody come by her house, except on Sunday when a black limo would come in the morning. It would drop her off later in the evening. Sometimes I wondered where her ex-husband was, because I never saw him, and she never mentioned him. He must have plenty money and still takes care of her, because every time I would try to pay her, she would never take it.

I knew Mamma had secrets. I had so many questions that I knew only she had the answers to. I just didn't know how to open the door to the past to ask them. I knew once it was opened, it would change everything. I knew mamma could feel

my longing for answers. Suddenly, she got up, went to the closet and pulled out an old musty blanket. Then she walked over to me. Our eyes met as if she was trying to warn me for what was about to happen next. I nodded my head in approval. I believed not knowing was worse than anything she had to share with me regarding my past.

She unfolded the dirty blanket and wrapped it around me. As the blanket conformed to my body, I was whisked away like traveling through time. A vision began to unfold right before my eyes of the most horrifying, beautiful secret I had ever seen. It explained my Mamma's world to me.

The whole scene played out in silence. I saw uncle Earl, James and Steve. James and Steve seemed angry. They were outside of this same house. Mamma was just a child. They slapped and kicked Mamma, till she fell to the ground. Then they ripped off her clothes. They all stood back pointing and laughing.

Earl went around the house and reappeared with a young boy. He looked like a younger version of the Pastor that married Eric and I. They slapped and hit him too. You could see the horror in his eyes! He pulled down his pants with tears in his eyes, while James and Steve held Mamma's legs open. He raped Mamma. I saw their very soul, and the love they had for each other bonded them as one. They were only children. My uncles stole their innocence and sold me into slavery. I could see my Mamma's beaten face. I could see the look of devastation. I could feel her pain. It was more than I could take. I felt the tears as they ran down my face. I needed the pain to go away. I had to do something. I couldn't watch this anymore. The weight of evil and sorrow was wrapped around me in that blanket. It was shocking the life out of me!

I jumped up throwing the blanket of pain to the ground. I ran into the kitchen, opened the draw next to the stove and grabbed a box of matches. I ran back into the living room, grabbed that evil blanket of secrets and ran to the back yard. I could still see where the whole event had played out. This was the place where they had hurt my Mamma. I laid the blanket over the ground where my Mamma's lifeless body once laid. I

struck one single match and lit the blanket on fire. I could hear the screams of pain as I watched it burn. When the flames died down, so did the pain that had engulfed me. I stood there until the last flicker of flame burned out, and the blanket was reduced to a small pile of ashes. I was at peace.

I couldn't change what happened that day many years ago. But that blanket became the sacrifice for the ungodly secrets, it had concealed for so many years. I fell to the ground and understood that little Syn was made that day. God forgave all that was done that day. The blessing produced was me. Through every pain, there is always a blessing produced.

I felt Mamma's touch on my shoulders. I looked up at her. She had this amazing glow of beauty and peace. I understood her beauty secret.

"It's not the life that is given to you that determines whether you are good or evil. It is the small choices you make along the way."

Mamma could have taken revenge on my uncles. She could have burned the house down and destroyed everyone and everything that reminded her of the past. Instead Mamma made peace with her life and released all power it had over her. Mamma was at peace. No one's life is perfect. Some people just have better ways hiding their secret than others, and the way they hide their secret is reflected in their character.

After the event, I looked at my Mamma. I mean really looked at her. She was brown- skinned like me, with big brown eyes and the same lips as mine. Why hadn't I noticed this before? I looked just like her and Pastor Jackson. I even have his last name Synthia Jackson. He wasn't trying to make a pass, at me. He just wanted to feel me. I was his daughter.

This day was the turning point in my life. All my unanswered questions were answered. Joyce was my Mamma and Henry was my father. I was made as the result of a rape and was named the Syn. I was sold to Big Mama. The Hood is where I am from, along with Ms. Mindy and Mrs. Annie. They

know who I am, and that's why they gave me free tuition to the school and a place to stay. All the pieces of my broken life were beginning to fit together. I was where I belonged.

I knew we both needed a pick-me-up, so I suggested we do a girls night. Plus, I wanted to do a much needed makeover on my Mamma. I wanted her to experience what it felt like to look and feel beautiful. I went out to my car to get some styling tools out of the car.

As I was returning back to Mamma's house, I saw a car parked in front of my house. At first I didn't think anything of it, except I had seen Eric getting dropped off in a similar car one night when he thought I wasn't looking. I went back to the house thinking to myself was Eric coming back? I shook it off and began doing a consultation on my client. I did a quick look-over and began telling Mamma my suggestions just like she was in a real hair salon.

She was tickled by the attention she was getting. Standing behind her, I pulled her hair away from her face showing the unsightly strands of gray hair.

I told her,

> "First, I'm going to give you a color. Then I am going to do your nails, facial, make-up and lashes and last but not least, a wax."

She just smiled with pleasure. I started on her color. While it was developing, I gave her a set of nails and a pedicure. I rinsed out her color and gave her a deep-conditioner. She had really let herself go. I waxed her under arms, legs, lip and chin, then put on some lash extensions. When I was finished, we both looked in the mirror. My Mamma was beautiful!

Before she looked like she was seventy-five. Now she looked forty-five. She stared in the mirror amazed. She looked like she had seen a ghost. She couldn't believe her eyes. It was like she couldn't believe the person who she saw in the mirror was really her. I went home and felt good about my makeover. I felt good that I could help someone who had been there for me.

The next day, I looked out the window, there was that same car again, sitting outside of my house. I couldn't see inside because of the extra dark tint on the windows. I was running late for school so I just let it go.   That evening I saw the car again. I started to get freaked out a little. I didn't know what type of people Eric was involved in. Were they violent? Did Eric have something they wanted, and they think I have it?

My mind was racing then my motherly instincts kicked in.

> "I need to do something! This fool could wait until me and my babies are sleep and come in with guns and kill us all. I need to know right now who I am dealing with!" I thought.

I took a deep breath and walked over to the car. I leaned over and put my face really close to the car window, trying to see if someone was inside. The glass began to fog up from my hot breath, so I couldn't see through the dark tint. I was startled as the window lowered. A dark, thin, wrinkled face man with bloodshot eyes and coffee stained teeth stared back at me.

> "Who the hell are you? Why are you looking through my window fogging up my glass?" The man said with a sharp and commanding voice.

At first he took me by surprise, and then the wheels in my head went into motion. My anger went from one to one hundred. He has his nerve! He has been sitting outside my house for the last couple of weeks, having me scared and acting like a crack head peeping through the blinds with the lights off, hoping no one can see me. Then he has the nerve to ask me what I'm doing?

I reach back to my Big Mama days and unleashed all my ghetto.

> "Well excuuuussse............ me!" I said, looking down at him with one hand on my hip and the other hand in his face.

Then, waving my little finger back and forth, I said,

"You are bold as hell. As much sneaking and creeping you've been doing, you gonna have the gall to ask me questions? I almost have the itching to call the police! Now tell me right now, what is your business here?"

Out of breath from my long speech and anger for the nerve of this man, I stood there tapping my foot waiting for a reply.

The man looked back at me in disbelief of my aggressive response.

"Who are you?" He asked with caution like he just disturbed mother hens nest, and he's not sure what could happen next.

I told him.

"I live here with my family, and I don't like people sitting outside my home that I don't know."

He answered in an apologetic tone.

"We are looking for Eric and his old lady. We have some business with them, so no disrespect. We got a tip that he lived here. But I guess we were given some bad information. You take care and have a good evening. Don't worry, we won't be coming around here no more."

I didn't move as I watched them drive off.

As the car pulled off, I stood my ground until the car disappeared into the horizon. It took a minute of me standing there before what he said clicked in my head. This is Eric's home, even though he hasn't been here in a while, and I am his wife!

So who the hell is Eric's old lady if it's not me? They must be talking about Angela? I haven't seen her either, since the whole fraud thing! Was she fired? That sorry ass bastard is messing with that good for nothing Angela. The sad part about all of this is, this time she's the one playing with fire because messing with Eric might cost Angela her life.

These men didn't look like the type who comes to your door to sit, talk and play games. He is the type of man who people hire to take folks out of the game all together.

I began to think to myself,

> "I wonder if he threats Angela better than me? Did he want her because she is prettier than me? Or is he with Angela because she has lots of money? I wonder if they plan on having any kids together, because I can send them these kids. He can sit over there and playhouse. I don't have the money to raise these kids. They can raise these kids right along with the clan he's making across town. I wanted to cry over the loss of Eric, but right now I hated him so much. If I had any tears, they would be tears of joy, just because I don't have to deal with that lying ass anymore."

I went in the house to get ready for the next day.

As I walked past the mailbox, it dawned on me that I hadn't checked it in days. I always dreaded checking the mail. There were always bills in there that I couldn't pay. Since I was on a new program and I had extra money plus tips from school, I thought "why not?"

I was what you call a baller in *the Hood*. I reached inside to find a certified letter from the courthouse. I opened it and read it as I walked into the house. It was a summons to be in court for the eighteenth at nine a.m.

I thought,

> "hell today is the sixteen--- that's in two days."

I knew Eric was going to have to be in court. He had to have been out on bail, because there's no such thing called a get out of jail free card for making counterfeit money. That's a federal court, he's dealing with. I wondered what they wanted

with me. I didn't know anything. I guess they need me in court to tell them about the statement Eric wrote saying that I knew nothing about his dealings in the streets.

As I walked into the house I saw the picture of Eric, me and the kids. If I wasn't so tired, I would snatch it off my wall and get rid of him once and for all. In the picture, all is perfect! The only thing perfect now is that I am finally happy with him not being in my life. I sat on the couch thinking about Eric. Sometimes I wished we could have a do-over. However, this time we'd get things right the first time. We would be a happy family for real. I shook those thoughts out of my mind and realized we were a happy family. I had my Mamma, my babies, and me.

Graduation day was soon approaching. I needed all my energy and concentration to be on school right now. Eric's trial was not in my plans. These past two years I have had beauty school blues, between Ms. Mindy and *Beautiful One*, the kids, Eric and his get rich scams that put my ass in jail, Angela, finding God and meeting my Mother.

I had managed to keep my personal life from interrupting school. No one needed to know I was married to a dog that was sleeping with my Caseworker Angela. They didn't need to know the hell she put me through because of her love of beauty. I guess in her case beauty was Eric, and he meant everything to her. She accused me of Welfare Fraud, then cut off all my benefits and never cared for a minute about how I was going to take care of my babies or what they were going to eat. I never did anything to constitute her hatred for me.

I must have had my own personal angel watching over me or else, I never would of made it this far. I wanted Eric and Angela's drama behind me. This way I could spend my time trying to figure out how to come up with the money to open my own shop and finally have my independence. The last thing I want is to finish school and then become a slave for Ms. Mercedes. I didn't want to work in her snoot-booty hair salon, where I would only see 50% of my profits. The other girls felt

they were special when she chose them as the gifted graduates from *Beautiful One Beauty School*. After all I have been through, I am strong enough to stand on my own. I just needed about thirty-thousand or so to get to my dreams, and nothing and nobody was going to stand in my way.

Everything was going my way, I felt invincible. I was strong and determined to keep hope alive. The next day at school, I went straight to Ms. Mindy's office, I wanted to tell her I needed to take the next day off, so I could go to court. When I thought about it, I didn't want her to ask me any questions about my business. Plus, I didn't know how long the trial was going to take, and I knew it could affect my graduation day.

Once I got there I told Ms. Mindy, I had been feeling nausea, and I had to go to the doctors for an appointment. When I left her office I felt so bad for lying. But if I had to express all that was going on in my life, and she said one thing wrong. I would have had a nervous breakdown or we would have had a stand-off.

I arrived at the courthouse. I wanted to meet with my attorney and get the scoop on the trial. The last time I was at the courthouse it was for some speeding tickets. But today it seemed so different. I looked for the information desk. There were so many people going in so many places. I was pushed from one way to another. I couldn't tell the front door from the courtroom doors. I was discombobulated. I reached out to grab anything and felt a wool suit coat.

I looked up at a very displeased young man,

> "Excuse me sir, could you please direct me to the Information counter?"

Realizing I wasn't a threat. I felt the tension in his arm lessen.

> "Sure," he said in a helpful manner. "I'll walk you over. It's not often that I am hooked by such a beautiful lady."

I gave one of those Alp-glow smiles as he took me right to the Information counter. He gave me a good-bye wink, walked away and disappeared into the blustering crowd.

There sitting on a small stool was the biggest ass that I have ever seen. His ass poured over the stool like hot fudge running from ice cream. He was an older gentleman. I was sure they gave him this job when he was skinny and could move around. Now retirement was not many years away. There was no way he could hoist his ass up any stairs or down these long hallways to catch a criminal. He wore a police uniform that needed to be about three sizes bigger. His shirt tucked into his trousers and somewhere in-between was a belt. He breathed heavy and out-of-breath. His expression was blank and uninviting.

I said,

"Excuse me sir, can you please tell me where the Prosecuting Attorney's office is?"

He looked at my small frame, gave me a good look over and a smile came over his face as he said,

"Hey pretty lady, what can I do for you?"

I thought to myself,

"Look at him trying to get his Mack on."

He was so entranced he forgot to respond.

"The Prosecuting Attorney's Office...?" I repeated again this time a little louder and aggressive and less like a damsel in distress.

He regained his professional composure and went back to his blank expression again. He stood up, pointed down the hall and said,

"You follow this hallway all the way down past those office doors, then you'll see another clerk's desk and tell them who you are looking for there."

I thanked him and walked down the hall with the pace of the crowd. As I walked down the hall to the Prosecutor's office,

I glanced into an office with an open door. There right before my eyes sat one of my greatest problems. It was Angela.

I hadn't seen that hateful woman since her random inspection of my house, when she stripped me and my family of our dignity and privacy. Now here she is sitting handcuffed to the table. She now knows what if feels like to have no privacy and have your dignity stripped from you. She turned her face in shame. I just stood there soaking up the moment. She wasn't so high and mighty now! Where was the high class job that gave her all the power to treat people like trash?

Then it dawned on me,

"Why was Angela here? What could she have done?"

I hope it wasn't because of that Welfare Fraud thing. I believe someone would have let me know something, if I had to testify against her? I wanted some answers. But right now I needed to handle my own business. I'll just call Mrs. Annie later and get the scoop.

I went to the clerk's office and gave her my summons. She looked it over and handed it back.

"Mr. Braxton has been assigned to this case. Have a seat and I will let him know that you are here." She said, picking up the phone to let him know that I was waiting.

I had a seat. I picked up a magazine to read, but my mind went right back to Angela, Before I could try and work on a solution about Angela's business, Mr. Braxton appeared from a hallway. I turned to see this beautiful stature of a man standing there all put together with his navy-blue suit and crisp white shirt.

"Ooh….. I love a man in a suit," I sighted under my breath.

As he stood there I looked at him with longing eyes. It had been a while, if you know what I mean? I took a deep breath to get my composure as I exhaled and the word,

"My!" Slipped out of my mouth before I could catch it.

Mr. Braxton was fine about five-ten, brown-skinned with perfect eyebrows, kissable lips, and a winning smile. My eyes absorbed his whole body and I fantasized that he would be my next baby daddy. For an older gentleman, this brother had it going on! He looked at me in shock!

"I'm sorry, " I replied. "I wasn't expecting someone who looked like you."

That was a stupid line I thought to myself in my attempt to salvage the situation.

I stood to my feet and extended my hand "Synthia Jackson?"

He looked back at me and looked at my hand. He put his hand to his chin like he was in deep thought.

"Yes, you are Synthia Jackson? I am pleased that you were able to show up. I have been trying to reach you for some time. When I didn't hear from you, I thought I might have to drop the charges and loose this case. I hope you have the information that I've been looking for? Let me show you into my office, so we can have some privacy and sit and chat."

As he turned to go down the hall a whiff of his cologne passed by my nose, I fell into his trance and followed him like a hunting' dog sniffing' a scent.

We went into his office. It was nothing to write home about. It had a wooden desk and two wooden chairs that sat in front. I have to say, it was only his presence that made the office appealing. On his desk were files stacked up as high as me. He pushed them to one side of the desk and made a space-way for me to see through. He grabbed a file from the top of the stack and began thumbing through the papers.

Then he said,

"So before we get started, I need you to tell me what it the relationship between Eric Davis and yourself?"

I didn't want to answer the question. It had been so long since I talked to a fine man that seemed to show some interest.

"I'm his wife," I answered in a whisper.

I was so embarrassed. Here sat a man with promise, and here I am having to confess to him that I am married to a good for nothing jailbird.

He looked at me unsure if he heard me correctly.

"Did you say you are his wife?" He asked.

I lowered my head in disbelief myself, shook it back and forth and reluctantly said again,

"Yes, his wife."

He sat back with a disgusted look on his face. He folded his arms across his firm chest,

"This changes everything," he said in surprise.

I sat there confused looking at his disappointment and not knowing why?

He replied.

"You can't testify against him because you're his wife."

He stood to his feet, removing his suit coat and exposing his fine, perfectly-shaped ass. When he turned to look back at me, I tried to gain eye contact with him again.

Mr. Braxton continued,

"He must have known that he was under investigation. Do you mind me asking you how long have you been married?"

"Just a couple of months," I replied. "And I haven't seen him since the day we got married."

"Of course you haven't, because he has been living at his girlfriend's house."

I acted like I was surprised and asked,

"What girlfriend?"

"The woman who's behind this counterfeiting ring, Angela Roberts!" He answered.

My heart stopped beating. I felt like someone had kicked me in my back and knocked all the wind out of my body. I didn't know what to say or what to think. I had so many thoughts twirling around in my head. I couldn't put anything in order. I was numb. The only word that made sense to me right now was,

"No, no, no, no, no, no, no, no." I screamed it as loud as I could.

Mr. Braxton jumped up and came to my aid. I began to sweat. Then I felt cold, then nausea. I couldn't get myself together! All the lies and the deceit were bad enough. She got my man, and now the woman had gone and put our family at risk with some counterfeit money. This is the same woman who wanted to put me in jail for doing some hair at home. That hypocrite.

Then Eric's dumb ass had the nerve to give me some of that fake ass money to buy groceries to feed our babies. They deserve each other. They are both two fake ass people going to jail for trying to push fake ass bills. I was brought out of my daze by the sweet smell of Mr. Braxton's cologne. I looked up to see him fanning me with one of the files from his desk.

"I owe you an apology Synthia." He said. "I thought you had something to do with the case. I believed you were the key to crack this case right open. I thought you had all the answers to the mystery Eric and Angela have been keeping from us all. I see now that I was wrong. You might be the biggest victim here. The money can be retrieved and restitution can be paid, but nothing can ever give you back what they both have taken from you. I want to let you in on a secret, there are some big time players involved named the *Associates* and the *Partners*. The *Associates* took the biggest loss. They put in money and

were promised a bigger payout in return for their investments. Somebody has got to pay for their losses."

He looked me square in the eyes as if to indicate my babies and I would be sacrificed as the payment for Eric and Angela's scheme. I turned away because I couldn't bare the thought of someone threatening to do harm to them or me.

He could tell that I was getting a little edgy and continued.

"They fronted Angela and Eric thousands of dollars in exchange for millions of dollars in counterfeit money. The price is thirty cents on the dollar right now. There are hundreds of thousands of real dollars missing. The *Associates* want compensation for their losses. The *Partners* on the other hand, are looking for the stolen counterfeit plates that were taken in the first place to make the money. Angela claims Eric has the money and the plates. Eric claims that Angela is holding out on him. The *Associates* are tired of the games. They want their money and the *Partners* want their plates back. The *Associates* and the *Partners* seem to think you are the missing piece of the puzzle. But now after my investigation, I see you are in the dark about the whole thing. I believe that if the money and the plates don't surface soon there is going to be a war. Unfortunately, you will be thrown right in the middle of it. If you know something or not, your life might be in danger. I can't let you go home. I need to keep an eye on you because you are my leverage if something goes down."

I sat there in disbelief! How could all this be going on around me, and I have no clue. Was I so excited about beauty school that nothing else mattered? Not to mention Eric and Angela giving me the blues! How could I have not noticed that my life was spinning out of control. Eric didn't give a damn about me and neither did Angela. They used me. It was all about what they could get from me, and my dumb ass just let them use me.

Just like Eric said,

"How much are you willing to pay to get what you want, and when you get it, was it really worth it?"

Eric and Angela were willing to sacrifice their life for money and power. Now that they sit in jail, I can't see that being worth it.

The only thing I am willing to sacrifice my life for are my babies. The overwhelming feeling to be close to them tugged at my soul. I felt like a desperate mother who has lost her child in the grocery store.

"My children, I need to get my children," I said in a panic!

Mr. Braxton stepped back from his hovered position over me, and said,

"Children, now that changes everything! You never mentioned children before. They aren't even mentioned in your file."

I thought to myself,

"My file? What file? And what does he really know about me? He didn't even know I was married and that's Public Record. Then he didn't even know I have children. That should have been in my police report when I went to jail?"

I stood up and gathered my things.

"Where do you think you're going?" He said with a forceful voice.

"I just told you that I need to see about my children. If I am in so much danger, I need to be sure that they are safe, they are my first priority. I could give a damn about Eric and Angela's asses. I hope they both die in hell together. Right now, I just want to get my life back and leave all this drama behind me. Like you said, I am in the dark and I prefer to stay there." I told him.

I headed for the door. Before I could turn the knob, Mr. Braxton was there standing between me and my exit. I looked

up into his mesmerizing eyes. They peered back at me full of rage.

"You're not going anywhere," he replied with a loud deep forced voice.

I stared back at him with eyes of steel and called him on his bluff. I pressed my small body up against his, wedging him between me and the door.

I gathered up my entire muster and said,

"Who is going to stop me? I hope you don't think you are? I don't know what type of game you think you are playing, but I am not the one to be messed with! I need to get to my children and you nor Eric, nor Angela, nor any of these street hoods are going to stop me. So--- MOVE!"

Shocked at my disregard to his threat, he moved from in front of the door. I walked out and quickly found the first bathroom. I went into a stall and sat on the toilet. I needed a place to think.

I needed to answer the hovering questions in my head. Who was Mr. Braxton, was he really my attorney? Was I really in danger? The car that sat outside of my house was it the *Partners* or the *Associates*? When they find out I am really Eric's, wife, are they going to expect me to pay for Eric and Angela's screw-up? Then it all started to make sense to me. I began to get focus, think back and remember what was going on around me all the time. I know who the *Partners* are, I grew up all of my life watching them going into the room to have their meetings. So many times, I would block out my past. But right now, I needed all those memories to come back to me. I know who Henry is. He is the leader of the *Partners* now that Big Mama is dead. Mrs. Annie was escorted to the house one day by Earl and Steve. I remember Big Mama sending out word to kill that woman for thinking she was more powerful than the *Partners* with her *Associates*.

Big Mama said,

"I will smash that hoe where she stands, before I will ever let her run what I have worked so hard to build."

I remember someone coming to Big Mama's house helping me with my lessons. They called her Barbra. That's how I learned. It wasn't until later that I found out others kids went to real schools. All of my clothes came from Mr. Roberts. They were always sewn custom clothes. I remember when Uncle Rubert was killed over some counterfeit plates. I remember Big Mama's grandsons: Earl, Steve, James and Charles. I remember the only one that was nice to me was Charles. His spirit wasn't like the other boys, and he didn't care what they thought. He was so big everyone was afraid to mess with him. Now life was crystal clear, I am the missing piece to the puzzle. I needed help, some back up and I could only think of one person who no one would mess with, Ms. Mindy. I left out of the bathroom, found the closest phone booth to call the school and ask to speak to Ms. Mindy.

She picked up the phone, and I started telling the scoop in a panic!

"Ms. Mindy, I need your help! I am at the courthouse and my attorney says that I am in danger. I need to get to my children. I am scared and I don't know what to do?" Silence was all I heard.

"Ms. Mindy do you hear me?" I asked.

In a calm voice she replied,

"Yes, I'm here. I need you to calm down. Where are your children now?" She asked.

"They are at my neighbors' house." I asked.

Then she said,

"Okay, I need you to go to room 304, and ask to speak to Charles. Tell him that Ms. Mindy sent you and he will take care of you."

She hung up the phone and I didn't know what to think, but she was my last resort. I went back to the Information booth where the same overweight police officer sat with the same blank expression on his face. The second our eyes met he perked up!

"Hey gorgeous you're back, can I help you with more directions?" He asked.

He looked at me and saw the terror in my eyes,

"Are you ok? He asked in concern. "Ain't nobody trying to do nothing to you are they? Because, I got a bullet for their ass if they do." He said, as he stood up to show off his gun like he was an old school gangster or something.

I told him.

"I'm fine. I just need to know where room 304 is?"

He sat down and pointed his finger.

"You take these stairs right behind me, then take a left and go down four doors. If you are going to room 304, you got all the help you need. Good luck and take care of yourself. I would hate to have to read about such a pretty young lady like you getting killed in a terrible accident or something." He nodded his head to say, well…..bye.

I could see from the smirk on his face, he knew he was no match for what I had going.

"Thank you for your concern," I sarcastically replied, and ran up the stairs.

When I got to the office, I walked right in. Sitting at the desk was a little woman smaller than me.

"Can I help you?" She asked.

"Yes, I am here to see Mr. Charles." I answered.

"Yes, he is expecting you, I'll show you right back." She said escorting me into his office. The receptionist immediately saw her way out and shut the door behind her.

I was shocked and relieved, when I saw his face. It was the officer I met the day I went to jail-- Mr. Charles. However, when I looked closer I saw his eyes and knew this was my Uncle Charles, the one with the kind spirit. Though age had changed his appearance, his loving eyes stayed the same. I wanted to hug him. I knew in his presence I was safe.

"I called Ms. Mindy, and she said that you could help me?" I said in a begging and asking voice.

He smiled at me with so much assurance. He was such a massive man, but his voice was so gentle, as he said,

"Synthia, you have been protected from the start! Big Mama told me to keep an eye on you before she died. Don't worry, the kids are fine. There are undercover officers living on your same block and they keep close tabs on you guys. The children are still with your Mamma, Ms. Joyce."

I sighed in relief.

"I didn't know what to do! Mr. Braxton told me that my children and I were in danger." I told him.

He reared back in his chair, shaking his head,

"Talking to him you were in danger. He is the connection to the *Associates,* and he is on their payroll. He didn't do anything to you, did he?" He asked.

"No, I just knew to get out of there." I answered.

"I'm going to tell you what is going on, so you will understand the position you're in. This might be a shock to you, but Angela is Mindy's and Samuel Roberts's daughter. She decided to team up with Annie and the *Associates,* which was a big mistake. Rodney, Annie's husband is so dirty. He is a stone-cold killer. He recruited his long lost son Eric to rebuild the *Associates.* Now you

need to understand you are Henry and Joyce's daughter. Henry is the leader of the *Partners*. Eric is Rodney and Mrs. Annie's son. They are the leaders of the *Associates*. By you and Eric being married, you have bridged the gap between the two. Eric will one day be the leader of both the *Associates* and the *Partners*, making him the most powerful man in this town."

"Mindy and I go way back, before the days of the *Associates*. This town was much different back then. Mindy and I are connected with the *Partners*. The *Partners* as you know, were started by Big Mama. She controlled the town. She had a little of everything from prostitutes to gambling to drugs to counterfeiting. Their operation went on for over twenty years, after Big Mama's grandson Rubert was killed she wanted peace in the city. All was well until Annie came on the scene with the *Associates*. She wanted all of the control and caused havoc in the city."

"First, she tried to threaten your father, Henry, but he is not easily frightened. Annie knew in order to have more control she needed money."

"The *Associates* found out that Mr. Roberts was the maker of the counterfeit plates. She ordered him to give them to the *Associates*, he refused and she put out a hit on his life. Mr. Roberts and Mindy owned *Beautiful One Salon and Beauty School*. The *Associates* set a bomb to blow in the salon and school, killing Mr. Roberts and his sister Mammy."

"The *Partners* all trusted Mindy. She was the type of woman that knew how to keep her mouth shut and not ask any questions. Mr. Roberts trusted Mindy also. When he was killed, he left her the plates because he knew they would be safe in her care. Whoever had the plates had the power. It started a war between the *Partners* and the *Associates*. The town was split. You either chose to be a Partner or an Associate. Mindy and I chose to band together with your father to rebuild this town and rid us of the *Associates*."

"Angela, she grew up knowing the *Partners*. They were her Godfathers and trusted her too. Well, Angela got caught up with Eric. She was in love. There was nothing she wouldn't do for him. The only problem was Eric loved you. This made Angela so jealous that she became out of control. Mindy told her to leave him alone, but she could see she was falling in the middle of her daughter's rage. So she called me to fix the situation. That's what I do, I fix things. When Mindy realized Angela had taken the plates her husband left in her care, she knew the whole thing had gotten out of control. That's when she called on her friends to help."

"Angela had gotten so out of control. She even got her job involved. The State is under investigation because of her accessing federal files to obtain the paper to produce the money. You were out of the loop, until you took that fifty dollars to the grocery store. That's when everyone thought you had a part in it too. Eric never wanted you or the children to be wrapped up in all of this mess. He tried to get you out of it by marrying you, and then he wrote a statement clearing you from all knowledge of the whole operation. All was going good until you checked the mail and showed up here at the courthouse to meet with Mr. Braxton. But you are safe now." He said.

He paused, then he continued,

"I have been honest with you, now I need you to be honest with me. The *Partners* are angry with Eric and Angela, but they are protecting them from the *Associates*. However, they would like to recover the plates and the money. I need you to tell me, where are they?"

I sat there like I was sitting in a theater watching a movie of my own life in amazement, anticipating the next scene.

I said in all sincerity.

"Charles, I am telling you the truth. I don't know where the money is. I never knew there was any money. I haven't seen or talk to Eric, since we got married over a month ago. I am clueless."

My look of sincerity softened his heart.

> "I believe you. If you knew where the money was, I'm sure you would have bought a new car and moved out of that little house. We have been watching you for a while. You haven't bought anything new for you or your children, since we started this investigation. Go on home and get yourself ready, I hear that you have a graduation coming up. Mindy always tells me how proud she is of you. Synthia, if no one ever tells you, I want to be the first to say that all your struggles, trial and determination will be you biggest rewards in life. Never look back, always keep moving forward and you will be fine."

I reached over his desk and hugged him. He knew me from a child. He was my guardian angel, when I thought no one cared. Tears filled my eyes. I was so thankful for his help and advice.

On my way home, I wanted to hate Eric and Angela. But I realized they were perfect for one another. Eric has been always so superficial. Angela would do anything for the love of beauty, and what a beautiful man Eric was.

Today was the day I had wanted to come for so long. All my sweat and tears were finally paying off. Today was my Graduation Day!

I arrived with my three children and Mamma. I looked at each one of my babies' faces and realized they were worth the sacrifice. If I had made them my main priority in the first place, I never would have had to deal with all the drama Eric brought into my life. As I walked into *Beautiful One Beauty School* for the last time, the name finally had a meaning to me. I came here as Ms. Know-it-all, full of attitude, rage and ghetto as hell, proud to just be a kitchen beautician. I'm leaving here, I am at peace with life. I wear a new title now, a Cosmetologist Professional Stylist.

Mamma sat down with the children. I walked over to speak with Ms. Mindy. I had so many things I wanted to say. She looked at me, and I could feel that she read my mind.

"You're welcome!" She replied, and a smile came across her face.

Then she walked over to Mamma. They were face-to-face. I could tell she could speak to Mamma just like I could. After a while, they hugged each other. I could tell that whatever beef they had between them was set to rest. They were at peace. I looked to the back of the room, and there was my Daddy, sitting next to him was Charles. Over on the other side was Mrs. Annie. As I surveyed the room, I realized I had a family, and they were all here to support me. When my name was called, I went up to the front to receive my certificate. I looked at all the other success stories, and I was so full. As I raised my head and thanked God, tears of joy ran down my face.

That evening I sat in my living room looking long and hard at the portrait of our family. I saw how perfect we all looked sitting there in peace. I could no longer stand to live the lie. Eric made his choice to be with Angela. He was the one who destroyed everything.

I got up and went outside to the shed. I came back with a hammer. With all my strength, I hit the portrait so hard that the glass shattered all over the living room. The first hit felt so good. I took another aim at it. With each strike, the pain and anger had found some relief. I hit it over and over, until I was tired.

I sat in the middle of the floor exhausted! I looked at what was left. The picture was scratched, the glass broken, the walls had holes where I had missed, but it was still attached to the wall. It was just a little tilted to the side, and a large tear ran down the middle separating Eric and I. It was no longer perfect. I thought to myself, now that is a better representation of our family. It was full of imperfections.

We have been struck, beaten and ripped apart, but we still managed to hold on.

Then I thought to myself,

> "That picture was only held by one nail, so why didn't it fall down with the first blow?"

I stood on the couch to see what was holding it. I reached my hand behind the frame and felt the uneven wall. Someone had plastered the whole frame to the wall. I took the hammer again, but this time I hit the same spot until I cracked the plaster. The hole got bigger and bigger, until I was able to reach inside. I felt around. My hand touched a soft cloth. I pulled the cloth out and unwrapped it. Three shiny steel plates were inside. I gasped. They were the money plates that Angela had stolen from Ms. Mindy. The very same ones everybody was looking for. I wrapped them back up and placed them on the couch. Then I reached in the hole again. This time I felt a paper bag. I pulled it out. When I put my hand back in the hole, I felt another bag and another. I sat each bag on the couch, until the hole was empty.

In all there were five bags. I looked inside one of the bags and found money. They were all filled with money. This must be the money the *Associates* paid Eric and Angela. Like I said before, my man sure knew how to steal. He took the money probably right in front of Angela. She was probably, so entranced by his beauty that the money was gone before she realized it. He had hid it here in my house.

At first, I screamed. Then I remembered Charles telling me my house is being watched at all times. I took the bags to my room. I sat up all night counting the money. In all, there was $100,000. Pinned to one of the bags was a note.

It said,

> "Synthia,
>
> If you have found this note, then I know I am either in jail or dead. Either way we are not together. I want you to know I do love you. I could never give you or my babies what you needed. I put this money aside just for you, so

you can open your own beauty salon with our name *Just Two Beauty and Cuts*. I've made too many mistakes and told too many lies for you to believe the truth. But please believe me when I say, I would have sacrificed the whole world for your success. Take care wife.

Love you always,

Eric."

I sat there speechless. The truth is… he was a dog. And he made mistakes, but the children and I were going to be alright.

I hid the money under the bed and cleaned up the living room to the best of my ability. I hung another picture of some flowers, where our portrait once hung. The next morning I got the children dressed and I put the money in the diaper bag and put the plates in a large purse. Holding the bag in one hand, I went next door to Mamma's house. I spoke to her heart. I told her what had happened, when I tried to destroy our family picture. She watched the children, while I went to the post office. While waiting in line, I thought of all of the good and bad choices I had made in my life. I tried to talk myself out of my next moves, but they all seem to feel right. I put the plates in a box and wrote a note,

"I hope these plates give you the freedom that they have given me. Thanks! I signed it. I could never repay you enough."

Then I mailed them to Ms. Mindy with no forwarding address or a name.

I came back home. I saw mamma and the kids working in her rose garden. I got out of the car and kneeled down next to Mamma. She was digging a hole, so without any questions I helped her dig. We dug most of the day. The hole seemed deep enough to fit a person in.

Then she went into the house and came back out with some pretty pillow cases covered with flowers decorations the outsides. She walked back over and placed them in the hole. She proceeded to cover the hole with dirt. I helped her until the hole was filled. She took some more rose plants and planted them right over the buried pillow cases. I never believed Mamma was crazy, but if she thought for one minute that a flower pillow case was going to root and produce a garden, she was truly out of her mind.

We went back inside and got cleaned up. Mamma fixed us some lunch. I began to look for the diaper bag that I had left with the children. I went over to the couch. There it was empty. Then, I understood what was buried under the rose bushes. I came to know my mother knew best.

Later on that evening, a limo came to the house. I peeked out the window and saw my daddy, Henry getting out. I ran to the door to welcome him in as he got close. I wrapped my arms around him. I knew he was here to make sure we were all safe.

He held me until I was ready to let go. His first words were,

"Syn, I am here to ask you, my grandkids, and my wife to come home."

I looked over at Mamma. She was here, so she must have had a reason for leaving him in the first place. She looked at him, but their communication was shielded from me.

He turned and looked at me,

"What about you? Will you and the children come with me?"

I didn't know what mamma had agreed to, and I didn't want to go against her wishes, so I responded,

"I'll go wherever my Mamma goes," a smirk came over his face. In a joyous voice, he said, "Then it's settled, you are all going with me."

I was happy because I wanted so much for us all to be together.

Over the next couple of months I learned everything I needed to know about myself. Daddy was open and left no questions unanswered. Ms. Mindy would come over often. Come to find out, she and Mamma were sisters. So the whole time, I was with my aunt. Angela is my first cousin. She and Eric got out of jail and separated. She said that she couldn't trust him. Ha! Who knew? Eric comes by from time to time, but he spends a lot of time getting to know his family, Mrs. Annie and Rodney.

The *Partners* and the *Associates* made a truce and decided to destroy the old *Hood*. We all met by the old dry cleaners and stood to watch as each house was destroyed by a bulldozer. I looked at Mindy's face as she watched the house that once concealed her secrets be leveled to the ground. Then I looked over at Annie, as the tears ran down her face when her old house went down. When Rodney's old house was being leveled, he fell to his knees because the pain was so great. Mamma and Daddy stood side by side holding hands, watching their houses being destroyed. Charles was there to make sure not one house was left standing.

We all looked at the once horrible neighborhood, filled with all of its nightmares. The place where beatings, meanness, rape, sex and prostitution once reign the minds of children. It was once a prison. This place was a hell on earth. Innocence was lost. It was all meant to steal, to rob, and destroy lives. But, the children grew up and got out. They finally took hold of their lives and worked to turn this same place into a refuge for some. Yet, the stories still lay in the buildings. Now when we all looked, we only saw a flat field. No more were the secret filled houses. In their place, I envisioned a beautiful perfect place for a park. I mentioned it to daddy and he agreed. Just like that, a beautiful, new park has taken the place of the Hood where so much pain and suffering was once housed.

Now it was going to be a place of laughter, fun and joy. It was a perfect and safe place for children. We decided to name it *The Secret Garden,* and they planted the most beautiful roses there. I opened my salon and named it *Just Two Beauty and Cuts.*

Mamma was so amazing. She went back and dug that money up one night, when all the hype had died down and invested it into my salon. Eric came back and worked in the shop with me. We became friends with benefits, because after all, my man was fine. I bought a house next to Mamma and Daddy and for once, I had everything I needed.

⋏ABOUT THE AUTHOR

Sylvia Hardie writes from a spectacular human experience. She was born in Nashville, Tennessee. The daughter of two Airmen stationed in Seattle, Washington, she was exposed to the arts all of her life. Her father was a writer and her mother a musician. As she grew up in Seattle, Washington, she was totally unaware of her own abilities. Yet her mother spent timeless hours molding her to be someone great.

Sylvia focused on creating a change for her family and herself, went to work and within 4 years finished school, saved all of her resources, and opened up her business, all while giving birth to 3 beautiful children.

Sylvia currently lives in Las Vegas, Nevada. She is a prolific writer who uses her creativity to create works of fiction that challenge the status quo and real life experiences to add captivating life to the characters.

In addition to writing, this mother of 3 and grandmother of 3 is a Cosmetology Instructor. She is a motivator to co-workers as well as students. She loves good movies and spending time with the special people in her life.

SYLVIA HARDIE

26937731R00162

Made in the USA
Charleston, SC
25 February 2014